WILD ZONE

ROUGH RIDERS HOCKEY SERIES

SKYE JORDAN

1

This sucked worse than lightning drills. He'd known it would. But knowing it and living it were always different.

Tate Donovan stuffed his hands into the front pockets of his dress slacks, wishing he were on the ice sprinting a succession of laps between the rink wall and the various blue and red lines until he puked.

Around him, Tate's teammates and their girlfriends or wives or dates had gathered at Dock 5 in downtown Washington, DC, to celebrate the engagement of Rough Riders' captain, Beckett Croft, and his fiancée, Eden. Also spilling into the warehouse-turned-chic urban event space for the formal dinner were loads and loads of Beckett's family and friends. Eden was estranged from her own family, but the Crofts had taken her in as one of their own, including Beckett's six-year-old daughter, Lily—also Tate's goddaughter.

Lily streaked by in a flash of sparkly purple, making Tate crack his first smile all day.

Isaac Hendrix, Rough Riders right wing, stepped up next to Tate at the bar and ordered another beer, his head swiveling to watch Lily speed past. "She hasn't stopped running since Beckett put her down when they walked through the door."

Tate managed a laugh, but his chest ached from an invisible stricture known as PTSD. Marriage-and-wedding-related PTSD. But Lily took the edge off. "Man, she's going to crash tonight."

"She's always been a happy kid, but since Eden and Beckett got together, she's had an extra spark."

Tate felt the blade of a knife beneath his ribs, but he kept his fake smile in place and nodded.

He'd always hoped he'd be well on his way to fatherhood by now. But here he was, freaking thirty-one and couldn't drum up the interest to date anyone. At this rate, he was going to be the oldest father in his kid's class. If he ever got around to having a kid.

"And speaking of spark," Hendrix continued, lifting his beer toward a seating area. "Mia and Rafe seem to be lightin' it up every time I see them."

Tate glanced that direction and found his sister sitting on his best friend's lap, her arms around his neck, her forehead against his. Mia and Rafe, not only Tate's friend since childhood but also a teammate, had been going strong for almost two months. Tate had hated the idea at first. With time, he'd come around to the realization that they made each other ridiculously happy. And Mia's love for Rafe had brought her to DC, closer to Tate. But that love was also very new and very strong and, for the time being, very exclusionary, reminding Tate he'd lost his two best friends. After losing his wife.

None of which, in the big picture, was as big a deal as it felt in the moment—like a bomb ready to implode. He'd been dealing with everything fine. Until this. Until tonight. The celebration just pulled the ugliness he'd managed to bury back to the surface. And with it came all the pain, all the anger, all the disillusionment.

To snuff the fuse on that bomb, Tate took another deep swallow of liquor and changed the subject.

"Can you believe this place?" He scanned the large round tables covered in white linen tablecloths dotting the unfinished cement floor. Strings of fat, bare bulbs hung along the exposed beams. Lush white floral arrangements with ornate light fixtures adorned every table, along with formal dinnerware. "Never imagined they could make a big old warehouse look this good."

"Amazing," Hendrix said. "Hey, you doin' okay? I know the divorce was hard on you."

Tate wanted to lie, wanted to tell everyone he was absolutely fine. That he never thought about Lisa fucking other guys in their house, in their bed, while he was on the road getting slammed around on the ice. That he never thought about what those other guys had been doing to his wife when she'd told him she'd been watching the game on television. Or when she'd been talking to Tate on the phone after a game before he fell into a hotel bed, in pain and alone, missing her. Sure as shit never took one hell of a hit to his self-confidence wondering if he fell so short in bed, he'd driven her to find satisfaction elsewhere.

Before his mind could even veer toward the thought of whether or not he'd fucked her after arriving home right after some other guy had just left their house after fucking her...

Oh, too late...

He forced his attention to the family and friends around him, to all the good in his life, and took a deep breath.

"It's not fun, but I can't escape reality. People still get married. Have kids. Move on with life. And I love you guys. I want you all to be happy. I'll find a way to deal with it."

Tate finished his drink. Alcohol might work tonight, but it wasn't going to work for the long haul. And he was going to have to find a way to cope relatively soon, because he'd agreed to be Beckett's best man, which meant Tate was going to find himself at a damned altar again. The fact that he wasn't the one getting married didn't matter. Just the thought made him go light-headed with anxiety.

He set his glass on the bar. A flash of light caught his eye, and Tate looked toward the entrance. The front of the building was all glass, and a woman wearing a sequined dress caught the lighting and sparkles reflected onto walls and floors. He didn't need to see her face to know she'd be just as beautiful as all the others here tonight. He was one of only a handful of guys who hadn't brought a date, which meant there were a lot of puck bunnies in attendance.

That thought made Tate ask the bartender for more whiskey.

"Wonder what that's about." Hendrix's comment pulled Tate's gaze toward the entrance again. Sparkles chatted up the kid they had working security at the door, son of the Rough Riders' owner.

Tate scraped a cynical laugh from his throat. "Can't she see he's under age? Christ, these women. They'll hit on anything with two legs that even smells remotely like money."

Matthew had a baby face, but at six-foot four and two hundred and twenty pounds with his father's stony expression, even Tate knew he looked older than his sixteen years.

"She's damned hot," Hendrix said. "Probably lookin' to crash and score."

Tate refocused on the woman. On her light hair, pretty face, the way she filled out that dress. "Probably."

Matthew continued to check invitations and allow entry to guests while the woman stood to the side, bending the kid's ear. But she didn't look mad. In fact, she was smiling. Yeah, she was flirting her ass off, hoping to get into the party.

Tate took a sip of his refilled whiskey and checked out the other guests. He knew almost every face—teammates, coaches, trainers, Beckett's family and friends, the team owner...

Arguably, this location held the most important people in Tate's life, yet he couldn't have been lonelier. He'd known this season break would be rough—his first since he'd divorced Lisa—but knowing it and living it were very different.

Another flash of light pulled his gaze back to the door. Guests lined the stairs to the entrance and Sparkles was still bothering Matthew.

"Poor kid," Hendrix said. "Bro, get over there and show some of those new-captain leadership skills. Either kick her ass to the curb so Matt can do his job, or paint a bull's-eye on your forehead. Maybe you could score tonight. I'd do it myself, but I asked one of the ice girls to be my plus one, and she'll be here soon."

Tate cut a frown at Isaac. "You're dating a Rider Girl? Which one?"

"Like you'd know the difference? The only reason you even know they exist is because they annoy the shit out of you. Oh, hey, there she is." Hendrix straightened from the bar, slapped Tate's shoulder, and met his gaze. "Put Matt out of his misery and think about tapping some of that. Dude, you need to score."

"I don't need a punk like you telling me I need to score."

"Whatever you say, boss." Hendrix walked toward the entrance, where a pretty brunette wandered in all wide-eyed at the decorated space. Tate took another sip of his whiskey and watched the Rider Girl's face light up when she saw Hendrix. She lifted to her toes to wrap her arms around his neck in a hug, then pulled back and smiled before she kissed him.

Heaviness collected beneath Tate's ribs. He knew he needed some of that. A lot of that, actually. But he was caught between a rock and a hard place right now. He wasn't a one-night kind of guy. For him, sex always included a relationship. And since

Lisa, Tate had an aversion to both relationships and women in general.

An aversion he needed to get over.

Tate glanced around the warehouse again. Dozens of beautiful women mingled throughout the space. Many were here with a date or spouse, but many were here solo or with family. And every one of them under the age of forty—okay and even a few above—was attractive. The majority of them were beautiful.

He searched all the women for something to interest him— their looks, their smile, something. But nothing flickered inside. He sighed and glanced toward the front door again. Sparkles was still bugging Matt. Still grinning. She had her hand on the rail, her body loose and relaxed. She said something to Matt, then turned to the couple handing over their invitations, and spoke to them. Now everyone was grinning, including Matt. And with one more comment from Sparkles, they all burst out laughing.

Curiosity stirred.

The couple stepped inside, and Matt continued taking invitations, but he still didn't let Sparkles into the party. Now Tate wanted to know the story. And if she was a puck bunny, he wanted to steer her away quietly. Those women were notoriously obnoxious. They'd do just about anything to get attention, and she was working that door hard.

Tate approached the entrance, stepping aside to let the flow of guests pass as he assessed the woman through the glass. Now, just a few yards away, he had his first good view of her. The fact that she was attractive wasn't a surprise. Tate hadn't realized how many gorgeous women existed in the world until he'd gone pro. Now they'd become commonplace, one almost indistinguishable from another.

Sparkles wasn't as petite as she'd looked from a distance. She was on the taller side, at least five foot eight or nine. She was long and lean with the kind of curves that made Tate's mind wander toward thoughts of wrapping his arms around them, feeling her up against him. The skirt of her sequined dress was short, and her tanned, toned legs went on and on, ending with matching sparkling spiked heels strapped to her feet.

Before his mind could wander again, Tate spotted Jake Tierney strolling across the parking lot toward the steps. This would be interesting. Tierney turned every female head within a five-mile radius. He was also one of the most eligible bachelors in hockey, with one of the fattest paychecks. If Sparkles was a puck bunny, she'd lock on to him instantly. And Tate would know exactly what to do with her.

As he waited for the two to cross paths, Tate scanned her again and realized she was holding nothing but a cell phone. No wrap. No purse. Where was she hiding her makeup? Her change of clothes for the morning after? Her condoms? Her sex toys?

Tate offered a hello to one of the Rough Riders' trainers and his wife while Tierney slipped past the guests in line. But at the door, instead of coming inside, he paused, eyeing Sparkles with interest. He smiled, turning on the charm that made most women swoon, and said hello. Sparkles offered a polite response, but then crossed her arms and paced to the opposite side of the small platform, staring out at the night.

Tierney gave Matt a shrug and turned into the warehouse, stopping when he saw Tate. "Hey, what's up?"

Tate lifted his chin toward the entrance. "She's been trying to get in, but Matt's blocking her. I'm gonna find out what her story is."

Tierney glanced at her again, and a big smile cut across his face. "Hell, yeah. Get the *whole* story. That is one prime cut of USDA—"

"Jake," Tate said with knock-it-off-already impatience.

Tierney chuckled. "Just sayin'. Mmm-mmm-mmm. Tasty."
He turned back to Tate, his gaze a little more serious. "Fuckin'
get some, would you? I know women suck sometimes, but
you've got to take care of yourself."

"Shut up."

Jake leaned in and gave him a deadly serious "*Get. Some.
Tonight.* Or face an intervention."

Before Tate could tell Tierney what to do with his order, his
teammate had disappeared into the crowd.

"Idiot," Tate muttered, edging toward the door. The early
July night air brushed Tate's face and made him want to take off
his suit jacket.

"Look, I totally get where you're coming from," Sparkles'
voice, even and congenial, touched Tate's ears, "and I've got to
give you kudos for taking your job so seriously, but if I tell my
sister I'm going to be somewhere, I'm going to be there..." She
trailed off as Matt smiled at another couple, took their invitation, and welcomed them to the party, then continued with "I'm
not sure how many ways I can explain this to you..."

"And *I'm* not sure how many ways *I* can explain this to *you*,"
Matt quipped back, more playful than brusque. "No invitation,
no entry." He gave her a shrug. "I'm sorry, but if I tell my dad
I'm going to do something, I'm going to do it."

Tate had never seen this snarky side of Matt, probably
because the kid was terribly respectful of authority. Tate braced
for the woman's explosion. Puck bunnies this insistent didn't go
down without a fight.

"I don't have an invitation, because my sister called and
invited me over the phone." Her voice remained light and
sweet. No attitude. No anger. In fact, she seemed almost overly
solicitous and good-natured, considering she wasn't getting her
way. "I'll let you listen to her voice mail. She's one of the event
planners—"

"And my mom is the DJ," Matt quipped back, grinning. "I'll let you listen to her latest voice mail too."

The woman dropped her head back and laughed. She *laughed*. The sound was light and fun and infectious, and Tate found himself smiling. Felt his chest loosening, his intrigue growing. She *was* trying to crash, but she wasn't flirting with the good-looking sixteen-year-old. Refreshing.

If her sister was the event planner here, then she was also the event planner for his charity banquet in three weeks, because Tate had hired the mother-daughter team on the advice of Beckett's bride-to-be.

"You are a-*dorable*," she told Matt, amused, "but, really, my sister is expecting me."

"Then she *really* should have left an invitation at the door."

The woman heaved a sigh and paced away from Matt. At the balcony railing, she looked out over the city.

For a long moment, she just stood there, and for a long moment, Tate just stared. Her dress followed every curve and dipped low in the back, exposing a lot of smooth skin and the sexy curve of her spine. He couldn't ever remember thinking of a woman's spine as sexy. But right now, his mind was drumming up fantasies of kissing his way down that spine until it ended, then continuing on...

Which was when Tate realized miracles did happen, because his cock was tingling with the long-lost desire to rub against soft things.

She turned sideways, leaned one elbow on the railing, and looked at Matt again. "Okay, then, I guess we're going to get to know each other really well, because I'm not going anywhere until my sister checks her phone, and with her running all over the party like a madwoman, that could take some time. I'm Olivia. What's your name?"

That was Tate's opening.

He put his glass on a side table and waited for foot traffic to clear, then walked out onto the metal platform. "Hey, Matt."

"Hey, Mr. Donovan."

"Matt," Olivia said with a nod and a contemplative scan of Matt's face. "It fits. You look like a Matthew."

Tate stepped toward her and offered his hand. "Hi, I'm Tate."

Her gaze turned on him, along with a warm, authentic smile. She took his hand, her hold firm. "Olivia."

Matt cast an uncertain gaze between them. "She doesn't have an invitation, sir."

"So I heard." Tate settled his gaze squarely on Olivia, and she held it with the kind of open, no-nonsense confidence Tate rarely saw in women. She also added a feisty little what-are-you-gonna-do-about-it umph to her grin, and Tate couldn't keep from smiling back.

Up close, everything about her was striking. Her blonde hair was shiny, her skin smooth and radiant, her eyes clear, sky blue. She wore light makeup and no jewelry. And she appeared as unimpressed by Tate as she'd been by Jake.

He liked that.

He released her hand. "What's your last name, Olivia?"

She cocked her head and queried with a puzzled "Why?"

"So I can confirm your relationship to the event planner."

"Essex," she offered without hesitation.

She was, indeed, part of the family. He nodded at Matt. "Olivia will be my plus one tonight."

"Yes, sir."

When Tate met her eyes again and extended a bent elbow for her, she looked a little stunned. "Thank you."

She slipped her hand around his biceps, telling Tate, "Matt is an excellent security guard. He needs a raise."

Tate laughed. And suddenly, looking down into this

stranger's beautiful blue eyes, he wasn't feeling so shitty about the night anymore.

He nodded confirmation at Matt. "I'll talk to your dad."

"Thank you, sir," Matt's chest puffed out a little with pride.

"He's just darling." She shook her head and walked inside with Tate. "What is he? Sixteen—" She stopped, put her free hand to her chest, and pulled in a breath. *"Oh, ce est magnifique."*

Her words came out soft, and when Tate turned narrowed eyes on her, still trying to figure out what she'd said, he found her taking in the space with awe.

"Was that...French?" he asked.

"Oh my. My, my, my." She released Tate's arm and turned in slow circles, her gaze taking in everything floor to ceiling. Everything except the people, which was novel when the guests were really the main attraction. And while she took in the warehouse, murmuring to herself in a mix of English and what he was sure now had to be French, Tate took another sweeping look at her.

She wore some exotic scent of flowers and musk that made his mouth water. Her voice caressed his ears while her slinky silver dress winked in the dim light. And for the first time in way too long, Tate's body continued to yearn after the initial flutter of attraction.

"They've done such an amazing job."

Her words dragged his gaze up her long legs, over her great ass, her flat belly, her full breasts, her sleek neck and rested on her profile. On her little nose. Her big eyes. Her plump lips. Slid over the fall of light hair. Hair that hung long and loose to her shoulders. The kind of hair Tate could sink his hands into and find traction.

Oh yeah. The whiskey was working. Because that thought led his mind down an extremely dirty path that included her head between his spread legs, his hands tangled in her hair...

Thick heat gathered in his pelvis. He tore his gaze away

from her face and cleared his throat. "So, do you see your sister?"

She scanned the crowd. "No...but there are a lot of people here." She sighed, turned to face him with a crooked little smile, and shrugged. "I'll find her eventually. She and my mom will be here until the very end, and I'm sure I'll be here helping them clean up. What's with the baby security guard at the door? There can't be anyone really important here, or you'd have armed guards and Secret Service. A celebrity would have bodyguards."

Tate grinned. "Baby is a second degree black belt in tae kwon do."

Her pretty face dropped in surprise. "Duly impressed. I wish I'd known. I would have given him a harder time. People like that make life hell for the rest of us."

That made Tate laugh.

"It's true," she complained with a half chuckle, pushing at his chest. "Don't laugh at me. My sense of humor is on Paris time, which means it's *sound asleep*."

He caught her wrist and held it gently. He'd forgotten how soft a woman's skin could be. "I bet a really good glass of French wine would make up for the jet lag."

Her gaze lowered to his mouth, and her smile burned a little hotter. "A little French *anything* cures jet lag."

She pulled back from his grip, flattening her palm against his, then threading their fingers. The move, while simple and harmless, struck Tate as intensely intimate.

"You're a nice surprise in my day, Tate."

That zinged through him, and vibrations radiated over his ribs. "Same here."

With her hand in his, they wandered toward the bar, and Tate couldn't help but focus on how odd it felt to have a woman's hand in his again. Odd yet good. So good. Which made Tate's mind wander to how good the rest of her would feel against the rest of him.

At the bar, the young server looked at Tate. "Whiskey, sir?"

"Please, and a glass of the Château Rayas, ninety-five, please."

Olivia lifted her brows. "That doesn't pour from any random spout." Then she glanced around again, only this time at the people. "Should I recognize anyone?"

Tate rested his butt against a stool, but he didn't move far. She hadn't taken her hand out of his, and he wanted to keep it that way. "Only if you like hockey."

"I used to love hockey," she said, her gaze returning to his with a spark of excitement. But in the next second, something clicked and sadness filtered in, snuffing the light. "In high school," she added, less enthusiastic. "My dad and I used to watch it. Then I moved overseas and, well...I got busy."

The bartender returned with his whiskey, a wineglass, and the bottle.

Olivia made a negligent gesture toward the bar. "Go ahead and pour. I don't need all that pretentious bull."

The young bartender tried to stifle a grin.

Olivia snuck a look at Tate. "Sorry if that offends you. But seriously, if a bottle of wine costs eight hundred dollars, you shouldn't have to do a sniff and taste test to make sure it's good."

The bartender choked on a laugh.

Olivia lifted her hands. "Am I right?"

Tate chuckled and shook his head. She was so fresh. Down-to-earth. Unpretentious. Too many women who gravitated toward professional sports players did it for the money, the status, the fame. Lisa had. A lot of the players' exes or current dates had. And they couldn't get enough of that bullshit.

"I don't know anything about wine," Tate admitted. "So to me, it sounds right."

"You do so. You just ordered the Château Rayas with total confidence."

"We have friends here tonight who love this wine, so I knew there would be a couple of bottles tucked away especially for them. I just lucked out that you like French."

She laughed. And man, she was...mesmerizing. Her eyes sparkled, her skin glowed. Tate couldn't look away. She had a spirit that was open and free and light. She lifted Tate. Let him see above those dark borders he'd been living inside.

"No worries," she murmured, lifting her free hand to his chest and hooking her index finger into the space between the buttons on his shirt, stroking button to button. "I love everything French."

Tate wanted to French every inch of her. "So you just came in from Paris?"

She nodded.

"Were you there on vacation?"

"No, I live there."

His brows shot up. "Really." Just his fucking luck. The first woman who'd interested him since his bitch of an ex-wife screwed him over, and she lived overseas. His excitement dimmed. "How long have you lived there?"

"Um..." Her eyes rolled upward. "Sort of off and on for years. I move around a lot."

"Why?"

"I just love traveling, experiencing different cultures, meeting different people. Life is short, you know? Gotta live all your adventures while you can."

There was a story there. One he'd like to know, but not one he wanted to get into now. Or here. "What are you doing in town?"

"I came to visit my mom and sister for a couple of weeks."

Couple of weeks. Tate's heart sank.

"So, what is this?" she asked, glancing around the space. "It's pretty fancy for a bunch of hockey players."

He followed her gaze, pleased to find his teammates too busy chatting with others to be watching him. He didn't need to catch any more shit about his love life than he already had. "Engagement party for one of the guys."

"Cool. Are you one of those guys?"

"I am."

She smiled. "Like your job?"

"Love it."

She nodded. "That's good. I believe in loving everything you do. Otherwise, it's not worth doing."

Oh yeah. He really liked her outlook. "What do you do back in Paris?"

"I work at a restaurant..." Something buzzed on the bar top. Olivia's gaze cut that direction and her hand drifted from his shirt to pick up her phone. "Sorry, it's Quinn."

Without letting go of Tate's hand, she answered. "Hey, I'm here, I'm—" She stopped abruptly. Her brows pulled together in a cute little scowl. "Wait, but you invited—" She pulled her hand from his and pressed it to her forehead. "I thought..."

Tate's hand felt cold. And the heat she'd created inside him started to drain as if his body already knew he'd lost his chance with her. He might have met her only fifteen minutes ago, but Tate already knew she was very different from the puck bunnies that swarmed the team. She was the kind of woman Tate had wanted to meet since he'd divorced Lisa.

"Are you serious?" she said into the phone with the first hint of frustration in her voice. "I just got off a plane, Quinn— No, I'm at the bar, talking to— Quinn— *Quinn*?"

She pulled the phone from her ear and frowned at it, growling. Turning off the screen, she settled a frustrated but apologetic gaze on Tate.

"I'm sorry. My sister..." She exhaled hard, and a slice of

anger cut across her face before it melted away into annoyance again. But her shoulders sank, and the light in her eyes had burned out. "Quinn, evidently, didn't invite me to *enjoy* the party. She invited me to *work* the party. And the only reason I'm not going to strangle her is because she's never traveled and she doesn't understand time changes and jet lag."

Tate instinctively reached for her hand to pull her closer, curving the other arm around her waist. And Olivia acted as if it were the most natural thing in the world. As if being touched by a stranger didn't alarm her in the least. As if leaning into him like they were already lovers was second nature. Which only made Tate want to seal that deal...like...now.

"Is there something I can do to help you get your job done quicker so you can get back to me quicker?"

She stroked his cheek and smiled. "I could tell you were going to be one of those guys as soon as I met you."

He braced for the nice-guy brush-off. "What kind?"

Her light eyes slipped down his face and rested on his mouth. "The kind I'd want to get to know *a lot* better."

The sexual innuendo in her tone seared a path through his belly and straight between his legs.

"I'd like that too." Tate couldn't quite believe the words had come out of his mouth.

Olivia swayed closer and looked up at him with those big blue eyes. "Maybe later, if you're still here when I'm done..." She gave a little shrug. "Have a great night, Tate. And thanks for getting me in. Quinn sounds like she's going to need a hand." She patted his chest and grinned a little wider. "Little sister to the rescue."

Then she pushed up on her toes, skimmed her fingers across his jaw, murmured something in French, and kissed him. Just a soft press of her lips.

Then she glanced around. "Can you point me toward the kitchen?"

Tate was still dazed when he lifted his hand toward a pair of doors toward the back. Then watched her walk away, her path to her sister followed by dozens of male gazes. She responded to greetings but didn't seek out attention.

And when she pushed open one swinging door, she paused and looked back. Her gaze found Tate's and held. And she smiled. The moment lingered while Tate's stomach flipped. Oh yeah, there was definitely something special about her.

"Who's that?"

The familiar voice dragged Tate's gaze around just as Olivia disappeared into the kitchen, and Tate turned to face Beckett. He was holding a beer and wearing a frown.

"The sister of your event coordinator. She came to help out," he said to make the explanation easier.

"If she looks anything like Quinn, I hope you asked her out."

"I haven't met Quinn yet. I arranged the event with Teresa. And I'm going to meet up with Olivia when she's done here to see if she wants to go out. But she just got into town, so she may not be up for it. Especially not after working tonight."

"That sucks. I was hoping she'd be back to hang on you some more."

"Why?"

Beckett made a face. "Because Lisa just walked in."

Everything inside Tate went cold. "*What?*" He knew neither Beckett nor Eden would invite her, so he asked, "How?"

"She's with Martin Kessler," Beckett said. "My dad invited Kessler. I had no idea—"

"Fuck." He sighed. "I know, Beck. I know."

Lisa was a publicist. When Tate met Lisa, she'd been digging for clients, struggling to grow her one-person company. Hooking up with Tate had changed all that. Looking back, he had a crystal clear view of Lisa's grand plan and how expertly she'd executed it, but at the time, he'd believed they held the same values and wanted the same things—marriage, kids, a family, a future together. But all she'd wanted was Tate's contacts to build her business. When that had only taken her half the way, she'd slept her way to the finish.

Now, three years later, she had a thriving multimillion-dollar company handling publicity for the majority of DC's biggest names in sports, politics, real estate, and business. Which meant Tate and Lisa would continue to run into each other. It had already happened twice since their divorce. Once at a charity event, once at a sponsor event. And each time, she'd been with a different man.

"Thanks for the heads-up," he told Beckett.

His friend was pulled into a conversation nearby. When he stepped aside, Tate had a perfect view of Lisa and Kessler. She looked as amazing as she always did, trim, coiffed, jeweled, her plastic smile in place. Tate's guts churned with emotions—anger, bitterness, hurt, betrayal. And here she was with man number three—or thirty, for all Tate knew—while he was so scarred over what she'd done, he couldn't even date.

Olivia's smile flashed in Tate's head. *Maybe later, if you're still here when I'm done...*

The stark difference between the emotions Olivia elicited and the emotions Lisa elicited struck Tate, and he made a decision right then and there: He was ready to move on the way Lisa had.

He might never have been a one-night-stand kind of guy, might have never had a fling, but if Olivia wanted him, he sure as hell wasn't going to walk away tonight. Because over the last year, he hadn't found anyone he'd wanted to move on with more than Olivia.

2

Olivia Essex wasn't short on men in her life. From the moment she'd moved overseas, they'd come easily. Being blonde and American had always been an attractive novelty. Over the last decade, she hadn't just learned a lot about men, she'd become a connoisseur. She truly did love them and all their eccentricities.

And as she smiled at Tate before letting the swinging door close behind her, she hoped the smokin'-hot American was still here when she finished putting out Quinn's fire. Olivia was a sucker for a wounded soul, and Tate Donovan was one big muscled mass of darkly charismatic, brooding man. She wanted to take him to bed and bring him so much joy, it took him months to remember what—or who—caused him the kind of pain she saw in those pretty chocolate eyes.

Her fingertips finally brushed the edge of the door, and it slipped from her grasp, cutting off her view of one of the best-looking men she'd ever met. And she'd met more than her fare share from all over the world.

Olivia smiled, sighed, and laid a hand over her heart. Turning, she floated deeper into the large space much like the one she'd come from, just not dolled up for guests. Cement floor, twenty-foot, open-beamed metal ceilings... Confusion filtered in. This wasn't a kitchen. It looked more like a storage—

A moan rippled through the air, chilling Olivia's spine and stopping her feet. A tortured, agonized moan followed by a choked sob. Then a round of insistent hushes while the moan was muffled.

What the...?

Olivia's mind darted back to Quinn's panic-edged voice over the phone, something Olivia had chalked up to tightly strung Quinn being tightly strung Quinn. Now, urgency drove her forward. "Quinn? Mom?"

She passed stainless steel shelving units and turned into a portable kitchen setup. A crew dressed in black pants and white dress shirts created a half circle around the source of the moan.

After a decade working in kitchens of every kind, from third-world huts to billionaire's mansions, Olivia's head filled with a hundred different scenarios for the injury causing the sounds of pain. Scanning the crowd for her sister and mother, she moved forward, pushing shoulders to make a path to the center.

"Quinn? Mom?"

They shouldn't be in here. They should be out among the guests, making sure everything was where it should be. That everyone had what they wanted or needed. Acting as liaisons to the kitchen to keep food stocked, but not working *in* the kitchen.

When Olivia finally reached the source of the moans, she stopped dead and stared, mouth open in shock. On the floor, a very pregnant woman in a white chef's uniform lay on her back. Quinn knelt on one side of the woman and their mother knelt on the other. The pregnant woman pressed her hand to her belly, scrunched her glistening face in pain, clenched her teeth, and groaned loud and long.

"Breathe, Charlotte." Olivia's mother's smooth voice attempted to focus the woman whose hand was cradled between Teresa's. "Come on, Charlotte, focus and breathe. One, two, three…"

"Quinn," Olivia said, alarm ringing in her normally controlled voice. "What the hell's going on?"

She hadn't seen her family in over a year, but when her sister looked up at her, it was still like looking in a mirror. "Oh, Livvy. Thank God."

Her mother stopped counting and glanced up too. Unlike Quinn, their mother smiled. "Olivia, baby."

Olivia dropped into a crouch beside her mother and wrapped her in a quick hug. "Hi." She pulled away and looked down at the woman on the floor. "I'm Olivia," she told her. "Are you hurt?"

The woman huffed a little laugh, but fear clouded her eyes. "Depends on how you look at it."

Olivia shot a look at her twin across the woman's pregnant belly.

"Olivia, this is Charlotte, our caterer." Then she told Olivia, "Charlotte's water broke. We called an ambulance, and her husband's on the way."

"An ambulance?" That seemed like overkill. "Maybe I'm used to the European way of doing things, but water breaking isn't generally an emergency when you have top-notch hospitals on every corner."

Her mother smiled. "She's only seven months pregnant."

"Oh." Olivia's eyes rounded along with her mouth. "Oh…my…"

Quinn pushed to her feet and waved Olivia to a corner while telling the workers, "You all have jobs. Do them."

The staff drifted to different areas of the kitchen. While

their mother stayed with the pregnant chef, Quinn paced in a small strip, one hand on her hip and one rubbing her forehead.

"This is a really important job," she said in a hushed tone. "It's an engagement party for the Rough Riders' captain and his fiancée. All the players and their wives and family will be here. The team owner, the coaches, the trainers..." She ran out of air and paused to take a shaky breath. "This is huge. If we blow this—"

"Okay, slow down." Olivia tried to get a big-picture view of the situation. "First of all, the place looks absolutely amazing, Quinn. It's a fucking fairy tale out there."

That made her sister laugh a little.

"The bar is flowing, so everyone is going to be half-drunk in about thirty minutes, which means anything that does go wrong will only seem half as wrong as if they were sober."

Quinn gave her a get-serious "Liv."

"Our prego is the caterer, right? Didn't she have everything prepared?" Olivia looked around the space, her gaze halting on the giant refrigerators. "There. Isn't everything nearly ready to serve?"

Quinn was so caught up in her panic, she didn't seem to hear the question. "The company hasn't been doing well. We really need this event to—"

"What?" Olivia's attention focused. "Mom said—"

A bubble of nearly hysterical laughter popped out of Quinn. Olivia's words died on her lips, and anger sliced a path through her body. Anger a decade old that still flared hot in seconds.

Olivia took a step back and crossed her arms.

Quinn panicked and grabbed Olivia's forearm. "No, no, no, no, no. It's not like that, Liv. That's not—"

Quinn exhaled and collected herself, but the cut inside Olivia already throbbed painfully. And the way it could break open like this made her wonder if it would ever heal.

"You know Mom," Quinn said, flustered. "She's a lot like you. You both want to do everything yourselves. She's not going to trouble you with her problems, especially not when she doesn't get to talk to you very often."

Olivia dropped her arms and glared at her twin. "You're really not making me want to pitch in here."

Quinn pushed her hands into her hair and squeezed her eyes closed. "God, Liv, just stop. You're so damned sensitive, I can't say anything right."

"*C'est le foutu bordel.*" Regret, hurt, anger swirled in her gut. She pressed her fingers to closed lids and rubbed tired eyes. She wanted to go find the sexy Tate, bury this fresh hurt, and get on the next plane back to Paris.

"I hate it when you do that," Quinn bit out. "It's so rude."

She dropped her hand and looked at her sister. It was two a.m. for Olivia. She'd worked a full shift at the restaurant before catching her seven-hour flight to DC. And in the face of this old, tired conflict with her family, exhaustion kicked in. This wasn't how she wanted to spend their short time together. "I said this is a fucking mess. Just tell me what you need."

Her sister huffed, pressed her hands to the sides of her face, and looked at the floor. Her hands were shaking and tears glistened in her eyes. And, dammit, just like that, love grudgingly pushed Olivia's anger aside.

She stepped in and wrapped Quinn—older by two minutes —in a bear hug, the kind her sister couldn't easily escape. Olivia instantly felt the bond they'd formed in the womb. They might have fought over the years, they might not be able to live together, but they would always be part of each other. "Shh, stop, Quinny. It's going to be okay."

Quinn pried her arms from between their bodies, wound them around Olivia's neck, and started crying.

Merde. Olivia's own eyes burned with tears. She squeezed

them tight and held Quinn close. *Merde, merde, merde.* She *hated* this. Hated this irreparable tear in her family.

"Shh, shh." She tried to calm her sister even while her own emotions were spiraling out of control. "I'm sorry, Quinn. I'm tired."

Quinn exhaled hard, sniffled, nodded against Olivia's shoulder. "I know. I'm sorry too. It's been a rough year."

Olivia rolled her eyes to the ceiling, stuffed the anger, and said, "Talk to me. What do you need right here, right now?"

Quinn pulled away, and Olivia let her. She felt the staff's eyes on them, felt the nervous tension in the room, but she ignored it. That, she was used to. That, she could handle. Her relationship with her sister and her mother had never been anywhere near as easy.

"This crowd is a *huge* foodie pack," Quinn said, wiping at her cheeks.

Olivia caught the eye of a young man leaning against a wall, lifted her chin, and patted her cheek. The kid was quick on the uptake. He grabbed a box of tissues and brought them over. Olivia gave him a smile and mouthed *Thank you*, and he retreated.

Quinn grabbed a few tissues and dabbed at her face. "Charlotte was preparing all sorts of specialty foods designed to impress."

Olivia thought back to the Château Rayas. And Tate.

"This isn't the kind of food I can just put on a plate and call it good." Quinn's panic rose as she described the complexity of the menu. "I can't even pronounce some of this stuff. Some has to be heated. Some is half-cooked and has to be finished in the oven or on the stovetop. Some need sauces. All of them need garnishes and decorations." Her blue eyes lifted to Olivia's, brimming with panic. "Olivia, you *know* I burn *water*."

Quinn covered her face with both hands again.

"Oh, honey..." She pulled her sister close. "I can handle

anything she had planned." Thoughts of catching up with Tate vanished, and Olivia sighed with regret, then opened her eyes and told Quinn, "I've got you covered."

"You do?" she asked, searching Olivia's eyes. "Are you sure?"

Quinn's insulting question made Olivia want to scream. She hated this familial roller coaster. Instead of being "sensitive," Olivia pretended her sister hadn't maligned her and said, "Of course. That's why you called, isn't it?"

"Well, yeah." Now that she'd calmed down, Quinn didn't seem so sure. "I mean, I know you cook and everything, I just... You're so good at fixing things."

Cook. And. Everything.

Don't explode.

Don't explode.

Don't explode.

She wanted to scream, *I'm good at fixing things because I work in kitchens where everything goes wrong all the time.* And *What the fuck do you think I've been doing with my life for the last ten years?* And *Do you listen to* anything *I say during our Skype calls?*

Instead, she gritted her teeth and focused on how much she loved her family despite their problems and getting that family *out of her kitchen* before she lost her shit.

Before she could banish Quinn, a woman rushed into the kitchen—definitely one of the guests. She was in a gorgeous salmon dress with sparkling straps and heels. Her honey hair was up in a pretty clip. Her only jewelry a slim watch on her right wrist and big diamond on her left ring finger. The woman's gaze searched the staff. "Where is she?"

"Oh shit," Quinn said under her breath, nerves shaking her voice. "The fiancé."

Olivia reached down and squeezed Quinn's hand. "Pull yourself together and act like you are totally in control. You're the only one who knows different. They can't see inside you."

As if the woman had radar, she moved directly to Charlotte and crouched at her side. Curious, Olivia followed.

"I'm Eden," she said, her voice warm and compassionate but direct. She circled the woman's wrist with her fingers and glanced at her watch, taking a pulse while she said, "I'm a paramedic. An ambulance is on the way. Are you sure this is amniotic fluid and not urine?"

"Yes," Charlotte answered, her voice labored with pain. "Contractions..."

"How far along are you?" Eden released her wrist, assessed her face, then felt around her abdomen.

"Thirty weeks."

"That's good," she soothed Charlotte offering a smile before looking up and asking one of the servers standing nearby for a few wet washcloths. Then to another, she said, "Find me anything we can use to prop up her legs. We need her feet higher than her head."

Both servers scurried off, and Eden returned her gaze to Charlotte. The paramedic reminded Olivia a lot of herself and the way she ran a kitchen, which made her smile.

"Oooooh," Charlotte complained, "another one..."

Eden picked up one hand, their mother picked up the other, and Eden coached her through the contraction with breathing.

"Eden?" The deep male voice drew everyone's gaze around to an attractive, athletic man in a suit. "The ambulance is here."

"Great." She took washcloths from the server and pressed one to Charlotte's sweaty forehead, folded another over her neck, then smiled at Charlotte. "Okay, sweetie, you're going to do just fine."

Now that she was out of pain, Charlotte's emotions went haywire, and tears streamed from her eyes. "What about the baby?"

Eden's smile remained warm and authentic. If she was

faking it, Olivia couldn't tell. "Your baby has an excellent chance of being perfectly fine as well. Babies are born every day much younger than thirty weeks, and you couldn't find a better hospital in the country to handle it."

The ambulance personnel entered through a back door with equipment and a gurney, and Quinn shooed the kitchen staff out for the time being. While the emergency personnel unpacked, Eden continued to guide Charlotte through contractions.

On the way out the door, Charlotte called, "I'm so sorry about the party..."

Then she was whisked away, and Olivia was left standing in stunned silence with her mother, her sister, and two strangers whose engagement party for about three hundred people was on the edge of falling apart.

Eden had one hand on her hip, the fingers of the other hand against her lips as she stared out at the now-empty driveway. Her fiancé, Beckett, sighed and slid his arm around her shoulders.

And Olivia prepared for a meltdown of epic proportions.

She pulled in a breath and took a step toward them just as Eden looked up at Beckett and started laughing. That stopped Olivia's forward momentum.

"Oh my God," Eden said between giggles. "This could only happen to us."

Beckett was laughing too. He dragged her into his arms and gave her a squeeze. "You know the best part about this whole thing?"

Eden wrapped her arms around Beckett's waist. "That it will be something that we look back on in fifty years and still laugh about?"

"That," Beckett agreed, "and that we could order a shit-ton of pizzas, and not one person in that other room would complain."

That drew a fresh round of joy-filled laughter from Eden and made Olivia break out in a grin so big, her cheeks hurt. Eden looked up at Beckett and sighed. "God, I love you."

Beckett cupped Eden's face as if no one else existed, as if they weren't standing in a room with three virtual strangers, and looked at her with so much love, it made Olivia's heart ache. Made something deep inside her tug. Something she barely knew even existed. "Love you too, babe." He kissed her. "Love you too."

Quinn leaned close to Olivia. "I'm going to touch up my face before they turn around and see a raccoon."

When she cut a look at Quinn, she saw the smudged mascara from her tears. "I've got this."

Quinn nodded and slipped out a side door.

When Beckett and Eden turned out of their embrace, Olivia finished what she started and offered her hand, first to Eden, then Beckett with a big smile. She took the jovial route, one that obviously fit their personalities.

"Hi, I'm Olivia Essex, and I'm here to tell you no pizza delivery will be necessary. I'll be taking over for Charlotte. Don't worry about a thing. I've handled parties all over the world of every size. The food will be a smash, I promise."

Eden's hand pressed to her chest. Her eyes were wide with surprise. "Oh my God. Are you serious? Teresa," Eden glanced at Olivia's mother, "where have you been hiding this gem?"

Teresa put an arm around Olivia. "Paris, most recently. In fact, she's just off the plane for a visit. If Olivia says she can handle it, you can absolutely be assured it will be done right."

That was an interesting comment coming from someone who'd never taken Olivia's culinary ambitions seriously. At least as seriously as Olivia did.

Eden's gaze returned to Olivia, and her breath whooshed out. Then, in one step, she enveloped Olivia in a hug. Correction—a bear hug, the strength of which made Olivia laugh. "I can't thank you enough."

Warmth suffused her, and Olivia hugged Eden back. "You just did." She released her, accepted the handshake and gratitude Beckett offered, then teasingly shooed them toward their guests. "Get back to your party now. Nothing to see here."

Once the couple was gone, Olivia was besieged by hugs from her mother as the kitchen staff started wandering back in. When Quinn returned, Teresa hurried back to the party.

Olivia turned to Quinn and searched her face—still so eerily identical to her own even at twenty-eight—for signs of meltdown, but her sister had done a good patch job. "You okay?"

A smile quivered on her lips, but she nodded. "Just threw me, you know? She shook her head. "The stress... It's just been..."

"No more stress tonight. I have everything in here under control. You've done a fabulous job out front. All you have to do is hover and relax."

"Okay."

"Just show me your caterer's menu," Olivia said, "introduce me to the staff supervisor, and don't think about the kitchen again tonight."

Quinn released a heavy exhale and spontaneously threw her arms around Olivia's shoulders, hugging her tight. "Thank you. It's so good to have you home."

Olivia held her sister tight for a few seconds with a familiar pleasure-pain constricting her chest, then pushed her away and gave her a stern look. "Enough. Big night. Don't mess up your makeup again. We have to get to work."

Quinn found Charlotte's menu and showed Olivia the fridges and shelves where all the food supplies and equipment were stored. With one more round of assurances for Quinn, Olivia sent her sister out to handle the party.

"Finally." Olivia could breathe. "What a way to start my so-called vacation."

Tying an apron around her waist, Olivia skimmed the menu. Now she felt like she was navigating a language she understood. Pregnant women, babies, medical personnel, mushy romance, panic—gah! Olivia didn't do that. Any of that. The kitchen staff had turned their nervous eyes back on her, but even that felt good. Here, she knew what to expect. Here, the rules were, more or less, established. Here, she knew what she had to do to achieve success, and that was well within her means.

Hosting an NHL team filled with DC foodies might seem like a big deal to Quinn and their mom, but for Olivia, after cooking at embassies, catering to dignitaries, feeding royalty, and satisfying the finicky palates of billionaires, this was the equivalent of serving hot dogs to kindergarteners.

The only firsts for Olivia here would be doing it completely on the fly and in four-inch heels. But she loved a challenge, and she'd endured pain far worse than sore feet over the last decade. Pain that included bruises, scrapes, stitches, burns, broken bones, and a concussion. Not to mention the shattered heart that seemed to follow her everywhere.

Once she'd read through the menu and looked at her watch, she'd settled. She was grounded. Secure. Confident. Olivia was ready to push through her fatigue and grab the rush a job like this always delivered.

She turned her gaze on the staff supervisor, a stately black man in his forties with a handsome face and a square jaw, and smiled. This in-charge thing was a rush. She was usually the sous chef or the kitchen manager. Time to step up. And Olivia was more than ready.

"Can you bring me the sous chefs, Marcus?" she asked. "We're going to be making a few menu changes."

The man's mouth dropped open. His eyes widened. "Changes? *Now?*"

Olivia laughed softly. She loved to surprise people by being something they didn't expect. Maybe she'd even surprise her mother and sister tonight. Maybe, once they saw what her life overseas had really been about all these years, their attitude toward her work and her life would change.

Everything happens for a reason, baby. Embrace it.

Her father's words softened her smile and gave her strength.

"Yes, Marcus," she told him, moving to the fridge to pull ingredients for the appetizers from the shelves. "Definitely changes. Definitely now."

3

Four nonstop, exhausting hours later, Olivia leaned against the metal railing of a small balcony off the prep area beyond the kitchen. She sighed and sipped the last of the wine one of the servers had brought her from the dining room and slipped off her heels to stretch her aching feet.

The last round of desserts was being served, which meant Olivia was officially done. Done cooking, done supervising, done fussing, done stressing.

What a night. Talk about putting out fires...

She'd finally banned Quinn from the kitchen after several terror-stricken visits over Olivia's menu changes. By the time Quinn had defied the ban and sought Olivia out again, the second round of entrées had been served. Her sister could have been wearing springs on her feet the way she bounced in and hugged Olivia, squealing with excitement over the success of the evening, and bounced out again.

Instead of bringing Olivia joy, this evening with Quinn and her mother had left her restless and unsatisfied. Even annoyed. Professionally, she felt great. Confident, creative, innovative, powerful, in control. She'd worked her entire adult life in this industry and could count only a handful of people she knew who could pull off what she'd done tonight with the ease and calm and quality with which she'd done it. That spoke more to her ability to manage staff and stress than it did her culinary expertise. There were many talented chefs. But, in Olivia's experience, never enough talented chefs others could work with effectively.

Personally... Personally she felt... She wasn't sure what to call this nagging feeling in the pit of her stomach. Unsatisfied? Lost? Lonely? Empty? Depressed? She'd felt it before. Felt it often. Usually in the wake of an intense or draining event when she didn't have the strength to hold up her walls.

Her quick fix of choice was sex with the hottest guy available in the moment. That usually filled the hollow feeling, at least temporarily. Sex was the fastest, easiest, most enjoyable escape without any of the ugly aftereffects of drugs or alcohol. Which had her mind drifting toward Tate. Tate and his mountain of muscle. Tate and his swaggering smile. Tate and those dark eyes that echoed the same ache she felt now.

Movement behind her drew her gaze as her mother stepped out onto the balcony.

"Everything okay?" Olivia asked. Her shift in thought made her fatigue register.

"Okay? Oh my God, Livvy. I don't even have words. The food... What you did here tonight..."

Her mother's pretty face crumpled much the way Quinn's had hours ago.

"*Oh mon Dieu.* Don't you start." Olivia turned to her mother and hugged her. "We're all tired. Take Quinn home, and you two get some rest. Tomorrow, we'll start fresh and catch up, okay?"

Her mother pulled back. "Aren't you coming? We'll wait for you."

"I'm pretty wound up." She shook her head at the worry in

her mother's face. "It's just the rush of the work. I need to relax, let the adrenaline drain before I'll be able to sleep."

"Honey, you're going to get sick."

"I'll catch up on sleep over the next couple of days. Really, it works for me."

"Where are you going to go?"

"You remember my friend Julie from high school?"

"From the culinary program?"

Olivia nodded. "She's got her own tapas bar on 14th Street. I'm going to Metro over and hang with her awhile."

Her mother stroked a hand over her hair. The familiar gesture infused warmth into that empty space inside her. But not enough to fill it. Too bad the only man who'd interested her tonight was probably long gone by now.

"Are you sure?" her mother asked. "I can make you chocolate milk. We can curl up on the sofa."

Olivia laughed. She needed a little more of a transition between France and home before she was ready to turn back into a daughter. "I will absolutely take you up on that tomorrow night." She clasped her hand around her mother's. "And I really want to hear about the company. Quinn said you guys had a rough year."

"Oh, don't you worry about that." She squeezed Olivia's hand. "I want you to enjoy your time home."

"I would enjoy hearing about the company."

"Absolutely, honey. And I can't wait to hear all about where you learned to do all the fancy things you did tonight. Are you sure you even need school? Maybe you ought to think about just coming home and opening up a catering business." Her eyes twinkled. "Wouldn't that be fun? You, me, and Quinn, working together?"

"*Ah, la vache, moman.*" She rubbed her eyes as a pained laugh escaped. *Kill. Me. Now.*

Neither her mother nor Quinn had ever bothered to learn

any French. The first few years, it had annoyed Olivia. It felt like one more way they rejected her life. But in more recent years, she was grateful to be able to say things out loud that they wouldn't understand.

Her mother pressed a kiss to Olivia's forehead. "Don't stay out too late. It's so good to have you home, baby girl."

Baby girl. The phrase twisted a place deep in her heart. Her mother had never used it until her father died. Until her father couldn't call her his baby girl anymore. In a lot of ways, Olivia wished her mother had let it go with him. It felt like a constant reminder of his loss.

Merde, she needed something stronger than wine tonight.

With more half promises, she said good-bye to her mom and looked out over the city again, draining her wine. More good-byes traveled on the warm air from the front of the building. Car doors closed, engines faded into the distance. She sighed, rested her elbow on the rail and her chin in her hand.

Christ, she was *so* lonely. At least back home, she had friends she could call on any time of day or night to hang out with. A dozen different men she could hook up with for a few hours of distraction. But even that thought didn't do much for her tonight.

At least not until she put Tate into the role of that man. Then her body perked up and got all kinds of interested.

She smiled and licked the taste of wine from her lips. He'd made an impression so quickly. That didn't happen very often anymore. After so many years in so many places, Olivia felt like she'd met every kind of man in every circumstance. Very little surprised her now. Very little impressed her now.

Something about Tate... Definitely his eyes. He was... hungry. Almost like a starving child. So eager to please, yet so guarded, so careful. Almost timid. All of which stirred myriad contradictions in Olivia's mind.

He was just so...interesting.

She heaved a sigh and let her mind clear. She was too tired
to try to puzzle out a stranger tonight. That was a perfect knot
to untangle during a long train ride through the Alps, not a
quick Metro ride across the city.

Olivia would love to see Julie. Her mind was still spinning,
but her body was dead beat. She closed her eyes, wishing she
were in New York, where she could find an all-night masseuse,
but as she drifted with that thought, she wondered where Tate
was right now. Wondered which beautiful woman at the party
had snagged him tonight after Olivia had disappeared into the
kitchen. Maybe he was undressing her. Running those big,
warm hands of his over her curves, his soft lips following in
their wake...

Olivia sighed, long and deep. "What a lucky girl..."

"Who's a lucky girl?"

The low voice startled her eyes open. The smooth, rough
timbre of Tate's voice registered and rippled along her spine.

Olivia swiveled, putting the railing at her back for support.

In one hand, Tate held a glass of wine. In the other, a closed
folding chair. He'd lost the blazer and the tie, unfastened a
couple of shirt buttons, and rolled up his shirtsleeves.

Holy. Hell. The man filled out his clothes like every inch had
been tailored just for him. His stance was easy and comfortable. He exuded confidence. Yet there was still a wounded air
to him.

"Well, hi," she said, smiling. "I was just thinking about
you."

"That's nice to hear. But...what was the 'lucky girl' about?"

She laughed, and it came out flirtier—and dirtier—than
she'd intended. "Um..."

A smile kicked up one side of his mouth. He leaned his
weight into one hip and propped his shoulder against the
doorframe.

The heat those simple moves whipped through Olivia's

belly was out of proportion to her experience with men. He simply shouldn't be able to look so sexy, so easily.

"Come on," he nudged, his voice soft. "I can take it."

"I didn't come out looking for you, because I was sure you'd be gone," Olivia said. "I haven't seen so many stunning women together at one time since I catered an event for the winners of the women's beach volleyball competition at the Olympics in Rio de Janeiro."

Tate's smile widened and his posture relaxed a little more. "Really."

"They don't call them Brazilian bombshells for nothin'."

He laughed, and Olivia reaped great pleasure as the shadow in his eyes lightened. "Good to know." He shook his head. "How did we get on that subject?"

"Me," she said with a smile, "thinking you would have been swept away by one of those bombshells in the other room within thirty seconds of my disappearance into the kitchen. Figured some smart girl would have you locked in her bedroom by now, all those fancy clothes stripped away, checking out the real you with her..."

Olivia caught herself before anything *completely* shocking spilled from her mouth. "Oops." She grinned at Tate's frying-pan-to-the-head stare. "I forgot...Americans work a little differently. My family always says I'm way too...forward...fresh off the plane."

Tate gave his head a shake and laughed. "Americans." He stepped onto the balcony and unfolded the chair. "That sounds strange coming from someone who is so obviously American. But the rest of it...the rest of it was..." He lifted his gaze to hers, paused a second, then shook his head wearing a puzzled little smile. "Exactly what I'd like to be doing. With you."

Excitement bubbled up out of nowhere, filling Olivia with joy, and she laughed. "Hell, you just made my whole night."

He still looked a little shell-shocked and didn't make any

move toward her, so she forced her excitement to a simmer. She should really let the guy move at his own pace. He'd been surrounded all night by all his hockey buddies in a very testosterone-ladin crowd. He might not like her heavy-handed skip-the-foreplay-let's-just-fuck style.

If he took too long to warm up, she'd nudge him.

He offered her the wine and gestured to the chair. "I figured you could probably use these after all the work it had to take to put that kind of food on those tables tonight. I'm not the only one who was blown away. It's all anyone could talk about all night, and in a room full of hockey enthusiasts, that's saying something. Doing it all without warning after flying in from Paris is nothing short of miraculous. I mean, maybe not to your fellow chefs back in France, but definitely to everyone here tonight. And I have to tell you, there were some damned high achievers filling that room. Not an easy crowd to impress."

Olivia's guts jumbled. All her thoughts of sex faded into the background. And now she was the one standing there with the frying-pan-to-the-head stare.

She was used to compliments on her looks, used to being wanted sexually by men. And yes, her culinary skills were praised...occasionally. Mostly in a you-got-the-job-done-well sort of way. But she wasn't used to being *seen* by men. Very few men saw Olivia for her talent. Very few people appreciated her skill. Yet Tate had just done both, so succinctly, so smoothly, so effortlessly, it humbled her. This man who owed her nothing, had validated her in a way she felt all the way to the bone. In a way even her own family had never appreciated.

"Thank you," she said, setting her empty glass on a small side table. She stepped forward to take the full one in his hand. "This is incredibly thoughtful."

His grin turned lopsided again. "I've spent my share of too many hours in skates. They may not be high heels, but..." He shrugged. "Your legs and feet can't be feeling too great right now."

Oh.

Wow.

She'd never imagined such minor considerations could make her want a man so badly. But those sexual urges were back—with a wild vengeance. Now she didn't just want him. She *had to* have him.

Olivia stepped toward him instead of turning toward the chair. Before she could reach out to touch him, Tate scooped an arm around her waist and pulled her close. Olivia sucked a breath of surprise and held the wine away from her to keep it from spilling. He'd surprised her—again.

She laughed at the surge of excitement rushing her veins. Then all his muscle registered. His sheer size and strength. His heat penetrated her dress and slid along her skin. And, God, his scent. He smelled like a mix of sandalwood, citrus, spice.

And every lick of humor melted into desire.

"Give me a little time." His quiet voice tingled over her skin and made her eyes roll back in her head. Made her sex clench. "I've been out of the game awhile. I'm...still getting the feel of things."

Her eyes fluttered open. All her blood had fled south, and her brain wasn't working. "Out of the game?"

"Divorced."

She nodded. "How long?"

"A year."

He dipped his head and nuzzled her temple, then kissed her there. Shivers skated across her skin, and desire squeezed her stomach. She stroked her hands up his chest, over his shoulders, loving all the muscle beneath the fabric.

"Bad?" she asked.

"Not fun." He exhaled. "And not something I ever expected to go through."

Oh... Her heart broke a little. And she understood that look she'd seen in his eyes earlier. She met his gaze directly. "Do you still love her?"

"No." His answer came immediately. With certainty. As if he'd given it a lot of thought. "I just haven't been tempted back into the game." His lips skimmed her forehead. "Until now."

Another wave of warmth surged inside her. She didn't realize how long it had been since she'd felt special until now. Relationships between men and women were so different in Europe. So fluid. So nonrestrictive. Only now, in this moment, did she realize that style of relating to men also left her feeling expendable. Disposable.

She tilted her head a little more to meet his eyes. "It doesn't have to be a game."

His arm loosened, and he lowered into the chair, then eased her to his lap sideways, his arms circling her waist, supporting her in a comfortable embrace. "No?"

"No." She leaned over to set her wine down on the table, then angled toward him. Sliding one arm around his neck, she rested the other palm against his chest. Then she smiled. "How long do you think you need? I'm going to be very European and tell you I'm ready when you are."

Surprise leapt in his eyes. Along with heat. His arms tightened around her. His gaze lowered to her mouth, and he murmured, "Never thought I'd forget how to do this."

She'd never imagined she'd find sexual insecurity a turn-on. But he was burning her up.

"I like the way I feel right here," she told him.

He relaxed and smiled. His lids dipped. "I like the way you feel too."

"See. No games. Just you and me, liking the way we feel together." She stroked his face and soaked in every handsome angle, feeling a little like she'd won the hunk lottery. "That's all."

Silence fell, and they settled into comfortable togetherness. One Olivia could get lost in. She loved the feel of his eyes on her. Loved the feel of his thick, hard thighs beneath hers. The way their heat soaked all along her backside. Between her legs. She was ready to sink into this man, right here, right now, and let him help her forget everything but him.

Unfortunately, they weren't alone. Which made her think of her mom and sister. And she wondered why he hadn't mentioned them. "Did you meet my family tonight?"

His eyes jumped up from the neckline of her dress. "Just your mom. Judging by how everyone was raving about the party, I imagine they're pulling in a lot of work."

She beamed at him. "Oh, that's awesome."

He lifted a hand to her face and cupped her cheek, another smile tilting his lips. "*You're* awesome."

Smiling, she relaxed against him, the collar of his shirt curled into her fingers. "That's so great. This is a competitive business. They needed a score."

"Mmm—hmm..." His thumb caressed her cheek, his eyes following its path, and the hunger there helped Olivia translate that hum into *Mmm-hmm, I need one too.*

His stubble seemed heavier now than when she'd first met him, and kept drawing her gaze to his lips. She knew from their quick kiss that his lips were soft. She licked her own, imagining how his would feel between her legs. Heat burst between her thighs, and she squirmed in his lap. Her hip bumped a prominent erection, releasing a surge of lust.

"Tate—"

"So, you're a chef."

They spoke at the same time, and Olivia realized her *"unzip your pants"* was way out of line with his *"Let's keep talking."*

"Sort of," she answered, trying to realign her thoughts when her body was dying to get this man naked and horizontal. For an instant, she wondered what he would do if she told him that, and a little smile curled her lips.

"Sort of?" he asked.

When he lifted a brow, she pulled her mind from the gutter. At least enough to hold a conversation. "I've been cooking for years, but I'm starting culinary school in a month. When I graduate, I'll—officially—be a chef."

"Do you just love to cook? Is that how you got started?"

"I've been cooking since I was a kid. My dad had me in the kitchen as soon as I could stand. It was a hobby we shared. When I first moved overseas after high school, I cooked American food in hostels and sold it to visitors. Word got out and soon I was selling to Americans living in whatever country or town I was in at the time. Along the way, I learned about local customs and cuisine." She shrugged. "It wasn't the least bit glamorous back then, and most of the time, it still isn't, but it's taken me on a lot of amazing adventures."

"That sounds fascinating. I hope I'll get a chance to hear about it while you're here."

She smiled. "If you're just saying that to get me into bed, everything you've said after 'Hi, I'm Tate' has been wasted."

It took him a few seconds, but the smile that finally broke out across his face rocked Olivia's world. Brooding, he was handsome as sin, but smiling, flashing a mouthful of straight, white teeth, his dark eyes sparkling, a damn dimple in his left cheek, the man was heart-stopping. His laugh was rich and smooth, and when he combed his fingers into her hair, Olivia was so blown away by the man, she was absolutely certain she'd never been so charmed in her life.

His laughter faded, but he was still smiling when he said, "You had me at 'a little French anything cures jetlag.'"

"Then why the hell are we still sitting here?"

His expression sobered, his fingers flexed and clenched in her hair, and his gaze turned hot and serious. The array of emotion he showed on his face made her eager to find out if it transferred to the bedroom. She hadn't had a multidimensional lover in...way too long.

She stroked the backs of her fingers over his stubble and found it softer than she'd expected.

"Want me to shave?" His question brought her gaze up. Such a simple question. And so direct. Yet so incredibly intimate, it tightened her throat.

"Would you?"

"Hell yes. I'll do anything you want.

"No." Her smile deepened. She shook her head, licked her lip, then dragged it between her teeth. She met his gaze and lowered her voice. "There's a good reason for the phrase 'bearded for her pleasure.' I want to feel it between my legs."

His jaw loosened, and his eyes glazed over. But in the next second, he went all warrior, with chiseled features, black eyes, and a voice from *Braveheart*. "Tell me you don't have a boyfriend back in Paris."

Damn, this guy just kept serving up curve balls. She didn't know one man in all of Europe who would give a shit at this point. A little laugh escaped her, and she feathered her fingers through the hair at his temple. "I don't—"

His hand slid all the way around her head and pulled her in, pressing his mouth to hers and turning her words into a hum of pleasure. "Mmm..."

The kiss ended as abruptly as it had begun, but cool air barely had time to whisper over her lips before he tilted his head and returned with more pressure, more demand, and the warm stroke of his tongue over her lips.

A thrill raced down Olivia's spine. She opened to him, and on the next hot, hungry sweep of his tongue, her mouth erupted with sensation. Her chest inflated with the excitement of tasting a new man. Her sex tingled with the promise of pleasure. He was a luscious mix of heat and need—exactly what Olivia needed.

She sighed and dropped her head back. Tate wasted no time taking over. He might not have been in the game for a while, but he certainly still knew how to play. His strong arms pulled her close, until her breasts rubbed his chest. One big hand cupped her head, holding her still for the pressure of his mouth. The other slid over her hip around her ass, and pulled her against the swell between his legs. His immediate, hot, aggressive show of passion surprised her—yet again. And damn, this man could kiss.

He was hungry and insistent. Serious and intent. A little dark. A little edgy.

Tate was starved.

And she wanted to be the woman who fed him all night and left him completely satisfied and sleeping like a baby.

But she wasn't near as patient as he seemed to be. She pulled out of the kiss and drew quick, shallow breaths. Tate lowered his lips to her neck and groaned, then kissed a path to her shoulder.

"I don't want to be too forward," she said, trying to catch her breath, "but to tell you the truth, I just don't know how else to be."

He lifted his head and looked into her eyes. His were heavy lidded and hot. "Just be you."

Thank God. She licked her lips. "How close do you live?"

A split-second smile fluttered over his lips. "Ten minutes. Did you drive here?"

"Took Metro." She pulled her lower lip between her teeth. "Told my mom I was going to visit a friend, not to wait up."

He lifted a brow. "Thought you said you were sure I'd be gone."

"Hey." She gave him a look laced with fake attitude. "I have friends."

He laughed, then kissed her again, and all the humor instantly evaporated in the sweltering heat. The slide of his mouth, the stroke of his tongue, the way he moved against her... This man was way better than any alcohol, any drug.

He broke the kiss, dragging in air and breathing out, "Holy fuck. Your mouth is wicked."

"Oh-ho..." She laughed the word. "Just you wait until you see exactly what I can do with this mouth."

He groaned, his lids fluttered closed, and his fingers clenched in her dress. "When are you done here?"

"Now," she said. When his eyes opened again, she continued, "I'm done now. This isn't my gig. The kitchen staff can clean up. Are you close to a Metro line?"

"Two blocks. Why?"

"So I can take it home."

"I'll drive you ho—"

She pressed her fingers to his lips and shook her head. That whole waking-up-together-morning after-driving-her-home thing...got really messy, really fast. She'd learned that young. "I don't want messy," she said, praying she didn't hurt his feelings. "I just want you."

He exhaled and held her gaze. When she lowered her hand, he asked, "Do you feel okay driving with me? I mean, now? To my place?"

"Why?" He didn't seem drunk. She'd developed an eye for that. "How much have you been drinking?"

"I stopped drinking hours ago. I meant safe. We don't know each other."

"Oh." She grinned. Laughed. Stroked his cheek. "I moved to Europe by myself when I was eighteen. Lived hostel to hostel for years. Learned Krav Maga on the streets of the countries where it was born. The question, Mr. Big Bad Hot Hockey Star, is do *you* feel safe with *me*?"

4

Tate was having a hard time focusing on the road with Olivia rubbing on him like a cat in the front seat of his truck.

She was twisted toward him with her mouth on his neck, her right thigh draped over the console and her hand under his shirt, roaming his skin. His mind kept jumping ahead—to getting her home and how he should handle that. It felt like forever since he'd treaded these waters, and sex etiquette changed so fast nowadays. She was so damn young and hot, he was feeling more on the old and slow side then he'd ever imagined.

Should he take it slow or fast? Should he be rough or gentle? Should he ask her what she liked or just go for it until she told him she wanted something else?

Every question tightened the muscles along his shoulders. His mind kept darting to his teammates and their locker room talk. If even half of it was true, those young guys did some nasty shit in the bedroom. Did Olivia expect that? Did Tate even want to go there? Maybe. With the right woman...

Olivia scraped his earlobe between her teeth. Chills ran down his neck and across his shoulder, and Tate shivered.

"What's your last name?" she asked, soft and sexy.

"Donovan." His voice sounded like sandpaper.

"Donovan, what's on your mind? I see wheels turning behind those sexy eyes, and if you keep clenching your teeth like this," she massaged his jaw in small circles, making Tate realize how sore he was right there, "you're going to need TMJ surgery in a few years."

She paused, pulled back, and looked at him, waiting. He felt the warmth of her stare on his face. When he didn't answer right away, her fingers combed through the hair on the side of his head again, her nails gently scraping his scalp. "If you change your mind at any point, I'm not going to be pissed. I know how bitchy some women can get, but I'm not—"

For the first time since they'd started the drive, Tate pulled his hand from the steering wheel and gripped her thigh. He cut a quick look at her before returning his gaze to the road. "I'm not changing my mind. I'm trying to remember my moves."

She laughed, the sound light and amused as she dropped her forehead against his shoulder and rolled it side to side. "Oh, Tate." She lifted her head. "You are so...God, I don't know how to explain it. You're just so...refreshing seems like a strange word, but it's true. You're so different, so honest. I just love it. I want to *eat you up.*"

The last three words could have been taken in any number of ways. But her deep, raspy tone made it clear she was thinking of the phrase with more hunger than affection. She confirmed that assumption after he put the truck into Park, when she pressed a hand against the opposite side of his face, pulled him toward her, and leaned in to kiss him.

He moaned into her mouth, groped for the seat belt release, and sprung himself. Then he turned, took her face in both hands, and kissed her. Hard and deep.

God, he could get so lost in this woman. *Hoped* he could *let* himself get lost in this woman. After what he'd been through, Olivia felt like fucking heaven. So he shut down that nagging good-boy corner of his mind. He tucked away all his misgivings over bringing home a woman he barely knew for the sole purpose of sex, and let his own needs roll to the foreground for a change.

And they roared in, taking over, like fire eating oxygen.

Next thing he knew, he had Olivia on his lap, his hands sliding up her thighs, pushing her dress over her hips. She was warm and smooth and toned. Their tongues spiraled as his hands curved over her ass.

Tate broke the kiss to pull in air. "Jesus Christ."

Olivia's hands were already working his belt open, yanking his shirttail from his waistband. Then her hands were on his skin, and *fuck*, he couldn't think.

"Olivia..." He grabbed her hands, squeezing them tight, more to keep his own hands still than to halt her movement. Because he wanted to feel her hands on him. Wanted to feel her mouth on him. Wanted—so badly—to feel her pussy around him. "God *damn*."

She made an impatient whimpering sound, dipped her head, and kissed him, hot and hungry. "Want you," she said between licks and kisses. "Can't wait... This is *insane*..."

Think, Tate.

Think.

"Let's..." he said, breathing hard. "Let's...slow down..."

That sexy sound came again, this time against his throat, where her teeth and tongue created tingles along his skin and opened a faucet of lust straight to his groin.

"Right..." she breathed. "Right..." She pulled back, and her hair fell into her eyes. "You make me crazy, Donovan."

"And you make me feel so fuckin' *alive*." He brushed her

hair aside and framed her face. "The only time I feel this electrified is on the ice, during a game."

Her smile softened. "That has to be the sweetest thing any man has said to me in...God...years."

He couldn't even fathom how that was possible. She had to have men all over her in Europe.

Chest to chest, arms wrapped around his neck, she leaned close and whispered into his ear, "Now take me inside where I can thank you properly." She bit his earlobe, shooting a sting down his neck, followed by the warm stroke of her tongue. "Or...not so properly. Which do you prefer?"

He closed his eyes, let his hands slide down her body, gripped her hips to hold her still while he gave in to the urge to rock against her. Pleasure spilled between his legs, and he gritted his teeth on a growl at the same time Olivia arched and echoed his pleasure. The synchronicity was electric.

When her lashes fluttered open and her pretty blue eyes landed on his again, he said, "I'll take everything you've got, baby."

He pushed the door open, and helped her to the ground before following. He looked down at the disarray of his clothes, and laughed.

Grinning, Olivia straightened the tail of his now-untucked shirt. She cocked her head and surveyed him with a look that made him grin like an idiot.

"Maybe just one last little fix right..." She leaned in, reaching for his head, but instead of fixing a few stray hairs, her weight shifted and she fell into him, pushing all ten fingers into his hair, laughing. With her face pressed to his neck, she murmured, "Yeah, right there. *Perfect*."

Her breath tingled against his neck. Her sweetness warmed his heart. And for the first time in way too long, he felt full. Content. Happy. She felt so goddamned perfect, it hurt. "Where the fuck have you been all my life?"

"Mmmm." She stepped away, then walked backward while Tate steered her toward his townhouse. "You'd have to name the year. I'm pretty nomadic."

"Okay...where were you in..." He named a year as she turned out of his path and fell into step beside him. He swung an arm around her shoulders.

"I was a junior in high school," she said, threading her fingers with his where they lay over her shoulder, then wrapped her other arm around his waist.

She was so loose, so easy, so relaxed. So comfortable in her own skin. She didn't worry about her clothes, her hair, her makeup. Didn't seem nervous about the night ahead. Tate was both mystified and envious.

"You?" she asked.

"First year of my minor career."

"How old were you?"

"Twenty."

"So you're about thirty? Thirty-one?"

"Thirty-one," he said, pushing away the uncomfortable thoughts his age always brought. How much further along in his personal life he thought he'd be by now. "What about..."

He named his first year in the NHL.

"Umm..." She had her eyes rolled to the sky as they walked through the gardens. "Must have been Yugoslav...no, that was the summer before..." She pressed a finger to her lips. "Cairo? No, no." She sighed. "I think I was somewhere in the Middle East. I have it all in a travel diary."

"Fascinating." He shook his head, again wishing they had more than two weeks to get to know each other.

But they weren't on a date. As they took the path to his front door, Tate reminded himself they were here to fuck, not talk. And as he climbed the stairs with her by his side, that was beginning to bother him more and more. Because he was beginning to like her more and more. He didn't know how the other guys did it—night after night. Woman after woman.

On the porch, he paused, leaned against the railing, and drew her into his arms. She came to him exactly the way he'd already come to expect, easily, fluidly, happily. She wound her arms around his waist, and smiled up at him. Tate brushed a strand of hair off her forehead and ran his knuckles down her cheek.

He just wasn't built for one-night hookups. And it seriously sucked to find that out here, now, with this woman, because he wasn't about to let her go, and he sure as shit couldn't keep her.

"First thing tomorrow," he said with a smile, "I'm sending that caterer the biggest damn bunch of flowers I can buy. Hell, I'm going to fill her damn hospital room *and* the nursery with flowers."

One of Olivia's golden brows rose with a little shake of her head. "Why?"

"Because keeping you in the kitchen also kept you away from the party, where there were dozens of guys who would have been on you in a hot second."

She chuckled low in her throat, her humor growing as the idea gelled.

"I'm serious." He lifted the hand holding his keys and searched for the one to the front door, then pushed off the railing. "You don't know my teammates. And, baby, you could have had your pick."

Olivia pushed Tate back against the railing, holding him there with a hand at his chest. She looked up at him with a no-fucking-around expression he hadn't seen yet. "I *got* my pick. I *always* get my pick. I *never* settle, Tate."

Her voice was compassionate but firm. Her gaze steady and serious. "So don't think for a second you were a fluke or a second choice or consolation to me being stuck in the kitchen. I had you picked before I ever got pulled away. I'll always choose to go home alone over going home with someone I'm not one hundred and fifty percent into just to be with someone. I'm not a woman who needs a man. I'm not a woman who settles for anything but exactly what I want. I'm here because I want you, Tate, not because I couldn't have someone else."

He felt something inside his chest melt. Felt his rough edges softening. Olivia never looked away. Never hedged. Never backpedaled.

"You are something really special," he said. "I know we just met, but…"

He shook his head.

Her hand relaxed on his chest, and she eased closer with an almost imperceptible nod of agreement. "But sometimes, you just know when you've found someone who clicks."

He lowered his lips to hers. Her tongue stroked his bottom lip, then dipped into his mouth and swirled lazily, sensually. But the heat rose, and in seconds, their sexy kiss had turned erotic and edgy again. The blood that had temporarily returned to his brain was back in Tate's pants. And there was a new intimacy between them that fueled the need.

Forcing himself to break the kiss, Tate had to clear his head with a shake to get the key into the lock. And with Olivia at his back, her hands all over him, Tate still struggled. The man with finesse and grace and lightning moves under pressure couldn't keep his hands from shaking while a woman he barely knew grabbed his ass with one hand and groped his package with the other.

By the time he pushed the door open, he was hard and throbbing again. He grabbed Olivia's wrist and pulled her hand off his cock, then had to take two full breaths before his vision cleared. When he focused, Olivia stood in front of him. She curled her hand into the front of his shirt and pulled him into the house.

5

W hat Olivia had told Tate was true: She had never been indiscriminate in choosing lovers. Still, she'd been with a lot of men. She'd always had an open soul and enjoyed sharing the pleasures of sex with another open soul. And Europe was chock-full of open souls, because Europeans were raised with an entirely different outlook on sex than Americans. Far more casual. Far more prevalent. Easy-come, easy-go. No commitment. No guilt.

Her personal issues fit in well with that model. If she didn't love, she couldn't lose. If she didn't trust, she couldn't be betrayed. And her nomadic lifestyle kept everything in sync.

Olivia was happy to hold on to her fluid, no-drama romances. She was proud of her sexual independence. Loved the way sex never interfered with her life or her goals. Liked the way she controlled whether or not a man came into her life and for how long, not the other way around.

Now, she was allowing Tate into her life, and while she was doing her damnedest not to look desperate, when the door closed and he didn't slam her up against the wall and fuck her right there, she knew she had to take action.

Olivia gripped the lapels of his blazer and pushed Tate back against the closed front door, wrapped a hand around the back of his neck, and lifted on her toes as she pulled his head down to bring their mouths together.

His hands stroked down her sides, up her back, down her spine and finally—finally covered her ass—pulling her hips into his. His erection indented her lower belly, and need surged. Olivia moaned, circling her arms back and around his neck.

Tate's hot breath bathed her skin on a similar sound. "Can you tell me what you like?" he asked, breathless. "What you want? I'll do anything...just tell me how you like it..."

Olivia pushed back, caught between frustration, anger, and heartbreak. What the hell had his ex done to turn a man so genuine into someone who didn't even know who he was anymore? How had she turned a man, who—judging by his career—had once had such high self-confidence and self-esteem into someone who needed to be told how to please a woman?

"What do *you* want, Tate?" she asked. "This isn't just about me." She stroked his face, slipped her hands down his chest, belly, then unfastened his pants. "I want whatever we find together as our perfect rhythm. I want the real Tate, when he's not worried about what someone else will think or what he should or shouldn't do. There are no judgments here, between you and me." She snuck her fingers under the waistband of his boxer briefs. "I want you to go after what you want, as hard as you want it. I assume that's how you play hockey."

To give him a nudge, she held his gaze and pushed her hand beneath the soft cotton of his briefs and took his thick cock into her palm. God she loved big cock's, she couldn't lie. Tate's eyes fluttered closed, his mouth dropped open on a sound of surprise and pleasure, and his head dropped back, hitting the door.

Olivia would have laughed, but Tate wasn't laughing. His handsome face was awash in pleasure. Intense pleasure. And, *God*, he was beautiful.

With one hand wrapped around his forearm for balance, she dropped into a crouch, and by the time she rolled to her knees, his eyes were open and disoriented. That worked for Olivia. He certainly didn't need to be coherent for what she had planned.

"Olivia...?"

"Oh, that voice." She moved his clothes aside, stroked him, and licked her lips. "I love the way you say my name."

He stroked a hand over her hair. "Oliv—"

She took the head of his cock between her lips, and the rest of her name came out of his mouth as a deep moan. His fingers closed in her hair, and his body jerked. A thrill raced through Olivia.

When she lifted her gaze, she found his eyes barely cracked, sparkling with fiery lust.

She pulled him from her mouth, murmured, "I already feel you at the back of my throat," and plunged him deep.

Tate bowed against the door, pushing him even deeper. "Ah, fuck, fuck, fuck..."

His hand twisted in her hair, and the sting sang across her scalp, giving her a dark thrill. "*Olivia...*"

He bent at the waist, put his mouth at her ear, and closed his hands around her biceps. "So fuckin' good... *So* good... Gotta—"

Before he could say "stop" and use that brute strength of his to pull away, she added suction and watched the big badass hockey player melt like butter.

He felt beautiful in her mouth. Thick and hot and smooth. He tasted clean. Smelled spicy and musky. And the power to make a man like this lose control created an unbeatable thrill.

When he was almost out of her mouth, she gave the head of

his cock a little extra attention until he was growling through his teeth, then pulled back, smiled up at him, and said, "This is me, going after what I want."

And she refocused on his thick, hard cock.

Tate's hands tightened on her arms, and he hauled her to her feet. Just lifted her like she weighed nothing. Like it took no effort. Before her mind could comprehend what was happening, Tate pivoted, banged her against a wall, and held her there at arm's length. He lowered his head, breathing fast to catch his breath.

"I don't want to scare you..." he said, voice rough and raspy. "I don't want to hurt you... And the way I want you is..." He shook his head and kept his eyes on the floor. "Vicious."

Lust surged through Olivia. Lust deeper and darker than anything she'd experienced before. There were things about Tate that tugged at something inside her. Something desperate that she'd never looked too closely at before. In Tate, she almost sensed a kindred lost spirit looking for both connection and expression.

She clenched her hands. "Show me. Show me how you want me. You don't scare me, and I won't let you hurt me. I want to taste that kind of passion, Tate. I want it bad."

"*Fuck.*" He bit out the word, lifted his head, and picked her up nearly at the same time.

Olivia grabbed his blazer for something to hang onto as he turned a corner, released her with one arm, and bent to make a wide, sweeping motion with his arm. Something crashed to the floor. Lights from the gardens filtered in through big windows. She'd just figured out they were in room off the kitchen when Tate dropped her butt on a table, hooked both his arms around her legs and pulled them wide, then dropped to his knees.

"Tate—"

He shoved handfuls of her dress up her thighs and covered her pussy with his mouth, panties still in place. The heat and pressure of his mouth made Olivia forget what she was going to say. His tongue wet the silk and teased, while his hands worked the fabric over her hips, down her legs and finally off. Then he hooked both thighs again and covered her with his mouth.

The contact and heat made Olivia gasp. His entire mouth moved over her. Ate and licked and sucked. Olivia's eyes crossed. She reached out and gripped the side of the table. Her back arched. Her pelvis rocked. Moans and disjointed words and pleas and curses rolled out of her. He never paused, never slowed, never gave her time to recover or even think. Just kept eating and eating and eating like he'd never get enough.

"Ho-ho-holy *fuck*..." Everything between her knees and her shoulders was on fire, bulging, aching, on the edge of implosion. "Tate... God... Fuck... *Yes, yes, yes...*"

She reached down and fisted his hair. Tate met her eyes, his dark and drunk. He released her thigh, slid his hand down her arm, covered hers and threaded their fingers. Then he held her gaze as he ruthlessly, mercilessly drove her straight over a cliff.

"*Fuck...*" She seized with ecstasy. Back arched, head thrown back, her mind went completely blank, blissfully floating in euphoria for those few long moments while pleasure shook her to the core. Shivered through her limbs. Rocked her foundation. And left her weak and panting.

Tate rested her thighs on his shoulders. "You blow my mind."

She blew *his* mind? Olivia rolled her head to look at him, but before her tired eyes could focus, sensation and pressure erupted between her legs again.

"Oh..." She groaned as he slid his fingers inside her, slow and deep, and she lifted into the pressure. "Mmmm, yeeeeees..."

Then he moved inside her, and whatever he did made pleasure sing through her pussy and contract the muscles around her spine. She arched against the tables hard surface, while the things he did with his hands made her eyes roll back in her head, her toes curl, her mouth water, and her body writhe.

He stood between her legs, watching the sight of himself finger-fucking her. Olivia reached for him, but he was too far away. And he watched her with those glimmering dark eyes. Olivia whimpered and gripped table edge for leverage to lift and rock into his touch.

"Crazy fucking good..." she murmured. "God..."

Another orgasm tsunami slammed into her, the initial spike of pleasure so sharp, it drew a scream from her throat and wiped her mind completely clear.

Panting, Olivia dropped a forearm over her eyes and sank against the hard table beneath her. "Oh *mon Dieu*..."

She felt like she'd been infused with champagne. Every cell buzzed and sizzled. Her muscles were spent. She couldn't catch her breath. Olivia tried to get her mind to work, but it refused. She couldn't begin to remember the last time she'd come so hard or in such quick succession or with nothing more than a man's hand and mouth.

Tate eased to his feet, and Olivia couldn't even gather the strength to sit up. He cupped her thighs behind her knees and rocked her side to side until her butt was at the edge of the table again.

"Jesus Christ..." She really couldn't offer much more. Truly, she was worthless right now. "Tate, you're...gonna have to give me...a minute. You've wiped out...a few million brain cells..."

His hand pressed against her belly, then slowly slid upward, pausing over one breast to squeeze and mold.

"Mmm..." She stroked his forearm.

His hand skimmed her chest, his fingertips grazed her jaw, then his hand slipped behind her neck—and took a possessive hold. One that sent tingles down her spine. "Your minute's up."

His dark voice sounded close and forced Olivia's eyes open. "Wrap your legs around me."

She obeyed, crossing her ankles at the small of his back to help her support weakened muscles. Then he was on the table with her, but she had no idea how he'd gotten there. His movements were smooth and effortless. With his hips deep between her legs, he eased toward her, and the unmistakable pressure of the head of his cock pressed against her. A little sigh escaped her lips.

With his eyes burning into hers, he tilted his pelvis, teasing her with the head of his cock. He dropped a kiss to her lips. "I put on a condom." Kissed her again. "I can't wait to feel you around me."

When the hell had he put on a condom? Jesus, she'd lost time somewhere. Maybe only minutes, but that had never happened before.

Tate's hand tightened on the back of her neck, and his hips rocked. His cock pushed inside, stealing her breath as he stared into her eyes. He was already drawing out again before Olivia had fully filled her lungs. His next thrust was deeper.

For a moment, he stilled. His eyes closed on a look so fierce and so sexy she thought she might climax at the simple sight. "So fucking perfect."

She reached up and stroked his jaw. "This is the Tate I was looking for."

He groaned, drew out, lowered his head, and kissed her on the next stroke. Her gasp broke the kiss, but it didn't keep Tate from moving. And fuck, he was powerful. Probably stronger than anyone she'd been with, but her mind couldn't catalogue any details while Tate was driving into her.

He easily pushed Olivia along the smooth table top. "Hold on."

It was an order, not a request, and Olivia reached overhead with both hands to grip the edge of the table above her.

With one hand on the table, the other tight around her hips, Tate brought his entire body into play—his knees, his thighs, his ass, his arms, his core. Every muscle tightened and flexed, and the arm at her waist dragged her toward him as he thrust.

"Fuck, so good..." She closed her eyes and soaked in his raw power, his intensity, his passion. God, he was even more amazing than she'd hoped. "Oh God..."

He hovered over her, his lips just above hers, his dark eyes owning her. He dropped a lick over her lips, and Olivia opened to take him, but he lifted his head again, leaving her hungry.

"Tate... *Dieu*...don't stop... Perfect. It's perfect."

A pinch at her waist pulled her eyes open. Tate's gaze waited, hot and demanding. "This is me, Olivia, going after what I want. *All of you. All night.*"

A fist clenched her chest so hard, it stole her breath.

He thrust deep and paused. She strained, on the edge of another wicked orgasm. "Do you understand?" he asked, deadly serious. "I want to own you. I need to *fucking own you* tonight, Olivia."

Her breath stuttered. And in that moment, looking into those dark, haunted eyes, his face shadowed in the dim light, she understood perfectly. For the first time in her life, she understood the intensity of two like people meeting and bonding. She understood the feeling of safety while being dominated. The comfort of being controlled. The pleasure of being completely taken.

"Yes," she told him. "Tonight, I'm yours."

Emotions she couldn't quite read flashed through his eyes. They were there and gone so fast, swirling among so much passion, she couldn't begin to guess what they had been. She only knew his thrusts came deeper, harder, and faster. His kisses grew more passionate. His expression darkened and sharpened.

"Olivia..." he rasped, dropping his forehead to hers. "So wet. Come for me, Liv. I want to feel it all around me."

Her body responded to his words, and the orgasm that had been hovering, crashed, shattering through her, twisting her muscles, and pulling cries from her throat. Olivia clung to him while he continued to thrust and thrust and thrust. And just when the orgasmic haze started to clear, another built. Before she had time to catch her breath, she was crying, "*N'arrete pas, n'arrete pas... Dieu...*"

When she shot into the stratosphere again, Tate came with her. His muscles hardened to granite beneath her hands, his guttural growls of release singing through her, heart, body and soul.

Panting, limp, and brain dead, Olivia release the edge while she melted against the table. Let her forearm fall across her eyes. And muttered, "*C'était incroyable.*"

Tate dropped his sweaty forehead to her shoulder and braced himself on his forearms. Their heavy breathing filled the silence. She slid her arm to her forehead and stared at the ceiling but she didn't really see it. She was searching her mind for the source of the knot lingering in her chest. A vague tension that was both familiar yet unidentifiable in the moment. Which was probably because Tate Donovan had just fucked the living stuffing out of her.

She laughed. Turned her head away from Tate's, lowered her forearm to her mouth, and laughed again.

"What were you saying?" he asked.

"When?"

He lifted his head and looked at her. His face was relaxed, his eyes sparkling again, and a little smile tipped his beautiful mouth. "What do you mean, *when?*"

She grinned and thought back. "Ummm... Hard to say. I sort of think in several languages now. Sometimes I don't know which one's in my head and which one's coming out of my mouth. Can you sing a few bars?"

He broke into laughter and laid his head against her

shoulder again. She brought her hands to his head and her fingers to his hair. His laughter faded, and he heaved a deep, satisfied sigh. Then tipped his head and pressed a kiss to her throat.

"Holy shit, Liv..." he whispered against her skin. "That was..."

"*C'était incroyable?*"

"It sounds so much better when you say it."

He dropped a soft, lingering kiss to her lips, and joy ballooned inside her. But as soon as she felt it, she knew what she'd feared moments ago. And right on cue, Tate pushed up on his hands. He was going to pull away. The perfect distraction was over. Olivia now had to deal with reality.

She braced for the void. The cold. The emptiness.

Tate made the familiar requisite moves, and Olivia used her hands to push herself up. She let her legs fall free of Tate's hips, and he stepped into the kitchen for cleanup while Olivia straightened her dress and picked up her panties from the floor.

As she straightened, Olivia looked out the dining room windows onto the gardens, silent and beautiful in the middle of the night. And she realized that instead of leaving a nagging ache inside her, Tate had given her a sense of... Of what? Calm? Peace? Wholeness?

All she knew was that when he stepped up behind her, wrapped her in his arms and lowered his head to kiss her neck, Olivia's heart felt light, when it usually felt heavy.

"What do you think?" he murmured. "Do you want to stay with me tonight? If it's too much," his voice dipped, "I... I understand."

Olivia was still waiting for the hole inside her to open. With any other man—*every* other man—regardless of who he was, how much she liked him as a person, how much he liked her, how great the sex was, the loneliness after sex had been almost instantaneous. But she wasn't feeling that now. What she was feeling was the stirring heat between her legs when she thought of Tate Donovan *owning* her for the rest of the night.

She tilted her head back, kissed his jaw, and told him, "If that's what happens when we're still fully clothed, I want to see what happens when we get naked."

6

A chime drew Tate from sleep. He reached out blindly, slapping at the nightstand to silence his alarm. But his hand hit the mattress.

Disoriented, he opened his eyes and found himself in the middle of the bed. Sprawled diagonally on his stomach. Naked. Confusion hurt his head. He hadn't slept naked since...

Almost before his mind touched on Lisa, it veered toward Olivia.

Instantly awake, he pushed up and looked around. He pulled in a breath to call her name, hoping she'd changed her mind about leaving in the early morning hours. But then he saw her sparkly heels missing from the floor—all she'd had on by the time they'd made it upstairs—and let the air leak from his lungs in disappointment.

He rolled to grab his phone and turn off his alarm, and his muscles ached in that deliciously well-used way that spurred wicked memories. Groaning, he dropped his forearm across his eyes. Last night had been—hands down—the best night of his life with a woman. And that included his wedding night.

"How fuckin' sad is that?" he muttered.

Even sadder, she'd stuck hard to what he'd discovered was her personal rule with men—one and done. Nothing he'd done had enticed her to entertain the idea of seeing him again—not withholding orgasms until her nails dug into his headboard and his sweat dripped on her chest. Not the foot or back massages. Not talking and laughing in the dark. Not finding utter bliss curled around each other as they fell asleep, arms and legs twined, bodies fused.

Nothing.

And he'd still never give it back.

Best. Fucking. Night. Of his life.

Over.

Dammit.

His self-esteem took another hard hit, just as Tate was pulling it to its feet.

He opened his eyes and looked at the angled ceiling of his bedroom. "What the hell am I missing?"

What didn't he have that other guys did? What made Faith stick to Grant? Eden stick to Beckett? Mia stick to Rafe? Tate was a good guy. After Lisa, he thought he might have been lame in bed. But last night cleared that up.

He sighed, edging toward resignation, something he'd gotten too good at over the last year. Maybe Olivia was right. Maybe a clean break early was for the best. Not that Tate would know anything about clean breaks. Lisa kept popping up in his life when he least expected it. But he had to admit, the thought of seeing her now didn't bother him so much. Knowing he wasn't broken, knowing he could still attract real, sweet, fun, gorgeous women like Olivia helped heal that particular festering wound, even if it was now replaced with a new one.

Tate sat up and swung his legs off the bed, groaning at the protest of all his underused muscles that had gotten a workout last night. He shuffled to the bathroom to shower. He couldn't be late to hockey camp if he harped on the kids for coming in late. It was time to get over the first one-night stand of his life and focus on the reality.

But that didn't keep his mind from wondering to all the things he'd do with Olivia if they had another night. Or how amazing it felt to have a woman in his bed again. He let his mind stray toward doing it again, with someone else. Maybe one of the puck bunnies so prevalent at the bars they hit after games or at the hotels where they stayed on the road. Just letting one of them follow him up to his room the way so many of the other guys did. The idea made Tate want to squirm.

Tate loved sex. In fact, he could become borderline obsessed with it if he had all the time in the world to indulge with someone like Olivia. But that was the thing—he loved sex with a woman he *connected* with. Which, he just realized, was why sex with Lisa had been so unfulfilling in those months before he'd discovered she'd been cheating. Because they hadn't been connected.

He forced his mind back where it belonged, dressed, and grabbed his gear. But on the drive to the rink, Tate found himself wondering how long it took to fly to Paris. How much it cost. And how often he'd be willing to make it for a night like last night.

Pulling into the parking lot, he laughed at himself. "Fuckin' long way to go and a lot of money to spend just to get laid, you idiot."

Only...

"Life is short, you know?"

Tate pulled his duffel over his shoulder with Olivia's words ringing in his head. He certainly wasn't getting any younger. The money for travel wasn't an issue. He could fly first class back and forth to France every week for years and never run out. But time *was* a problem. During the season, there was rarely two days in a row when he could get away to make that trip, and the season took up between eight and nine months of his year.

And what in the hell was he doing, thinking about flights to France after one freaking night with the woman? The woman who didn't want more than one night? This was exactly why he'd never been cut out for one-night stands. Because if he was into a woman enough to sleep with her, he didn't want to stop at one night.

"Hel-lo."

Tate startled at his friend's voice, singing the word. He stopped in his tracks and swiveled toward Beckett.

"Your head was in the clouds." Beckett was looking at Tate like he'd grown a second head. "What's up?"

"Nothin'." He reached for the door to the practice arena and held it as Beckett entered, then followed. "Man, what a turnout last night. You'd almost think people liked you or something."

Beckett grinned. "I think they love my daughter and soon-to-be wife most."

They said hello to the guys behind the desk and passed into the locker room designated for the Rough Riders.

That whole whirlwind romance between Beckett and Eden still made Tate uncomfortable. But he'd warned his friend plenty of times. Tate even pointed out how he himself hadn't listened to the warnings from friends and family before he'd married Lisa. But Beckett was adamant about tying himself to Eden after dating her only six months.

And Tate had to mentally smack himself for judging Beckett when not five minutes ago, Tate had been considering flying to fuckin' Paris to get laid.

"What in the hell's gotten into you?" Beckett asked over his shoulder as he continued to his locker. Both men dumped their duffels, grabbed their helmets, skates, and sticks, and headed toward the ice.

"What do you mean?" Tate followed Beckett into the rink, settled by the familiar, refreshing

whoosh of cold air on his face.

A handful of kids was already on the ice, supervised by a camp coordinator. Tate and Beckett dropped to the bench, toed off their shoes, pushed into their skates, and started lacing.

"I mean that look," Beckett said, glancing sideways at Tate. "That grin. The extra bounce in your step. From the moment you got out of your car, you've had some fuckin' swagger going."

"I don't fuckin' swagger."

"You do today. You didn't even look this happy when you heard you were going to the Olympics. Me, I was swaggering for weeks. You just thought it was cool." He waggled his finger at Tate. "You didn't have any of this shit going on."

Tate laughed and shook his head. "What shit?"

"That, right there." Beckett started on his other skate. "Any other day, you'd have told me to fuck off."

"I would not."

"Not in an asshole way, just in a don't-bug-me way."

"Whatever." Tate grinned down at his skates as the laces moved effortlessly through his fingers.

He did feel different. He'd felt different from the moment Olivia had entered his life the night before. Lighter. Brighter. Happier. If he just kept the whole "I'll never see her again" thing out of his head, Tate felt great.

"Thanks for making the right move with Quinn's sister last night." Beckett's words snapped Tate out of his thoughts.

His smile dropped, and his chest chilled. He had nothing to be ashamed of. He knew that. Still, he felt...weird about everyone knowing he'd had a fling with Olivia. "What?"

"Quinn's sister. The cook? She saved our asses last night. I'd hate to think about what would have happened if Matt had kept her out and she'd gone home. God, what a disaster."

Tate relaxed a little. "Yeah, you got lucky, and she's more of a chef than a cook."

"Oh yeah?" Beckett tied off his skates and sat back, giving Tate a speculative look. "Well, cook or chef, she impressed the hell out of Eden. She wants to fire our wedding planner, who screwed up the scheduling of our engagement party in the first place, which lead us to Quinn and her mother, and hire their family to handle the whole wedding."

Tate lifted his brows. "Wow, that's great. But you should tell her you guys can hire Quinn and her mother, but you can't hire Olivia."

"Why not?"

Tate felt Beckett's eyes burning into him as he tied off his laces. He straightened and scanned the ice where all but a handful of kids had arrived. "Because Olivia lives in Paris. She's only here for a couple of weeks."

A moment of silence filled the space between them, peppered with shouts and laughter from the kids echoing through the enclosed rink.

"Huh," Beckett finally said. "You sure know a lot about a woman you barely met before she got dragged into the kitchen. How long—exactly—did you talk to her?"

"I don't know." Tate laughed it off and shrugged. "I wasn't checking the clock."

More silence followed. More staring.

Tate rolled his eyes. "God, I hate the way you do that."

"Do what?"

"You know what." When he cut a look at Beckett, he found his friend grinning. "Fucker."

"So?" Beckett nudged with too much hope, too much anticipation. "Did you ask her out before she left? Take her for a drink after? What?"

Tate knew his friends and family wanted to see him happy,

but sometimes he got confused between what he wanted and what he wanted to do to please them.

Tate leaned forward, resting his elbows on his knees. Flashes of his night with Olivia teased him with the first taste of her warm mouth. That first press of her curves against his body. The first real flutter of life back in his heart.

If he was going to tell anyone about it, Beckett was the person he trusted most.

"Yeah." He exhaled, and with the secret on the tip of his tongue, Tate's stomach clenched with a weird anxiety. "I, uh...I took her home."

"Cool," Beckett said. "So you talked to her on the drive? Did you get her number? Did you make a date with her?"

Tate laughed softly. He had such a reputation for not sleeping around that even when he admitted to it, no one believed him.

"No, Beck, I didn't drive her home. I took her to my place." It took an extra push of effort to get the next words out. "She spent the night with me."

The mix of shock and disbelief on Beckett's face made Tate laugh, but he was grateful when he saw most of the missing boys arrive on the ice. He started to stand. "Kids are here—"

"Hey." Beckett grabbed his arm and pulled Tate back to the bench. "They'll wait. This is important. Bro, talk to me."

A little of that guilt Tate was trying to get rid of snuck in. "Everyone does it all the time, including you before Lily and Eden. I'm not gonna be telling you anything you don't already know."

"I'm not judging you, man. I'm just surprised. It was never your style, not even before Lisa. And there's been no one since Lisa. Then, bam, you meet a girl, talk with her, what? Thirty minutes, tops? And take her home the same night? I'm just checking in with you. Making sure everything's okay."

"Yeah, sure," was Tate's automatic response, because on the

surface, everything was okay. "I mean..." He shrugged. "We just...she's just..."

"Special?" Beckett finished for him.

Tate let the air he was holding release. "Yeah, I guess."

"What do you mean, you guess? You fuckin' took her home, Tate."

"It just sounds, I don't know, juvenile, I guess. I liked her. We clicked. I took a chance." He shrugged again. "She made it easy."

"No, this doesn't have anything to do with what she did. I've seen women literally fall all over you—as in, you had to physically unhook them to get away—and you still didn't take them to your room. Dude, remember those twins that sat in the hall outside your room in Tampa?"

Tate started laughing and rubbed at tired eyes. "Crazy women."

"I met her," Beckett said. "I went into the kitchen last night after I found out our caterer was rushed to the hospital to give birth and met Olivia."

Tate's head came up. "Rushed to the hospital to *what*?"

"She didn't tell you?" When Tate shook his head, Beckett said, "Our caterer went into labor right before the party started. Olivia didn't go in and help out. Olivia went in and *took over.* Eden gave the family a ridiculous tip that was more like a second freakin' payment."

Tate's mouth hung open as his mind replayed the night. He couldn't remember hearing anything about the caterer, which wouldn't have been unusual when he'd been hanging out with the guys most of the night. Olivia sure hadn't mentioned it. Tate had hung on the woman's every word and that was certainly something he would have remembered.

"You know Eden," Beckett said. "She admires anyone who'll run toward a problem instead of away from it. After it was all said and done, Eden wanted to canonize the woman."

That made Tate smile. As a paramedic in DC, Eden saw her
share of rough situations. "I could see that."

"Hold on," Beckett said, frowning. "Did you just say she
lives in *Paris*?"

"I know how to pick 'em, right?" He shook his head, and
another wave of disappointment tried to drag him down. "It
doesn't matter. It was just one night."

Beckett stood and parked his butt on the half wall between
the rink and the bench, facing Tate. Crossing his arms, he
settled a smile of anticipation on Tate. "So? How was it?"

Olivia filled his mind, and his heart responded. He couldn't
keep the fucking smile away. He dropped his head and rubbed
at the burn in his cheeks with both hands. "Oh my God." He
laughed. "Best fuckin' night of my life."

Beckett broke into laughter. "Yeah?"

"Yeah." Tate grew serious and glanced up at Beckett for a
second. "I didn't know it could be like that." He refocused on
the floor, a little hard to believe it had really happened now that
he was mired back in everyday life. "She's..."

Everything I never knew I wanted.

And she lived in Paris.

"She's great. But, again, it was one night. And she doesn't
want anything more. I'm just a fling for her." On a deep breath,
he looked at the ice. "Come on, the kids are waiting."

"Nah, nah, nah, hold on." Beckett put a hand on Tate's arm.
"You deserve a good woman in your life."

"Dude, I can't change—"

"I'm not saying you can or you should," Beckett said. "I'm
just saying that if it was that good and if she's here for two
weeks, then why don't you think about getting as much of that
as you can while she's here?"

"Because you know me, Beck. You know after two weeks
with her—"

"That's not true. If you fell deep for every girl you slept

with, you'd have been married fifty times." Tate sent him a look, and Beckett amended, "Okay, twenty times. Whatever. My point is that you don't fall hopelessly in love with every woman. Look what you've already done. You had one hell of a night, and you're already resigned to putting her into your memory banks. You have the ability to have a short, casual relationship with a predetermined end date without heartache if you frame it that way in your mind ahead of time."

Maybe with someone he hadn't connected with so immediately. Or so completely. Maybe with someone who wasn't quite so delicious. Or so sweet. Or so devilish. Or so sexy. Or a hundred other things he'd already come to either love or admire about her. But Olivia was a little too much of everything all wrapped into one woman. Sure, he knew there was a lot to learn about her. But he'd also been around long enough to know how to spot the important things. Not to mention his painful divorce to a shitty woman, which taught him all those things to watch out for.

All in all, Tate's gut knew that seeing Olivia again was dangerous to his heart.

He also knew his heart was flipping somersaults at the idea.

One of the kids skated past them backward, imitating Tate's and Beckett's frequent threat in a comical attempt at a baritone. "Gonna make you do sprints if you're late, boys."

"Good idea, Blake," Tate called after the kid, his own true baritone echoing through the rink and drawing all the kids' gazes. "Blake wants to do sprints. Great warm-up. Everyone, go."

All the kids groaned, slowly falling into line, starting sprints across the ice.

"That'll teach him to be a smartass," Tate said, grinning at the kids ribbing Blake.

Beckett gripped Tate's shoulder and shoved him out on the ice with a good-natured "There's my team captain." He tossed

Tate a hockey stick, and they glided toward center ice. "Just think about it. And it wouldn't hurt if you could talk her into taking the wedding job either."

Tate rolled his eyes and reached out, hooking one of the kids around the waist and pulling him from the sprint, as the ten-year-old laughed so hard, the kid fell on his ass.

That made Tate feel better. To get Beckett to leave him alone, Tate offered a noncommittal "I'll think about calling her."

Which would be difficult given he didn't have her number, and getting it would require conversations he'd rather not have with people he'd rather not have them with.

Nearby, Beckett hooked another kid, and another young boy fell into a laughing mess onto the ice. God, Tate loved this camp. But he knew it wasn't just the kids bringing out this joy. Olivia had broken through some wall inside him, allowing it out.

Beckett grinned over at Tate. "For a woman who put a smile on my face like the one you're wearing right now, I'd do a lot more than call."

7

Olivia was jerked from sleep when her bed rolled like a boat in a storm.

"I can't wait anymore." Quinn's voice immediately oriented Olivia.

She was home—in the States. In DC, sleeping in the room she and Quinn had shared their entire young lives. Right up until Olivia had left home for Europe after their dad had died. And Quinn was bouncing on her bed to wake her up, the way she had for years.

"You can't sleep all day," Quinn said. "I haven't seen you in a year. *Wake. Up.*"

"Oh my God," Olivia groaned and pulled the pillow over her head, laughing a muffled "Go away."

But she couldn't deny the sweet sense of nostalgia swamping her as Quinn continued to bounce, and Olivia continued to laugh.

"Mom," Olivia yelled, "make Quinn stop!"

"Mom's not going to save you Livvy. *You...need...to...wake... up.*" She punctuated each of the words with a bounce.

"Oh, Quinn." Their mother's amused voice entered the

room. "Let her sleep. She got in late, and she worked hard last night."

She'd also been *worked over* hard last night. Olivia had never realized so much pleasure could be so exhausting.

"I'm awake. Stop bouncing, or I'm going to puke on you." Olivia threw the pillow at her sister and said, "What do you want?"

Quinn just grinned at her with that million-fucking-dollar smile. The one Olivia lost when their dad died and their family fell apart. The one she hadn't been able to find since, no matter what corner of the world she'd searched.

Though, she might have caught a sparkle of it last night.

A little spark lit up in the middle of her body. She'd never been loved the way Tate loved her last night. She should really call it fucking, but somehow, that description didn't quite fit. Last night, Tate had made Olivia feel like nothing mattered outside his townhome. Like he had nothing on his mind but becoming so tangled up in Olivia, he could never get out.

From the way he held her gaze while he drove her to multiple orgasms, to the way he curled around her after, slipping into sleep with his face buried in her hair, Tate had given her the intense experience of being deeply cherished beyond anything she'd ever felt with any other lover, though the *why* of it still escaped her.

"Olivia." Quinn shook her leg.

"Stop it." Olivia smacked Quinn's hand away, annoyed at being jerked out of her warm memories of Tate. "Mom, make her leave me alone."

Teresa wandered toward the bed with a familiar smile on her face, the one that told Olivia just how happy she was to have her home. The one that was so happy, it tipped the scales toward teary. Sometimes, Olivia thought coming home caused her family more pain than joy. And that cut at Olivia's heart.

Their mother sat on the corner of the bed. "Just let her tell you the good news, and she'll leave you alone."

"Hardly." Olivia rubbed both hands over her face and moaned. She knew her family. If they didn't have to work today, they'd want to do something with her—go shopping, have lunch, take in a movie, wander the museums, walk the river. And as much as she wanted to do those things too, right now she really just wanted to lie here and think about Tate. Remember every minute of their night together. Maybe find something about him she could use to pry him off the pedestal she'd mounted him on after last night.

Since that obviously wasn't going to happen, Olivia rolled to her side, propped herself up on her elbow, and rested her head in her hand. And prepared for a long-drawn-out tale about Charlotte's baby. "Fine. Talk, Quinny Quinn."

She got that I-can't-stand-it giddy grin, cast a look at their mom, then said, "We picked up six new jobs last night, Liv. *Six.*" Quinn was almost coming out of her skin. "And one of them is Beckett Croft's daughter's birthday party. Did you meet her last night? She was one of the kids there. A gregarious little blonde angel zipping all over the party."

Olivia laughed at Quinn's description, so full of affection for a little girl she barely knew. But Quinn had always had an affinity for kids. "Um, nope. There weren't any kids running around my kitchen."

Quinn deflated a little. "I hate that you didn't get a chance to come out and meet everyone." She glanced at her mother. "What a great group, weren't they, Mom? Really neat people for being so famous and wealthy."

Their mom agreed. "They'll go down as one of my favorite jobs to date."

"Who came?" Olivia asked, only mildly interested.

They both looked back at her, but Quinn was the one to ask, "What do you mean?"

"The famous and wealthy. Who was that?"

Quinn's face broke into another smile. "All of them. You're the hockey fan. You should know how much that franchise is worth."

Olivia pushed herself upright and combed her hands through her hair, pulling it off her face, then dragged her T-shirt—one of the many she'd stolen from her father's dresser after he'd died and still slept in—over her knees. "I just used to go to the games with Dad. I don't know anything about the franchise. Or even about the sport, for that matter. Not anymore."

Though she could attest to the intensity of one particular player in the bedroom.

"They make anywhere between half a million and eight million *per year*."

Olivia frowned, resting her head in her hand. "I guess. I mean they're professional athletes."

She thought back to Tate's townhome. It was in a nice part of DC. It was on the new side. It seemed roomy, though she hadn't seen much beyond the dining room and Tate's bedroom. With the prices in DC now, it had to have cost somewhere around a million and a half. But as her mind woke, the implications of Quinn's information in relation to her family sank in. "And you've got six new jobs with these people?"

Quinn's eyes rounded, and she nodded, sending Olivia an "exactly" message.

"That's fantastic," Olivia said. "Great crowd to be networking with. What kind of jobs?" After ten years in the industry, Olivia's mind started calculating and arranging at lightning speed, and within a nanosecond, she found a few *huge* potential problems. "Do you guys have the cash to float you in case something falls through? Because when you've got events back to back like that, they can drain your finances really quick. And if your books aren't so tight they squeak, one late payment can send the company's financials into a tailspin. And, crap, I hope none of them come up before Charlotte's ready to start working again."

When she didn't get an instant response, Olivia's stomach tensed. "Okay, well, I hope you at least have a backup caterer."

Quinn glanced at their mother. Teresa reached out and patted Olivia's knee. "You're just like your sister, worrying about money. Just leave that to me, sweetheart. As far as a caterer goes, everyone we spoke to at the party last night wanted you."

The tension in Olivia's stomach coiled up her spine.

"We explained that you're not here long, and we are looking into other options, but Quinn and I were hoping you could stay, just a little while longer than you planned, and help us out. It would be fun, and it might be the last time we get to see you until you're done with school, or we have the time and money to take a break and come visit you."

That was the first mention either of them had ever made about visiting her, regardless of what country she'd been living in at the time or how often she'd asked. So teasing her with a visit in an effort to get her to work while she was here on what should be a break from working three jobs in preparation for school, created a sliver of resentment. One she didn't feel fully entitled to since she'd been the one to move away.

Olivia exhaled. "I don't know, Mom."

"Well, think about it." Smiling, her mom pushed from the corner of the mattress. "I'm going to meet a potential candidate. Maybe it'll all work out and none of us will have to worry about anything."

The knot in Olivia's gut loosened enough to allow her to breathe easier, but Quinn didn't look convinced. After both of them gave their mother a kiss and promised to meet up with her in a few hours for family girl time, they stared at each other until the front door closed, securing their privacy.

All the unspoken problems they should have talked about

last night weighted the air between them. Olivia crossed her arms and leaned back against the wall. "Spill it, Quinn. What's really going on with the business?"

"It's just been slow. We have calms and storms, but we don't have the cash to just let things idle when it's slow. Then we'll get a big job, or a couple of big jobs in a row, and we have to leverage credit cards for deposits. We always pay the cards off when the client pays us, but sometimes there's a lag. Sometimes the client makes a change, and we don't get paid as much as we think. Sometimes there are cancellations, so the money we think is coming in, doesn't. We've been managing with lots of small jobs. And the money you send every month has saved us more than once. But last night was a *huge* step forward."

Quinn shook her head and smiled. "We caught the engagement party as a fluke. Beckett and Eden's wedding planner is a part-time space cadet and dropped the ball. A friend of a friend recommended Mom, and we scooped it up and ran with it. The only reason Charlotte was available was because her husband insisted she take some time off before the baby. But when she drove him crazy climbing the walls with boredom, he let her go back to work. So, we snapped her up for a couple of big events."

Quinn stood, crossed her arms, and paced the room. "Eden's enthusiasm over our work on the party has carried through the team."

"How many events did you have Charlotte booked for before last night?" Olivia asked.

"Just one, but it's a big one—a charity event in a little over three weeks. One of Beckett's teammates." Quinn rolled her eyes to the ceiling. "Mom pointed him out last night, but I didn't get a chance to meet him. I can't remember his name. There are *so many* of them."

"Twenty-three," Olivia said, remembering what Tate had told her about his team the night before while he'd been giving her a foot massage that turned into much, much, much more.

She rubbed her tired eyes. "There are twenty-three players on a team."

"Anyway, this guy puts on one of those five-thousand-dollar-a-plate dinners to fund his charity every year, After-school Advantage. It's black-tie, the whole team goes and brings their wives or girlfriends or dates. Sponsors and donors and season ticket holders will be there. Some are buying full tables for family and friends. He says it funds the entire year of the program—"

"Three weeks?" That sliver of resentment jabbed her beneath the ribs. Why was it so hard for her mother and her sister to remember something so major in Olivia's life? "I won't be here Quinn. I have *school*."

"You said it starts in a month. This will happen right before. You can fly back the next day. Mom and I will handle everything after the party."

"You want me to start full-time school and go back to work jet-lagged?" Her anger rose. "Do you even realize I worked my *ass* off for two years to save enough money to offset my scholarship, partially because I was sending money home? Now you want me to work while I'm here *and* extend my stay so I can work some more? To hell with how that affects everything I have planned for my life back at home?"

With a heavy exhale, Quinn flopped down on the bed, reclining sideways and propping her head in her hand. "I'm sorry, Liv. I'd love to tell you we don't need you. That we're solid—"

"I don't want you to *lie*." Old anger from the past flared, and bone-deep hurt flowed in its wake. "Don't tell me what you think I need to hear, Quinn. Just tell me the truth, or I'll get back on a plane right now."

Identical anger and hurt flared in Quinn's blue eyes, and she sat up. "And don't you act like I'm trying to hide secrets that are messing with your life. I'm telling you right now, we're struggling and we could use your help. If you choose not to help, fine. If you want to leave, fine. But don't you dare threaten to leave like that in front of Mom. Abandoning us both the first time when we needed you the most hurt us enough for a lifetime."

"And both of your lies hurt *me* for a lifetime."

Quinn turned her gaze on the floor and shook her head. "I'm so sick of this. I'm sick of living in the past."

"It's not the past if you keep doing it. Why have you been telling me everything is fine when I call?"

"Because Mom didn't want you to worry. You were already sending money, what more could you do? We all know you wouldn't come home."

Her anger burned hotter. "Just because you never went after what you wanted in life doesn't give you the right to judge me because I did."

"I *am* where I want to be. I stayed to help Mom get on her feet."

And Olivia had left because they'd made it impossible for her to stay. "I'm not going to feel guilty that neither of you asked me for help over the years. Did all my experience in restaurant management just slip past you? Did you think it was irrelevant? Or could you just not bring yourselves to ask my advice about anything?"

"We may have not given you the credit you deserve, but you live across the goddamned world, Liv. Last night was the first time we've ever had the opportunity to see what you do first-hand. And you were out so late—or early, depending on how you want to look at it—neither of us could tell you how impressed we were with everything you did last night. You didn't even give us the chance to thank you. Honestly, Liv, you don't make it easy to appreciate you."

"Oh, perfect." Olivia closed her eyes and rested her head

back against the wall. "Now it's my fault. I feel like I've stepped into a time machine."

"Stop living in the past. We have a very real problem right now. Mom gave us eighteen years of her life when she could have been out working, creating a career for herself, one that could be supporting her now. Dad's life insurance is all wrapped up in that company. She doesn't have anything to fall back on. I can always find work, but Mom's not as flexible. Finding a job that will cover health insurance and retirement at her age is impossible."

Quinn pushed from the bed, crossed her arms, and paced across the floor, then back before meeting Olivia's eyes again. When she did, her anger had mellowed into frustration and fatigue, much like Olivia's.

"We need to do what we have to do to make this work," Quinn said. "I know this is bad timing for you, but I need you to pitch in here. Dad would want us to do this for her. So I'm asking you now. I'm asking you to stay and help so that we can hold on to this forward momentum and keep Mom on her feet."

Well, shit.

What the hell was she supposed to say?

Olivia exhaled, and her shoulders sank under the work ahead of her. "Fine. I'll stay. But only until school starts. I'm not going to lose that scholarship."

Quinn gave a nod, but she looked more resigned than happy about it. "Great." She turned and wandered toward the door. "Then get dressed, sis, we've got work to do. We have to check out the kitchen at a new venue, negotiate a menu with a new client, and talk ponies, fairies, and flying dragons with the most adorable almost-six-year-old you'll ever meet."

At the door, Quinn paused, and her mouth quivered into a fragile smile. "Thanks, Liv. We really miss you. Every day."

And she turned the corner toward the kitchen.

Olivia fell back on her bed and stared at the ceiling, wondering if she was more of the reason their family was broken than her father dying.

Then she wondered what Tate was doing, if he'd want to see her again, and how she would get in contact with him.

"Don't be an even bigger loser than you already are." She rolled to her feet and sighed heavily as she pulled clothes from her suitcase.

8

Tate slowed as he approached the open warehouse door of Essex Elite Events with sweat collecting on his palms. A sign hung above the door, a cursive "x" in Essex adding flair to the name and logo.

He'd waited three days for the company to open for regular business hours, hoping he'd hear from Olivia before then. He'd gone as far as leaving a Post-it on his apartment door any time he left with a note for her to call him with his cell number, only to come home to the note every time. So he was feeling pretty vulnerable right now, putting himself out there to tell her he wanted to see her again when a: she'd made it very clear she was a one-and-done kind of girl, and b: she hadn't made any effort to contact him.

Tate took a breath before he stepped into the shadow cast by the industrial building and rubbed his hands down the sides of his jeans. Then he exhaled and tried to settle. But, man, his stomach felt like a wild bird in a cage. This was way harder than getting out on a rink in front of eighteen thousand people.

The wide metal doors were open, but inside, the warehouse was quiet and dark. Tables and chairs were stacked along one long wall and the middle of the space was stocked with supplies alongside a forklift.

He'd only met Teresa once, when he'd spoken to her in person at length about taking over the project from the previous planner. Tate had fired the other woman after she'd messed up one too many times on Eden and Beckett's wedding plans. After the engagement party, Tate was glad he'd followed Eden's gut on the Essex mother-daughter team and hired them off her recommendation alone. Though he couldn't help but wonder what they would have done if Olivia hadn't come in at the last minute and saved them.

None of that mattered now. It was all just something to busy his mind, because he knew Olivia was working with her family while she was in town. Which meant, involved or not, Tate and Olivia would see each other again. He was hoping that would happen sooner rather than later and more often than not. But he was still nervous as hell about how she would react to him now.

Tate cleared his throat, and the sound echoed through the space. He lifted his hand to the wall and rapped a few times, then called, "Hello?"

His voice vibrated in the darkness but got no response. Tate's hopes dropped, but his tension ebbed too. He walked deeper into the space, looking around. Row after row of rolling wardrobes were draped in material Tate could only guess was used for decoration. Oxygen tanks lined a short section of wall space. Shelves and shelves were lined with folded linens. Glassware. Tableware. Vases. Candles. Mirrors.

The sheer amount of inventory gathered gave him a whole different scope of this event-planning gig. It was massive.

A female voice in the distance touched Tate's ears and made his stomach flutter. He moved through the warehouse, focused on the tone, trying to figure out if it was Olivia or someone else. He had two different spiels worked up—one for Quinn and one for Teresa—if he needed them. But he hoped he found Olivia here first.

The clip of heels joined the woman's voice growing closer, but Tate still couldn't tell. And dammit, after hearing Olivia giggle and moan and scream for an entire night, he should be able to recognize her voice.

Then she laughed. A soft, sweet sound that flipped Tate's heart so hard, he covered the pain with his hand.

And he stepped back.

Three times.

He finally stopped himself when the woman walked into the warehouse from an open side door.

Olivia.

She wore a suit. A straight business skirt, a blazer, and heels. It didn't seem like her style—other than the color. Red. Deep, sensual red. It fit her curves like a fucking glove. And Tate ran his tongue over his lower lip. Even days later, he could remember exactly how good those curves tasted. And exactly how much Olivia loved being tasted. His grin widened, and his cock tingled with the memories.

Her head was down, her gaze on notes in her hand. Pausing at a small desk just inside the door, she set the papers down with her back to Tate.

He approached and paused ten feet away, hoping to catch that sultry floral scent of hers, but couldn't. Crossing his arms, he waited. Her hair lay in loose curls against her shoulders, and he wanted to role one around his finger while she laid stretched out on top of him, naked and sated. The thought made him smile. Started his mind down a path to surprising her when she got off the phone, lighting her up, because he knew exactly how to do that in about three seconds flat, and taking her right here, quick and hard. An appetizer to a multiple-course meal to stretch through the night.

Olivia laughed. "That sounds great. Okay. Fantastic."

Tate started forward, relaxing into the rightness of just being in the same room with her. Beckett was right, Tate did deserve a good woman in his life. Even if they only had a little over a week left together. Based on their one night, Tate was pretty sure Olivia could bring him as much happiness in that short amount of time as all his other relationships combined.

But he had to put himself completely out there if he expected to get any return. Life was like that. Every reward he'd ever reaped in hockey had been because he'd thrown himself on the mercy of the ice—sometimes literally.

He was four feet behind her when she said, "Yes. I'll have her call you as soon as she's free."

Two feet. He could smell her now. Fruity shampoo. Clean body wash. Not what he expected based on how sexy she smelled the other night. But that slipped out of his mind as she said, "Okay. Sounds good. Thank you. Bye."

She bent to write something, and Tate said, "That sounded good."

Her head came around as she glanced over her shoulder. She was smiling, bright, happy. Her hair slid over her suit jacket, reminding Tate of the way it slid over her shoulders when she'd looked at him that night while he'd taken her from behind.

"Oh, hi," she said, then turned back to what she was writing. "I didn't see you. It was good. That was—"

He didn't care, he needed to touch her.

He closed the distance and slipped his arm around her waist. She gasped, straightened, and grabbed at his arm. "What—"

"Just one second." Tate pressed his face to her neck. "I just need to feel you for a second. I've missed you."

"Mr....Donovan...?"

Tate laughed, nuzzled her ear, and kissed her neck. She didn't taste the same. That had to be his imagination. But something didn't feel right. He wasn't sure what. Was almost afraid to look too closely. "I think I liked Sir better, but I guess we could try Mr. Donovan if you want."

"Uh, no." She was still stiff against him. Her voice wasn't the warm, teasing, sexy voice he was used to.

Dread gathered in his gut. He drew in a breath and pulled back, meeting her eyes. They were... Damn. Maybe the alcohol had lingered longer than he'd thought that night. Or maybe there hadn't been enough light. Because she just didn't look the same. No, she looked the same, but not the same.

"I know that look." She stepped out of his arms and turned to face him at the same time. "You're not going crazy. This has happened before." She held her hand out to him for a shake. "I'm Quinn Essex, Olivia's sister."

His jaw unhinged. He stepped back. Way back. His stomach dropped to his feet. He rubbed a hand over his mouth. "Oh my God. I'm...*fuck*..." As soon as he said the word, he slammed his eyes shut and put up both hands. "I'm...*so* sorry." He covered his face and paced away, filled his lungs, and turned to face her again. "Wow, I couldn't have messed that up worse if I'd tried." He stuffed his hands into his back pockets and focused on the concrete at his feet, but he couldn't keep his gaze off her face, unable to believe... "You've got to be—"

"Twins," she said with an apologetic attempt at a grin as she wrung her hands. "Identical. We used to get mistaken for each other all through childhood. Still would if she didn't live in another country."

"Oh my God..." He hadn't felt this foolish since he'd found out Lisa had been screwing guys for months behind his back.

"It's really okay," Quinn said. "I'm sorry as well. I hope this won't make you want to change our working situation. My mother and I are really looking forward to planning your event for Afterschool Advantage."

"Oh, God no." He held up his hands. "As long as you still

want to do it. I hope you do. I'd have a hard time finding someone at this late date."

"Yes, yes, absolutely." She laughed the words, and it seemed to put them on even ground again.

He smiled. "Wow, awkward way to meet, huh?" He was scraping a hand through his hair when her earlier words registered. And now he wondered why she hadn't hauled off and slapped him. He looked up at her again and gestured between them. "What did you mean *this* has happened before?"

"Oh, um..." She tucked her hair behind her ear and crossed her arms. "Well, you know, sometimes when Olivia comes home, she meets someone, and, like you, they hit it off..."

She left it open-ended. Just dangling there for Tate's mind to grab and run with. Anyone who knew anything about Tate knew you never left anything dangling if you didn't want him to grab it, take control, and own it.

He might have owned Olivia for a night, he'd known that going in, but it sure looked damned different in the light a few days later. He'd never imagined himself as one of the many schmucks who'd come looking for her afterward, but it was crystal clear that he was just like every other guy she picked up. No different from the puck bunnies his teammates took up to their rooms, fucked, and never thought about again.

That realization kicked him straight in the gut with absolutely no warning. It stole his breath like a sucker punch from the league's biggest defenseman.

"Right." His word came out rough. He felt like he'd swallowed gravel. He dropped his gaze to the concrete again, and it took all he had to dig up enough composure to even make the attempt to look like this wasn't as big a deal as it was. "Well, again, I apologize for mistaking you for Olivia, Quinn, and..." He gestured to her and finally pushed out, "for uh...you know."

She was giving him that puppy-dog-at-the-pound look. The one bleeding hearts turned on the one mutt everyone passed up. "And I'm really sorry about Olivia. She's a beautiful person. And she doesn't intentionally mean to hurt anyone. She's just..." Quinn shrugged. "She's just...a little lost."

Yeah. Well, so was he. Now even more than his normally pathetically lost state.

"Sure," he said. "Well, I guess I'll just— I think I have an appointment schedule with Teresa to follow up on the banquet details. I might see you then?"

She nodded and smiled. "I'll check the calendar. Hey, did you want me to have Olivia—"

"No." He said it too forcefully and put out a hand. But, *no. God no.* Talk about mortifying. "Please don't."

Quinn pressed her lips together and nodded. "Of course."

"Hey, I'm sorry. I didn't mean to snap at you. This isn't your fault. I— This just really threw me, you know?"

"Sure." She nodded and chewed her lip. "I understand."

She looked so uncomfortable that he couldn't stand to just leave her like that. He stuffed his hands into his pockets and looked around the warehouse. "This is...a big operation."

"Yeah. Some days it feels overwhelming."

"Sounds like you had some good news on the phone."

She perked up. "Yes. A possible wedding job for friends of someone who was at Beckett's engagement party."

"That's great."

"It is. We've been struggling to get it to run in a way that will support my mom until retirement. I don't know if Olivia told you, but our dad died some time ago."

"No, she didn't." Nope, Olivia didn't say much about her personal life. Every time Tate had asked, she'd done something to make his eyes roll back in his head. "I'm sorry."

"Thanks. We were a really tight family, and he was our core. I doubt Mom will ever remarry. They were that once-in-a-lifetime for each other, you know?"

Nope. Tate didn't know anything about that. "That's got to be tough. How long ago?"

"Ten years now. Hard to believe he's been gone that long. Sometimes it still feels so raw. We all still miss him so much."

Tate nodded, calculating the years. "You had to be young."

"Eighteen." Her gaze went distant. "He got sick early in our senior year." She focused and smiled. "Made it to watch us walk across the stage, though. Passed a few days later."

Holy shit. "I can't even imagine how hard that would have been."

She sighed deeply and nodded.

"It sounds like that's about the time Olivia went to Europe."

Quinn smiled again. It wasn't a happy smile, but it wasn't sad either. And it wasn't bitter. It looked more like acceptance or resignation. She shrugged. "We're all coping...in our own ways."

Right. Quinn was coping by dealing with the issues, struggling through the obstacles, and sticking it out by her mother's side.

Olivia was coping by running away. Jumping from man to man to man.

Just like Lisa.

Did Tate have "Big Fat Sucker" stamped on his forehead? Or was his judgment in women really just that shitty?

"Well, thanks for understanding," Tate said. "It was good talking to you."

"It's not a problem. It's forgotten. And, again, about Olivia... I'm sorry."

Tate worked up what had to be a lousy smile. "Me too."

9

Olivia was in trouble.

She knew when she saw the grocery list Quinn had given her mother before sending her out the door. It had been as long as Olivia's arm.

She crossed her arms, leaned against the kitchen doorjamb, and rested her head there. She was tired. She wasn't sleeping well, and she'd been planning food and a cake for Lily's party in between helping her mother interview caterers to take over the smaller jobs so Olivia could focus on the two bigger ones.

Lily's party wasn't a problem. Eden was extremely easy to please. She liked clean eating and basic ingredients with lots of flavor. Right up Olivia's alley. The cake Olivia could do in her sleep, even if Lily wanted some bizarre winged dragon creature. And the kitchen in Beckett's parents' Arlington home where they were holding the party had been sent directly from the heavens above. Olivia could throw a wedding reception for five hundred people out of that kitchen.

But the charity banquet was hanging a lot heavier in the back of her mind. She didn't want to tell her mother and Quinn that, but she'd made sure they'd secured Charlotte's sous chefs for the day before and her entire staff for the night of. The only problem she could see running into would be bizarre menu requests, ingredients she couldn't get or that would be out of season and ridiculously expensive. She didn't want to do anything that would eat into her mother's budget.

As Quinn called a few last items out to their mother, Olivia rested her eyes. She'd figure the banquet out soon enough. She was scheduled to meet the client at the end of the week, before Lily's—

"Olivia."

She startled awake. "*Oui, quoi? Quoi?*" And found Quinn glaring at her from the dining room. Olivia exhaled and rubbed her face with both hands. "Shit."

She'd just fallen asleep on her feet. Not exactly new. She'd done that numerous times over the years working double shifts, but it wasn't how she wanted to spend her time off.

Olivia pulled her hair back, and wound the band she'd been wearing on her wrist around the ponytail. "You haven't sent Mom to the store so you could yell at me since that Christmas when I borrowed the car and dented the bumper. I'm doing exactly what you wanted me to do, and I'm doing it well. So *why* are you mad at me *now*?"

Quinn gripped the back of a dining chair, propped her other hand on her hip, and settled that look on Olivia. The judgmental one. Olivia thought she'd gotten over the irritation that brought, but evidently it still raked a few fingers across a blackboard somewhere in her psyche.

"You slept with Tate Donovan," Quinn said with absolute authority and censure. "That's what you did."

The fact that she knew hit Olivia sideways. "How the hell—"

"Not only did you sleep with him the first night you were in town, but then you dumped the poor guy. Now the immediate future of *our* business hinges on the referrals of *his* buddies and the buddies of his buddies. So I sent Mom out because I didn't want to talk about this in front of her. You're welcome."

Hurt from the past came rushing to the surface. All the animosity between them they'd failed to get past sizzled. And Olivia was reminded that real love caused bone-deep pain.

"I didn't thank you. And I *won't* thank you. First, because you're acting like a bitch. Second, because you didn't do it for me. You did it for Mom. Everything you do is for Mom. It's like I don't exist. As soon as Dad got sick, I ceased to exist for both of you. Nothing I wanted or needed mattered anymore."

Olivia pushed off the doorjamb and took a step toward Quinn. "If you ever want to know why I don't come home more often, record just one conversation with me and play it back. That judgmental tone of yours gets old really fast, Quinn, and you've already used up your quota of my patience. So if you want this stupid birthday party and this goddamned banquet to go off perfectly, don't push your luck."

Instead of backing off, she matched Olivia's step forward. "You hurt him. You hurt him like you hurt everyone who cares about you. You and your cavalier European attitude. Why can't you ever just leave that behind when you come home?"

"Everyone else who cares about me? If you're talking about you and Mom, try looking in the mirror. That's where you'll find the person you really care about. People who care about someone stand up and do the right thing even when it's hard. They say what needs to be said even if someone else doesn't want to hear it, because they know the alternative will hurt so much more. People who care about you don't take the coward's way out, and don't steal the most precious thing in your life."

"*We. Didn't. Steal. Him,*" she said with barely controlled impatience. "*Cancer* did."

"But you took his last months from me. You and Mom stole all that time I could have spent with him. You stole my chance to say good-bye. To tell him how much I loved him one more time. To support him through the illness. Through the therapy—"

She choked on emotion. It took her so by surprise, she shut down. She held her breath, tightened her muscles and clenched her hands to hold the ripping sorrow and the fiery rage inside.

Quinn said nothing. She stood completely still, staring at the floor.

This was a ten-year-old tear in the fabric of their family that no one and nothing could repair. This kept Olivia living on the other side of the country, feeling like half of her was missing because her family was somewhere else, yet knowing she couldn't live with them.

A never-ending spiral that left Olivia feeling incomplete.

She did everything she could to make her visits home brief and enjoyable, but inevitably, every second or third visit, things between either her and Quinn or her and her mother blew up.

In a more controlled voice, Olivia told Quinn, "Tate and I both knew what we were doing. I don't know why you think what you do, but I assure you, he's not hurting over our one night."

Quinn crossed her arms. "And I assure you, I don't need dozens of men in my background to recognize the feel of an erection pressed against my ass when a man pulls me close from behind. Or the signs of affection when he whispers, 'I've missed you' at my ear and kisses my neck. Or the look of pain in his eyes when he realizes he's just like all the rest. Because that's what happened, Olivia, all because *he thought I was you*."

Quinn yelled the last words in anger.

Olivia's mouth dropped open. Her heart skipped two full beats, then hammered hard and fell straight to the pit of her stomach. "When? Where?"

"Today. At the warehouse." She dropped her arms and drew herself up. "So I may not take as many risks as you, but *this* is why. Because I have Mom to think about." She stabbed her finger at the floor. "Now, you're going to go find him, talk to him, and do whatever you have to do to make sure he doesn't badmouth our family into bankruptcy or fire us from his job."

Olivia was already shaking her head. Tate would be humiliated. He would be livid. He would hate her. She wasn't eager to face six feet of muscle furious with her, or see how far his opinion of her had fallen.

"He's not going to—" She started. "Wait. What job?"

"The banquet, Liv. Tate is *our client* for the banquet. So you're going to talk to him, because not only do we need that job, but you have to work with him."

"I— But—"

"You make sure that Tate Donovan has nothing but good things to say about *all* the women in this family before you board another fucking plane."

10

T ate pushed toward the net with a puck on the blade of
his stick.

Wait. Fire. Score.

Wait. Fire. Score.

Beckett came at him and reached in.

Waaaaait.

Tate let the puck glide just beyond his teammate's blade.

Beckett's reach tipped his weight past the center point,
creating space on the ice for Tate to shoot without interference.

Fire.

Tate slammed the puck, rocketing it toward the net, right
past Beckett. His teammate was way too far off balance to
recover in time to block.

Score.

"Yes," he hissed as he let the forward momentum swing him
around the goal.

Beckett picked up one of the many stray pucks on the ice
with his blade and took up Tate's previous position as offense.
Tate claimed defense and did what he could to crowd Beckett,
messing with his attempt to master calculated hang time.

They'd been running drills like this for over an hour. All after already picking up a practice game earlier that day with eight of their teammates and chasing after a bunch of rambunctious ten-year-olds for four hours that morning. But Beckett didn't complain. He didn't bitch. He didn't beg off and tell Tate he had to go home to Eden, who had the day off and was home with Beckett's daughter, Lily.

Even when Tate knew Beckett would rather be home with them, he was still sweating his ass out with Tate because Beckett understood the therapeutic value of working out your frustrations on the ice. And Tate needed it because even two days after mistaking Quinn for Olivia, he still felt like an absolute fool.

Beckett scored and Tate picked up another puck, switching positions again.

"All right." Beckett wiped his sweaty face on his shirtsleeve. "I'm done takin' it easy on you now."

Tate laughed, though it sounded more like footsteps on gravel.

"No net for you pretty boy," Beckett said, putting force into his skates and coming at Tate hard.

Adrenaline spiked, and muscle memory had Tate maneuvering to get past Beckett. But his teammate was as good as they came, and when Beckett kicked up the heat, he was like a cement wall. The only thing Tate had on the man was speed. So he poured on the juice, used a little fancy footwork, added some well-honed stick work, and still couldn't get past him.

"Goddammit," Tate complained. "You're a pain in the ass."

"Bet you say that to all the boys," he said as he blocked again. And again. And again.

"Motherfucker."

"Can't go through me." Hip check. "Can't go around me." Another block. "What are you gonna do?"

Go under you. Tate tapped the puck between Beckett's legs, then reached around him and dove for it, stick outstretched. The edge of his stick tapped the puck a second before Tate landed chest-first on the ice. His momentum propelled the puck into the net.

Score.

Tate pounded the air with his free fist, "Yes!" Then he rested his helmet on the ice, laughing.

Beckett skated a circle around Tate, also laughing. "You lucky son of a— Oooooh..."

Tate didn't need to look to know someone had walked into the rink. And by the language shift, that someone was female. Tate's stomach might have been numb from the slab of ice beneath him, but that didn't keep the butterflies from taking flight.

He tried to catch his breath while he constructed those walls Lisa had taught him to build. Walls that worked relatively well against the woman who had lied to him and cheated on him within a year of their wedding vows. Not so well against a woman who'd made no promises, given Tate nothing but pleasure, and pulled him from a darkness he'd been wallowing in for far too long.

"Hey, Olivia," Beckett said. "I was just using Tate as a Zamboni."

"It's been a while since I've seen a game"—her voice touched his ears, and a pleasure-pain sensation cut through him—"but it looked to me like Tate smoked that puck past you."

In any other situation, Tate would have found that both hilarious and sweet. But there were too many emotions dogging him. And hearing her voice now, he didn't know how he could have mistaken Quinn's voice for Olivia's. They were very similar, no doubt. But Olivia's held an intangible quality of...seriousness wasn't quite right. Maybe worldliness. Olivia's voice held a certain sultry, mysterious, knowing, jaded edge.

Where Quinn's was straightforward, open, compassionate, and sweet.

"It's not always about the score," Beckett told her. "We're working on techniques. Donovan's mastering the 'corpse on ice.' While he's trying to figure out how to get back on his feet, I promised Eden I'd talk to you about our wedding."

Tate rolled his eyes, pulled his knees in, and only now realized how the last week had caught up with him. He hadn't been sleeping, and he'd been working out like a lunatic. All of which he was feeling now.

He shook the ice from his jersey and looked up, tensed for the sexual punch at the sight of her. But she wasn't the vixen he'd been expecting. Maybe the one he'd built up in his mind. She'd wandered into the bench area, where a half wall separated her from the ice. She was wearing faded, worn jeans and a sweater, one with an uneven hem and a thick fringe all around the edge. Her hair was pulled into one of those, loose messy knots that were so popular with women now, stray strands fell across her forehead and around her face.

And man, what a face. He hadn't been drunk that night. It hadn't been too dark. And she was even more beautiful in full fluorescent lighting.

Those big blue eyes shifted from Beckett to Tate, and they were filled with apprehension. Her lips turned in a cautious smile, but it was real. And warm.

Fuck me to hell and back.

Like a boxer guarding one area, he'd left another vulnerable. His heart took the brunt of this kick, and the pain put enough fear into him to spur some self-preservation. Because Tate knew in his gut Olivia hadn't come on her own. He'd bet his next signing bonus—God willing he got one—that Quinn had given Olivia a piece of her mind.

He should have known Quinn would tell her. And God... Mortification burned through him in a thick swath of fire.

Beckett was asking her about catering the wedding, but Olivia never took her eyes off Tate. And Tate never moved from center ice.

"We chose the last Saturday in August," Beckett said, "because that still gives us ten days for a honeymoon before training camps start."

When Tate didn't move toward her, the sparkle in her eyes dimmed. She returned her gaze to Beckett. "Thank you for the offer. I really appreciate it, and if I were going to be here, I would absolutely be all in. But I'm starting school soon, and in late August, I'm going to be learning to use blades as well as you do, but for a whole different purpose."

Beckett turned on the charm, pulling out the playboy smile he hadn't used on anyone but Eden since his fiancée walked into his life. "I'll make it worth your while. Next to Lily, Eden is the most precious thing in the world to me, and I'd do anything to make her happy."

Olivia's shoulders softened. Her head tilted. She pulled her hands out of her pockets to cross her arms against the chill. "That is so sweet, it makes my heart hurt, but the truth is, I've been working ten years for this forty-thousand-dollar scholarship, and if I don't use it, I lose it."

Beckett propped a hip on the wall of the rink a few feet from Olivia. "Forty grand? Where are you going?"

"Le Cordon Bleu."

That soft, fluid French accent cut through Tate's chest like a sharp knife and set his groin on fire.

"Tate... N'arrete pas, n'arrete pas... Dieu..."

"Tate... Don't stop, don't stop... God..."

He'd ended up learning a little French that night. And even though the memories still thrilled him, they also hurt. As did the fact that they'd spent eight intimate hours together and she hadn't once mentioned a fucking forty-thousand-dollar scholarship. He'd tried to get her to talk about herself, but she'd always turned the conversation back around to him or to sex, and he'd fallen for it, thinking he'd be able to talk her into a date, another night, or something...

But she'd bailed before the sun came up. Such a player move. And he couldn't legitimately be mad about it, because she'd gone into it in an up-front and honest way. He'd known she was all about casual sex. He'd known she'd be returning to Paris. And this fucking heart of his just would not cooperate with his head.

Which only made this thing twice as frustrating.

Regardless of what happened, how it happened, or who it happened with, Tate was done. The bottom line here was that he liked her entirely too much and he honestly couldn't take another heartbreak. He'd been through this. This trying and hitting a brick wall. He wanted to escape to the locker room, but she blocked his exit.

"Do they do four-year programs there?" Beckett asked.

Forget it. He wasn't staying for this conversation, blocked path or no blocked path. He started toward the bench.

"No. Three months to two years, depending on the program. The scholarship is for the one-year track. Tate," she said as he headed toward the door at her left. "I need to talk to you a minute, *please.*"

Beckett glided over to Tate and pushed him back a ways. "Let me take your gear." His friend reached out to take Tate's hockey stick, but grabbed Tate's glove as well, holding him there. He met Tate's gaze deliberately, and kept his voice low. "She may not be perfect, but no one is. Including you, bro. But she's real. She's got a good heart. And she is two hundred percent zeroed in on you."

He didn't want to hear that. Beckett was one of those guys who could get a sense of a person within ten minutes of meeting them. He could read their true nature through things like eye contact, word choice, body language, facial cues, voice tone, and other intangible, unquantifiable characteristics. And he'd been so dead-on accurate over the years, guys on the team often asked him to vet women before they invested emotionally or financially in them.

Beckett had told Tate several times he didn't think he should marry Lisa. But he'd never mentioned it again once they were married. And never once rubbed the breakup in Tate's face.

"Doesn't matter," Tate told him. "Remember? The whole France thing?"

Beckett jerked the stick out of Tate's hand. "*Get. Over. It.* Get over it, or you're going to spend your whole goddamned life alone and miserable. Is that what you want?"

"No. But I don't want to spend it getting fucked over either."

"Then put up some goddamned walls, take the hits, get a few scars, and get your ass back in the game, just like you do out here. This is only half your life. Don't *live* only *half* your life. Stop being a pussy and take some control."

He skated off the ice, said good-bye to Olivia, and disappeared into the locker room, leaving Tate and Olivia alone in a huge arena, staring across the ice at each other. And Tate got that sick feeling in his gut, the one that always came right before he and Lisa started fighting.

So he did what Beckett told him to do. He put his head down, planted his hands at his hips, and glided her direction while he shored up the skeletal barriers he'd put in place over the last week. Because he knew how freakishly sophomoric it was to be twisted over a woman he'd known, what? A day? Could he even say he'd known her a week when they'd only spent one night together?

He was disgusted with himself when he slowed near the

wall where she was standing with her hands piled on the ledge. When he met her gaze, he found her grinning, a silly little grin that lit up her pretty eyes with a familiar mischief. One that did all sorts of crazy things to him.

"Hi," she said, soft but chipper. Then she pulled the corner of her lip between her teeth and bent over the wall, grabbing for his jersey.

"Whoa…" Tate shot backward, hands up, then realized how stupid he looked and skated a circle as if he hadn't just acted like a first grader trying to get away from a girl. "Been there, done that. Learned my lesson."

"Tate," she complained, leaning on the wall with her forearms. "Come here. I just want to say hello."

"Hello." He skated random slow patterns just out of her reach. "Are we done?"

She sagged, propped one elbow on the wall, and dropped her chin in her hand. "I'm sorry about what happened with Quinn."

"So am I." He still felt the mortification of the moment burn across his skin. "But it was my own fault. And she wasn't supposed to tell you."

"*Pffft.* She couldn't wait to ream me."

"Is that all?" he asked, trying really hard to keep his voice even, cool, unemotional. "'Cause I've been working all day. I really want to take a shower, get food, and pass out."

She straightened and frowned at him. He could have handled it if that damned pouty lip of hers hadn't come out. "Can't we talk a minute?"

"I don't want to cut into the little time you have left here." He started toward the exit again.

And, sonofabitch, she stepped in his path. "You know we need to talk."

Fuuuuuuuuuck.

"We really don't," he said, skating backward figure eights. "You were up front with me. And it was my fault I didn't confirm Quinn's identity before I..." He blew out a breath. "Never mind. It's over. Everything is just like it should be. We had one night and you're on a flight to Paris in a week. We're all good. Nothing to talk about."

When he turned toward her again, he found her sitting on the half wall, her legs hanging into the rink, plain white Keds with no laces on her feet. He had no damned idea why he found that so freakin' adorable, but it pulled at his heart in half a dozen different ways.

He scraped his skates to a halt, pulled up his big boy pants, met her gaze, and waited. Memories pressed in from all sides. Split-second video clips of their night. Olivia arching into him as he sucked her nipple into his mouth, moaning and riding him faster. Tate lying sprawled out on his stomach, still panting when Olivia sauntered back from the bathroom, draped her still-sweaty body across his back, and released a handful of condoms on the mattress in front of his face with, *"Catch your breath, stud. I want more of what you're dishing out tonight."*

Olivia's exasperated exhale pulled Tate back as she glanced toward the hundred-foot ceiling and straightened. "Can we, I don't know, go for a drink or something?"

"That would break the one-night rule."

Her face fell into a belligerent expression that reminded him a little too much of Lily when she didn't get her way, which was just another layer of adorable.

"Fine. I guess we'll just get this over with then," she said. "Quinn is terrified that word of our night together is going to spread through the team and reflect badly on the family." Olivia gestured absently to the rink, indicating Quinn was over-reacting. "She's afraid that potential jobs Essex could get from the team or connections to the team could be ruined because of *this.*"

She gestured between herself and Tate in a way that seemed to make what had happened between them a throwaway event.

He shook his head, repeated the gesture, even more flippant. "There is no *this*."

Olivia's hands came out, palms up, and she offered an exaggerated "*Right?*"

That diffused his tension again and brought up his urge to laugh. But dammit, he didn't want to laugh. He didn't like her coming in here, acting like his embarrassment and his feelings were things she could push aside with a little charm, a little flirtation.

"That's what I told her," Olivia went on. "But she insisted—I swear, that girl is so melodramatic sometimes—that I'd hurt you, and that your hurt feelings were going to ruin everything. No joke, you'd have thought the world was ending."

She was teasing, trying to lighten a potentially touchy topic. Tate could appreciate that. But it didn't change the underlying situation between them. And it didn't help Tate feel any better about being one of her puck bunnies.

But he was ready to let this Quinn thing go, so he matched her flippant tone with, "Some people."

"Some people," she repeated with a smile in her eyes. She braced her hands on the ledge at her hips and looked at the ice, shaking her head and swinging her crossed feet. "She's a bleeding heart, that one. Means well, but... Anyway, can I tell her that you promised not to say anything bad about me to anyone involved with the team so it will settle her nerves about losing business for the company?"

"You can tell her I'll think about it."

She game him an excuse-me look. "You'll *think* about it?"

"You're in *my* rink, interrupting *my* practice, wanting *your* way. And it's not even for you, it's for Quinn. So I'm not particularly eager to make concessions. I'll *think* about it."

Her expression fell along with her shoulders. "Since you won't sit down and talk with me, I'll just tell you that Mom and Quinn won't have time to vet a caterer with the ability to handle your banquet, so I'll be doing it. If that's a problem for you, let me know now. I can reach out, make some calls. See if I can find someone qualified to fill in."

He narrowed his eyes. "That's two weeks from now. You're not supposed to be here that long."

"Nope, I'm not."

"Is that going to screw with school?"

"I'm not going to let it."

"Why'd you say yes? Why didn't you tell your family you had to go back?"

She looked down at the ice and didn't answer for a couple of long moments. "I've been asking myself the same question. If it was just my mom and Quinn, I might have said no, told them to figure it out. But I have my doubts about your ability to get another caterer at the caliber you need to pull off a celebrity dinner for thousands of dollars a plate on such short notice."

That chipped away at the barriers around his heart. "Why would you have said no to just Quinn and your mom?"

"Because the same old bullshit that always happens between us when I'm here is already happening again. And I'm just done with it all. I have one of the most important things in my life happening in a very short time, and all they care about is themselves." She looked up with a furrow between her brows, pout still in place. "Sorry, that was probably way too much information."

Tate hesitated. It *was* too much information. He didn't want to get into any family drama. Still, he couldn't keep himself from asking, "What's that about?"

She sighed and shook her head. "I've done a lot of charity work overseas, and I don't want to see the kids you help suffer just because I've got issues with my family."

Beckett was right. She had a good heart. A really good heart. She just hid it well. As someone who'd done the same since Lisa had trampled all over his, Tate recognized the signs. Which made her willingness to help him even sweeter.

"Thank you," he said, sincerely grateful. "That means a lot to me."

Her mouth flickered into a smile, and she nodded. A second of silence lingered between them. Her gaze slid over him, and when her eyes returned to his, a familiar little gleam hinted there. "I must have been too young to appreciate how hot hockey players are when I was in high school, because watching you fight for that puck was a serious turn-on."

Just like that, fire spilled through his lower body. His automatic response for any other woman would have been some dry brush-off, a response that made it seem like he hadn't even picked up on her interest. But with Olivia, his lips formed the words "Oh yeah?"

"Oh yeah." Her smile heated, her voice grew heavy and languid, and her lids lowered as her gaze slid downward again. "Reminds me of our night. Of the way you—" She cut off the last word and Tate found himself hanging on the edge, waiting to hear the word *fuck* drop from her lips. Instead, she teased him with, "The way you are in bed. Passionate, driven, intense. Relentless."

Memories depicting all those words flooded into his head. Pressure built across his hips, and his temperature spiked.

"The way you go all-out. And even when you score, it's not good enough. You go after it again. The way you push and demand. The way your total and complete focus made me feel like I was the only person on the planet. The only thing that mattered. The only woman you wanted. Or had ever wanted. Or would ever want."

Her eyes fell closed, and she tilted her head back with a

long hum of desire that pumped blood directly into his cock. "Mmm, what a rush. Rush after rush after rush."

When she opened her eyes again and he saw the wicked light there, he knew what she would do next. Which was the moment he realized he'd drifted too close. But his brain was too slow, Olivia's hands too quick. She reached out and snagged a handful of his jersey, yanking him toward her with an evil little giggle.

"Oliv—"

His blade tips hit the wall, stopping him. But she already had her thighs open, and she wrapped her legs around his hips, pinning him there. Tate caught her biceps and pushed away.

"If you're goin', I'm goin'," she said, her voice husky and serious but her eyes sexy and playful. "So if I go down, you go down." Her grin glinted with an extra spark. "And you know how I love to go down."

Another memory rushed in, of Olivia on her knees, offering her warm, soft, wet mouth to fuck. Excitement coiled tighter, but Tate didn't want to find her amusing or fun or flirty. Because that made him want her. Hell, who was he kidding, as long as he was alert and breathing he wanted her.

"Liv, I smell like a locker room."

"No, you smell like sweat. You did plenty of that our first night together," her voice dipped, and her lids lowered, "and I like it."

He exhaled slowly, purposely refocusing on why he *shouldn't* stroke his hands down her arms. Why he *shouldn't* wrap his arms around her waist. Why he *shouldn't* press his lips against hers. Why he *shouldn't* sink his tongue into her warm mouth and take a long, deep, slow taste of her to quench what felt like an endless fast.

"I was just thinking the same thing," she said, as if she were reading his mind, her voice another silky reminder of that unforgettable night.

"I doubt it."

"Really?" she asked softly. "Because I was thinking about stripping you out of these sticky clothes, stroking every inch of your amazing body under a hot shower until you were squeaky clean, then feeding you with your choice of delicacy until you were absolutely sated, and rocking you so hard, you'd sleep for days. Isn't that what you said you wanted to do shower, eat and pass out?"

Just like that, Tate's partial hard-on turned to rock. If he hadn't been wearing a jock, his sweats would be tented right now.

It was the *only* thing he wanted. Tate heard Beckett's words again. *"Take the hits, get a few scars, and get your ass back in the game."* The problem was that Tate couldn't just change the way he thought about women and relationships overnight. And in truth, he didn't really want to. He was proud of the way he treated women, which was probably why he was having such a hard time accepting that he was just another boy toy to Olivia.

But that was his problem, not Olivia's. And if he wanted to love Olivia while he could, he was going to have to find a way to get over it.

But Olivia seemed to finally read Tate's silence for disinterest, because the flash in her pretty eyes vanished and her expression fell into a little pout. "But, unfortunately, unless we can do that in your locker room, it won't happen tonight."

He almost jumped at the bait. Almost. Before the *Why not?* fell from his lips, exposing his keen interest in executing her plans, he caught it and just lifted a brow instead.

"I have to prep for Lily's party tomorrow. Mom and Quinn are picking up the food. I'm making and assembling the base of the cake tonight, prepping some of the food, then finishing everything tomorrow before her party while Mom and Quinn are decorating."

Tate slid his arms around her waist and eased closer,

frowning at the fact that Beckett hadn't told Tate about this. "You're catering Lily's birthday party?"

"I am."

"I didn't know Eden and Beckett were having it catered."

"Guess they asked after the engagement party." She lifted a shoulder. "They're key clients for Mom and Quinn. They tell me the Crofts' family is a potentially big referral base all through the District and Metro."

Tate nodded. "The Crofts do know a lot of people."

"At least the work will have purpose, then."

"This hasn't turned into much of a vacation for you."

She skimmed her fingers through his sweaty hair, and her smile returned, along with the light in her eyes. "Oh, I don't know. My time with you feels like a vacation." She tipped her head. "When you're not mad at me."

He smirked, wishing he could take her home and have her in his bed all night. "I think Quinn's right on the mark about one thing."

Olivia's gaze angled up to his.

"I think there's a softie inside this pretty shell of yours," Tate told her.

"Oh no." She leaned back and shook her head with an obstinate frown. "Uh-uh. Not me." She fisted her hand and tapped her chest over her heart. "Stone right here, dude. Granite. Quinn stole all the good stuff in the womb. Left me with nothing redeemable. Just ask her."

Tate was grinning, completely against his will. "I didn't have to. She volunteered the information."

"Oh God." Her shoulders sank. "I'm afraid to ask."

Now, so close to her in the light, Tate saw all kinds of things he hadn't seen before. Like the darker rim on the edge of her light blue eyes. And the length, curl, and golden color of her lashes without mascara. Like the little scar above her right brow and the smooth texture of her skin. "She said you're a beautiful person."

She waited, and when he didn't go on, another brow winged upward. "And in the same sentence she said...?"

"Why do you do that?"

"Because I know her. She's my *twin*. So tell me how that sentence ended."

He sighed. "She thinks you're just a little lost."

Olivia broke out in laughter, and when her head tipped back, it was all he could do to keep himself from pressing his mouth to her throat.

"You're not lost?" he asked.

When she looked at him again, she was smiling, but the sparkle of laughter didn't reach her eyes. "Quinn thinks I'm lost because her version of happiness and mine differ. Because I don't follow American norms. Because I'm not striving for the American dream."

"What are you striving for?"

She stared at him an extended moment, gaze distant, lips parted. After a second, her walls went up. She closed her mouth, thought about it some more, and said, "That changes as my life changes. We're not all born knowing where we want to end up. I'm sure you've heard the saying, 'Not all those who wander are lost.'"

"My sister is one of those."

"Where does she live?"

"Here."

"Are you close?"

He nodded. "We had a rough patch recently, but we're getting past it."

"Good to know you can forgive." She slid her hands up his sweaty chest to his shoulders and ran her fingers over the stubble on his jaw. "Gives me hope. I really don't like it when you're mad at me."

She slid one arm behind his neck and pulled his head down.

Tate resisted until she said, "Just one kiss good-bye. I have to get going."

As soon as her lips pillowed beneath his, Tate moaned. Olivia opened. Her tongue reached for his, circling, circling...

And Tate was fucking gone.

He lost all reason, all logic. Lost all willpower, all resistance. He wrapped his arms around her, one low on her hips, the other high on her shoulders, using his hand to keep her head right where he wanted it. Positioning her mouth right where he needed it. And Olivia responded exactly like he remembered, like liquid fire. They flowed into a rhythm that amped the heat between them in seconds. Enough heat to melt the rink beneath his skates.

Tate was spiraling. Fast.

He broke the kiss and pressed his forehead against her temple. "How do you fuckin' do this to me?"

"It's not me. It's *us*." She pulled back, framed his face with both hands, and he had no doubt that the emotion he saw in her eyes was real. "I'm sorry if I hurt you. I'm sorry I'm not more...traditional or American or whatever." She shrugged. "This is me. I love sex. I happen to really, *really* love sex with you. More than I've loved sex in a long time. And I know we have a limited opportunity. That makes me hungry. Feels like it might make you hungry too."

He clenched his teeth and flexed his fingers in her waist. "You know it does."

Part of his jaded mind knew she could be doing this to boost his ego so he'd stay on with Essex. But that same damaged ego really wanted to believe she *did* enjoy sex with him more than with other guys. Only he couldn't ignore the fact that either way, the major problem between them still existed.

"But you've confirmed something I already knew about myself," he said. "Something I was trying to disprove because I wanted you so badly."

"Which is?" she asked.

He exhaled, frustrated with the ache between his legs. "I'm not a one-night, sex-with-a-stranger kind of guy."

She lifted her brows, and a hot little smile turned her lips. "Well, another night would be night two, and we aren't strangers anymore."

He laughed, but it came out as pained as he felt. "Really? Because I learned more about you from Quinn in five minutes and listening to you talk to Beckett for three than I learned directly from you in bed over eight hours."

"Oh, *mon dieu de sexe*," she purred in a way that made Tate light up like a struck match, "I promise you that's not true."

Calling him her sex god nudged him closer to her way of thinking but didn't make him cave. The last week and its turmoil were still too fresh.

"You have the ability to have a short, casual relationship with a predetermined end date without heartache if you frame it that way in your mind ahead of time."

Maybe Beckett was right. At least half-right.

Voices broke the spell between them, and Beckett straightened, glancing toward the lobby where a dozen preteen boys flooded through the doors. He groaned, released Olivia, and pushed backward, gliding a short distance away.

"Club practice," he told her.

She swung her legs over the wall toward the bench. "Okay, well…"

"Hold on." He skated to the mat, threw the guards on his blades, and curled his hand around hers. "If you wait for me, I'll drive you home."

As soon as he said the words, Tate flashed back to their first night together and that moment when he'd tried to offer the same. Remembering the skittish look in her eyes then made him cringe internally now. Another faux pas. He walked her toward the hall that connected the lobby, the locker rooms, and the lounges, expecting that any second, she'd pull from his grip and get the hell out of Dodge.

Instead, she threaded their fingers, smiled up at him, and said, "I'd love that."

Tate damn near wobbled on his skate blades.

"Wow," she said, "You were tall to begin with, but you're really tall in skates."

He laughed and led her down the corridor to one of the private lounges accessible only to the Rough Riders' staff. "You can hang here. I won't be more than fifteen minutes."

"This is incredible." She released his hand and wandered toward the twenty-foot glass wall that looked out onto the rink.

The boys and their coaches were on the ice, warming up, but Tate's gaze was on Olivia's ass and how delicious it looked in those jeans.

She smiled over her shoulder where she'd stopped behind one of the leather lounge chairs, her hands on the back. "Is that the age of your boys?"

It took him a second to figure out she meant the kids in the summer camp. "Mine are a couple of years older. Just as rowdy."

"Look at the goalies," she said with a smile in her voice. "You can't even see the kids behind all that equipment. How do they even move?" Tate was smiling but figured it was a rhetorical question, so he didn't answer. Then she glanced over her shoulder a second before returning it to the ice. "What are the colored lines for? I can't remember."

"They split the rink into zones of play." He wandered up behind her. "Between the goalie line and the blue line is either the attack zone or defense zone. Between the two blue lines is the neutral zone."

She leaned back against him, without any concern over getting his sweat on her clothes. The woman was beyond low-maintenance. She was so easy to be around, the maintenance seemed to come in being *without* her. Warmth nudged his barriers down a little more and he slid his arms around her waist, flattening his hands low on her belly, aching to slide them between her legs, and Olivia ran one hand over his forearm, closing her fingers around his wrist.

Which reminded Tate of that night, when he'd rolled her to her stomach, pushed into her from behind, and worked his hand between her legs. He closed his eyes, remembering the way her back had arched, the way she'd tilted her pelvis to take him balls-deep. The way she'd tightened her hand on his wrist, loving the feel of him moving between her legs while she gripped the headboard with the other, bracing herself for his thrusts. Using it to push back to meet him.

Her laughter snapped him back, and he focused on the ice, where a gaggle of kids lay tangled in a heap.

"Oh my God," she said, her hand stroking back up his arm. "They're so cute. I'll have to come watch you one day before I leave. I bet you're great with them."

His barriers slipped a little more. "Really?"

She looked over her shoulder. "Really what?"

"You want to come watch the kids?"

"I want to watch *you* with the kids, but yeah, I do. Is that okay? Do I need to tell you when I'm coming, or can I just drop in?"

A strange icy-hot tingle swirled in his gut. "You can come anytime."

She turned to face him. "What's that funny look for?"

He shook his head. "I guess I just realized that no one's ever been interested before. I've been running this camp for six years, and aside from my family or teammates, I can't think of anyone who's ever wanted to come watch."

Her smile dropped. "Not even your wife?"

"Ex-wife," he corrected, even though he knew Olivia was referring to the past. "And no. I guess I never expected anyone to be interested."

"Tate—" She broke off abruptly with a frustrated huff. "I can't talk to you like this. You're too damn tall." With her hand fisted in his sweaty jersey, she used him for balance while she toed out of her little Keds and climbed on the arm of a leather lounge.

"Jesus, Liv, be careful." He was watching the chair to make sure it didn't tip, until Olivia put her free hand to his face and guided his eyes to meet hers.

"All right. Listen to me. Your ex was a selfish, angry, mean, unhappy person who didn't know how good she had it. And she missed out on an amazing life with an amazing man."

Tate stood there, staring into her beautiful blue eyes, speechless. Not only did he have no idea how to respond, he had no idea where that had come from.

"Promise me—right now—that all future women you date have to pass the hockey-kids charity test. If they don't want to come watch you with the kids..." She hitched her thumb over her shoulder. "They're *out*."

Tate laughed and reached for her waist.

"You think I'm kidding." With her arms wrapped around his shoulders, her belly against his chest, she looked down at him. "I'm not. If a woman isn't open enough to be involved in what you do, in who you are, then they don't deserve you. *You're* the prize in the deal. I think you forget that because your ex was—" Anger flashed in her eyes, and she stopped suddenly. "Your ex had issues. But I'm reminding you right now, *you* are a prize. And coming from a woman who's met a lot of men over the course of her life, I can guarantee I know a prize when I see one."

Tate closed his eyes and pressed his face against her chest.

He tightened his arms and just held her a long moment, lost in complex emotions.

When he lowered her to the floor, kissed her, and left her there watching the kids, all he could think on his way to the locker room was *Fucking France.*

11

Olivia stood behind the small bar in the lounge, her forearms pressed to the counter. With her chin resting in one hand, she used the other to tap the face of her phone to check the time.

"So much for fifteen minutes."

If Tate didn't get in here soon, Olivia was going to freeze her tush off. The room wasn't exactly cold, but the temperature from the rink seeped through the glass, so it wasn't exactly warm either.

She shifted on her bare feet, straightened, and pressed her hands against the edge of the bar, smiling at the joy and concentration on the kids' faces.

The door to the lounge swung open. "God, I'm sorry," Tate said, striding in wearing fresh jeans and tee, hair wet, a duffel on his shoulder. He stopped short and scanned the room. "Oliv—"

"Here," she said, drawing his gaze.

"Oh, jeez, thought you left." He started toward her, distracted. "Glad you found the bar. I forgot to tell you there are drinks and water in the fridge. One of the trainers caught me and—"

His gaze finally stopped jumping around and focused. His dark eyes dropped from her face to her open blouse, where she'd unbuttoned the front and left it open to show her lacy bra and lots of skin.

All his air whooshed out. His gaze jumped back to hers and his lips twitched with a smile before he scanned her open shirt again. "Did you change your mind about going home?"

The look in his eyes exposed just how hungry he was, and boosted Olivia's need. There was definitely something about Tate. Something that pulled at her. Something that tied all her loose ending into knots.

"Unfortunately," she said, "I do have to go back to my mom's. I have a lot to do for tomorrow, and I never disappoint a client."

The excitement in his eyes dimmed a little, but he nodded. "I respect that."

Since he didn't come around the bar to her as she'd hoped, Olivia eased back. Her shirt fell open a little more, and Tate's gaze slid downward.

"What the..." he murmured and took one step forward, then planted his hands on the bar and leaned in, looking down. She was naked except for a pair of clinging lacy panties. Tate slammed his eyes shut. "Holy. Shit."

She laughed. "Welcome to the *wild zone*, Mr. Donovan."

A look of desire flashed over his face before he dropped his forehead against the bar with a groaned "*Olivia.*"

She pulled her bottom lip between her teeth. "I figured if the room had cameras, they wouldn't catch much behind here."

He didn't move. Just groaned again.

"Does the room have cameras?"

"No," he breathed.

"In that case, get your sexy ass over here and warm me up."

He exhaled heavily and lifted his head. The want flashing in his eyes stoked the heat between her legs. "Jesus Christ, you're going to give me a heart attack."

Her grin grew. "I don't want to do that, but I would like to get your heart beating really, really fast."

Tate pushed up and looked over his shoulder at the rink, where kids and coaches sped across the ice.

"You've never had sex in a semi-public place, have you?" she asked.

He returned his gaze to her. "Fuck, no."

She took his face between her hands and pulled him toward her for a kiss. She licked his lips, then into his mouth, and curled her tongue around his. Pulling back, she found his dark eyes dazed and hungry.

"I haven't been able to stop thinking about you for days," she said. "I'm sleeping like shit, and I have to be coherent enough to function tomorrow if I'm going to pull off this party. Take one for the team, Tate. Go lock the door and get back here."

Without a word, he strode to the door, opened it a couple of inches, and looked down the hall. When he closed and locked it, a thrill shot through Olivia. Anticipation launched her temperature. Excitement spiked her heart rate. And when he returned to her behind the bar, she jumped into his arms.

He caught her effortlessly, and she wrapped her legs around his hips. With one arm tight at her waist, one behind her head, he covered her mouth with his, and the hunger between them swept her away from everything but him. Relief, hunger, and need vibrated in his throat.

Both physical need and their location infused Olivia with urgency. She unclasped her hands from his neck and broke the kiss to reach for his pants. Tate's mouth moved to her cheek, her jaw, her neck, shooting shivers over her skin.

"Baby," he rasped, "you blow my mind." Then his teeth bit into her shoulder. The sting made her gasp and shot lust between her legs. "Fuckin' want you so bad."

He lowered her butt to a stool she'd pulled behind the bar, and he leaned back. While Olivia struggled to get his zipper down around his erection, Tate stroked and squeezed her breasts, pinched her nipples.

She finally got his pants undone when Tate released the clasp between her breasts and her bra fell open. He groaned, bent, and covered one breast with his hot mouth.

Sensation melted between her legs. Tate's hand followed, his fingers sliding over the silk fabric of her panties in firm circles.

"Yes, yes, yes." She found the rungs of the stool with her feet and lifted into his touch. "Oh yes." All she could do was pull at his shirt and wind her fingers in his hair. He was too far away to grab. She bent her head close to his. "Come here. Let me touch you. Need—"

He moved his mouth from her breast to her lips, cutting off her demands. Then he was stroking the other breast with one hand, while his opposite hand slipped beneath her panties and slid over her sex.

She gasped, broke the kiss, and opened her eyes to his. Then his hand moved, Olivia's eyes crossed, and her head dropped back. Everything was happening so fast. She wanted to slow down and savor it, but knew they couldn't.

Before she righted her head, Tate had her panties at her knees. Olivia pressed her hands to the cushion of the stool to balance as stepped out of them, then he parted her thighs to take his hips. Instead of pushing his hips between her legs, he dropped and slid her thighs over his shoulder, then covered her pussy with his hot mouth.

"Oh... Fuck..." The pleasure was instant and intense. And Tate had to feel the time constraint too, because he worked her hard and fast. Licking, sucking, rubbing, he whipped Olivia to the edge of orgasm so quickly, it startled her. "Jesus Christ... Tate—"

Olivia grasped his head, gripping a handful of his hair as the climax ripped through her. Her muscles contracted, and she curled toward him, only to be hit with jolt after jolt of pleasure. She clenched her teeth against the urge to scream. And when the orgasms finally subsided, Olivia's head swam.

"Fuck," she whispered, trying to catch her breath as Tate pushed to his feet and tossed his wallet on the bar.

His expression was sharp and intense, and his eyes were black. He darted a look toward the glass before searching for a condom. Olivia used his jeans to pull herself upright, moved his clothes out of the way, and found his thick, hard cock waiting. But she'd barely licked her lips when Tate rolled on a condom.

She was still making a sound of disappointment in her throat when Tate wrapped an arm around her waist, pulled her off the stool, and turned her to face the glass.

"Kneel." His husky order warmed her ear, but it wasn't his breath that tingled down her neck, it was the hunger and demand in his voice. "I need to get *deep.*"

Olivia shivered. She *shivered.* A full-body tremor of raw excitement.

She balanced her knees on the stool's leather pad and pressed her hands to the edge of the bar. Tate's big, warm hand stroked her skin from her thigh to the middle of her back, pushing her shirt toward her shoulders. When she looked back at him, his dark gaze ate her up. Every intimate inch of her.

"So fucking gorgeous," he murmured, his hand continuing to sweep over her, creating and endless swath of heat. "Next time, we're turning on all the lights and taking our time, and I'm going to look at every inch of you."

Next time?

A bubble of emotion swelled somewhere inside her and drifted toward the surface. But she had no idea what those emotions were.

Tate's hands were everywhere now, stroking her abdomen, sliding down her back. He circled her waist, flattened his hands on her belly, and moved upward. Over her ribs. Covering her breasts.

He groaned and drew her back against him. His erection teased the crease of her ass and made her pussy clench. Tate pressed a path of openmouthed kisses along her spine, sliding her shirt a little higher for each one.

Olivia couldn't take it anymore. She reached behind her, found his erection, and lifted her hips to nudge the head of his cock against her opening.

"Hungry for me?" Tate rasped in her ear.

"Starved."

He sighed, the sound carrying a satisfied growl. Wrapping one arm low across her hips, he used the other to stroke her pussy and place himself. By the time he was ready to push inside her, Olivia's mouth watered with anticipation.

Tate slipped a hand between her thighs and lifted her leg to the side. Slowly, slowly, slowly, he opened her until she was completely vulnerable. Only then did he push inside. And he entered her just as slowly. Inch by exquisitely thick, burning inch until he filled her beyond capacity, making her breath stutter, her heart quiver.

There, he paused, and Olivia lowered her head, letting it drop between her outstretched arms braced against the bar.

He pressed a kiss to the top of her shoulder and said, "Feel me, baby?"

She didn't understand the question, just knew she wanted him to move. To rock his hips. To pull out and thrust home. To fuck her until she screamed.

He seemed to read her mind, drawing out of her so

completely, she lifted her head to look over her shoulder. But before she ever got that far, Tate drove back in. All the way in. Swift and hard.

The finish stole Olivia's breath. The instant explosion of pleasure pushed a cry from her lips.

"This is all I've been able to think about," Tate rasped at her ear. "Getting so deep inside you, the only thing you feel is me. The only thing you can think about is me."

"Yes..." It came out in a whisper.

The arm around her waist loosened, and he slipped his hand between her legs. Her sex clenched.

"Mmm, so soft." He gently worked his fingers into her folds, until two fingers snuggled on either side of her clit.

He released her thigh, and when she closed her legs, his hand was wedged against her sex, rubbing her in all the right places. Pleasure spilled in, and Olivia moaned, long and low.

He wrapped his free arm around her, cupping her breast.

"Tate." She moaned his name, lifting her hips to push him deeper. But it also made other parts tug against his hand... "Oh God..."

Tate thrust gently, a quiet move, but one that sang through her. Each stroke grew longer, deeper, and harder. Each stroke delivered a double jolt of ecstasy. And Tate seemed exquisitely talented at spacing his thrusts just far enough apart to hold off Olivia's orgasm until she was shaking and panting.

"Want to feel you come," he murmured at her shoulder. "All around me."

He thrust and Olivia's back arched, but she couldn't move because Tate was right there, a wall of muscle. "Yes, yes..."

"Mmm, Liv, feel so good."

He thrust and his breath pushed out of his chest on a growl.

"Ah..." She jerked, shivered, but didn't break. "Mmm..."

"So good right on the edge, isn't it?" His voice was like

whiskey, smooth, dark, suggestive, erotic, a little edgy. "Makes you want to just linger here."

He thrust again.

Olivia bucked, cried out, soaked in the pleasure flooding her pelvis, and clenched her teeth against the white-hot lust.

"You need it, baby?"

"Yes."

"Mmm." He pulled out a little, pushed in a little, pulled out a little, pushed in a little. The lazy, scintillating, maddening rhythm made Olivia's pussy relax and open and reach for him. Ache for him. And he knew it. He felt it. Because once the tension ebbed and she was breathing easier...

He thrust. Hard.

Stars sparkled behind her lids. "*Fuck*," she bit out. "That's so good." She huffed air, shaking again. "Why is that so good?"

"Because it's *us*," he murmured and bit her earlobe. "Remember?"

She pulled an arm away from the bar to catch his head and kissed him. Opened fully to him and rolled his tongue with hers. When he groaned, she pulled back and whispered, "Give it to me."

Even as he pulled out, he asked, "How bad do you want it?"

"Really bad."

Thrust. *Zing. Bang.*

She squeezed her eyes as the pleasure ripped through her. "Ah..."

"How bad?"

Olivia fisted her hand in his hair. "So bad."

He thrust again.

Olivia whimpered. Tate swore, kissed her hard, and hammered out strokes in quick succession.

Olivia rose and rose and rose... And finally flew. Before she broke, Tate covered her mouth to muffle her scream. Her brain went numb, her vision went white, and her body flexed and twisted with ecstasy.

Distantly, she felt Tate's last few thrusts before he too found release. He turned his head and pressed his mouth to her hair, muffling his own deep sounds of pleasure.

Olivia bent one arm on the bar, and rested her head there. Tate's weight felt like lead, but she didn't complain. And as they caught their breaths, Olivia's mind kept circling around a dumbfounded sort of shock at how intense, how fulfilling, how damn good this sex was. She had enough experience behind her to know there was something special between them making the sex so spectacular. It wasn't simply physical.

"Holy shit..." His quiet words dragged her back to reality and everything that still faced her. Including going back to Paris in a very short time, just when she was beginning to want more time with him.

He pressed a kiss to her shoulder and pulled away. Olivia groaned, crossed her ankles, and dropped back on her heels. While Tate cleaned up and washed his hands in the sink, Olivia pulled her bra into place and buttoned her shirt.

She was a little depressed about heading back home to deal with her family now. And she wasn't thrilled about having to work a party that wouldn't pay her a dime. But that vacant feeling that always engulfed her after sex was notably absent. Again.

Olivia wondered if that hollowness went away when you found the right person.

Tate stepped in front of her with her panties. He was still breathing hard, wiping his face on the shoulder of his tee while he righted the skimpy lace. In the moment, she was sure she'd never seen a man do anything more adorable. Then he outdid himself when he lowered to one knee and held her panties so she could step into them. "Here you go."

Emotion expanded inside her, the kind of emotion that

both alarmed and confused her. She slipped off the stool and stepped into the panties, using his shoulder for balance.

When he stood, his mouth kicked into a grin. "What's that little smile about?"

She leaned in and kissed him. "It's all about you, Tate Donovan. It's all about you."

12

Olivia rested her head against the seat and gazed out the windshield, but she didn't see the DC streets or the traffic. Tate had wrung her out and left her blissfully sated. She tilted her head, laid it on his shoulder, and let her eyes close.

Tate squeezed her hand where her fingers were threaded with his. "You okay?"

"Mmm, perfect." She pulled in a breath and let it out in a slow sigh. "But I'm going to have a hard time keeping my eyes open until I get all my work done tonight."

"Can I help? I'll let you boss me around and everything."

She laughed and lifted her head. "That sounds fun, and if I were in my own kitchen, I'd do it, but I'm already out of sync in my mom's kitchen, so I'd end up walking over you. It'll be easier for me in the end if I do it on my own. She rested her chin on his shoulder. "Thank you for offering, though. That's sweet."

She kissed him just below his ear, and his head leaned her way. At a stoplight, he turned his head, met her eyes, and smiled. They were almost nose to nose, and he eased forward, pressing a kiss to her lips. His lashes fluttered closed and he let his lips linger. The moment felt so intimate. So perfect.

He pulled back and glanced at the light, which had turned green, and continued down the road. Olivia nuzzled his neck, breathing in the clean, male scent of his skin.

"Do you know what you want on the menu for the banquet?" she asked.

"Are you available?"

She laughed. "Only for you."

He squeezed her hand. "I think I'll leave that up to you. It's a complex group of people. We'll have players who'd really rather be at a bar with a burger and sponsors who are more interested in talking than eating. Then there will be true donors, who are really the ones who pay the most attention to the food. And I'm not going to be any help because I'm not one of the people who knows anything."

"So, no froufrou food?"

He grinned. "Good start."

"Are we talking steaks? Do you want to get really simple with a gourmet burger?"

"I'd lean toward steak, considering how much they're paying."

"Okay. What options do you want for vegetarians and vegans and gluten-free—"

He groaned.

Olivia laughed. "You want me to handle it?"

"I really do. Is that okay?"

"Of course. That's my job." She thought a minute. "Okay, let's play the either/or game. I'll give you choices, and with the banquet in mind, you choose. It's just to give me an idea of what I'm going for."

"Okay."

"We already did burgers versus steaks. How about four-course or five-course?"

"I don't know the difference."

She smiled. "Warm spinach salad with bacon and feta or cold wedge with blue cheese, bacon, and tomato?"

"Spinach."

"Filet mignon or New York strip?"

"Ooo, that's a tough one," he said. "Up to you."

"Arctic char or wild salmon?"

He cut a look at her. "Arctic char? What in the hell is arctic char?"

She laughed. "A fish."

"You can pick."

"Okay, what about dessert? Do you want to go with decadent chocolate or light and fruity? Cake, soufflé, tiramisu?"

He groaned. "So many choices."

"You sound like you're in pain. Okay, how about this, what's your favorite dessert?"

He thought about it a second. "I really love key lime pie."

"Okay, done. It may not be a pie, but I'll make you something sensational in key lime." She rubbed the tip of her nose along his neck. "See, not so bad."

"You make it easy." After another moment of silence, he said, "I love this part of DC. All the old trees. Every house is different from the next. All stately with big yards and beautiful gardens. Have you always lived here?"

"From birth to eighteen. And every year was wonderful, right up until the end. But I've got lots of great memories. Did you grow up here?"

He shook his head. "Colorado. Moved for my first farm team and kept moving. I've been here six years and really love it. Love the area, love the people." He lifted a shoulder. "But you never know. One day I could go into work and the coach could call me in and say, 'Sorry, buddy, you're playing for the Blackhawks now—or the Devils or the fucking Ducks—pack up.'"

"Really?" She frowned. "That's got to feel so unstable."

"Says the nomad."

"True."

"I guess you get used to it. Easier when you don't have a wife and kids. Beckett's contract comes up in July. If the teams here want to sign him, they're going to have to add a no-trade clause, because he's not uprooting Lily and Eden."

"You can do that?"

He cut a sidelong grin at her. "If you're good enough, you can do anything. Just gotta stay on top of your game."

"Sounds like a lot of pressure."

"Your job sounds like a lot of pressure to me."

"How do you stay on top of your game?"

"There are so many aspects to being your best that there's always something to work on," he told her. "If it's not your skating, it's your handwork. If it's not your focus, it's your leadership. I'm taking over as captain next season, so this summer, my regular trainer is pulling in some guru to coach me on effective leadership, motivation, stuff like that."

"That sounds cool. Where is it?"

"Canada. Ontario. That's where my trainer lives. He works out of a college rink up there. It's a sweet setup. During the day, I get top-notch hockey training. At night, I get counseled in leadership to polish up my versatility. I leave right after the banquet."

"Man, to have those kinds of experts at your fingertips. That's what I love about Bleu."

He turned his head. "Bleu?"

"Le Cordon Bleu. I just shorten it." She grinned. "They hate it. Sometimes I do it in front of them just to get a rise."

Tate laughed and kissed her temple. "You can be pretty damn sassy."

"The instructors there are so amazing. And the school is always having seminars and short courses where chefs from all over the world come to teach. Food and culture and people fascinate me."

They fell silent again. Olivia's mind wandered toward things she normally didn't ask men she slept with. These were discussions for friends and coworkers or acquaintances, and even though she knew she should be demarcating a more rigid line between friend and lover, for the first time in her life, she didn't want to.

"Can I ask what happened with your ex-wife?" When the happy look on his face fell, she regretted the question immediately. "Never mind. I'm sorry. It's none of my—"

"It's okay." His voice was gentle. "She was cheating on me."

The answer was so unexpected, Olivia didn't have time to stem her shock. She sucked air and blurted, "*What? For fuck's sake, why?*"

Which made Tate burst out laughing. And he kept laughing until tears filled his eyes and he had to wipe them away with the back of his hand to drive. "Oh, baby, that was priceless. I wish I had that on video."

His humor over her reaction lightened her own feelings, but she shook her head. "That's just unbelievable."

"Thank you, but..." He winced. "You haven't lived through a hockey season."

"Why? What's hockey season like?"

"It's sort of indescribable. One of those things you have to experience to understand. We play about three or four games a week. Half our games are at home, half are away. We practice most of the days we don't play. And in our spare time"—he put the word spare in air quotes—"we're expected to do charity work and attend team events. But it's really the emotional roller coaster that I think is the hardest on wives and girlfriends and kids. We're all so passionate about each game and our overall ranking. Your team could win, but you could have had a shitty game. If you're hurt, you're cranky. If you're tired, you're cranky. If you lose—"

"Let me guess," she said.

"All in all, hockey season can be grueling."

"Sorry, maybe I do have to experience it to understand, but it sounds a lot like my last year, flying all over the damn place for one event or another. There's the travel, the work, the required socializing and schmoozing. Sure, it's stressful and exhausting, but it certainly doesn't make cheating okay."

"Amen."

"I mean," she added for levity, "unless you're a closet serial ax murderer or Cheetos addict or you snore or something."

He slammed his hand against the steering wheel, and Olivia jumped. "It was the fucking Cheetos. I *knew* it."

And it was her turn to burst out laughing. She was just catching her breath when they pulled in front of her mom's house.

Tate turned off the truck, and Olivia had one of those knee-jerk reactions. "Oh, you don't have to—"

"I want to talk to Quinn."

Alarm bells buzzed in Olivia's head. "You don't have to talk to her. I will."

"I think it should come from me." And he opened his door and climbed out.

"Tate. Tate—"

He closed the door and walked around the front.

"Shit." She opened her door and stepped out just as he met her there. "Really, don't. It will only piss her off."

With his hands braced on the door, he met Olivia's eyes. "She'll give you nothing but grief. But I guarantee she won't give me a sliver."

"To your face. She'll give it all to me behind your back."

He tipped his head. "Can you trust me on this?"

"Oh my God, Tate—"

"Please?"

That cut off her next argument. She pressed her eyes

closed, then glanced at the house and returned her gaze to Tate. "I swear, Donovan, if you make things worse—"

"I'll become your sexual slave in perpetuity." He held up his hand. "So help me God."

She smiled grudgingly, turned, and started up the stairs toward the house.

13

Tate felt Olivia's tension ratchet higher with each step toward the house.

He slipped a hand beneath her hair and stroked it down her back, looking up at the majestic historical brick home. "Wow. This is amazing."

She smiled. "I've always been so in love with it."

Pausing on the porch, trimmed with a white banister and rails that had seen better days, she looked around the yard with its overflowing flower beds, lush lawn, and mature trees.

"My parents bought it about forty years ago, right after they got married. It was in foreclosure and had been abandoned for a long time. My dad renovated it from top to bottom over the years. He did the historical research on the house, so whenever I'd help him, he'd tell me all the stories. It was fascinating." She ran her hand over the peeling paint on a banister and watched the flakes flutter to the porch. "So sad to see it falling into disrepair. This would have driven my dad crazy."

Tate leaned against the column. "You sound like a daddy's girl."

She grinned, but it was sad. "Two hundred percent." Her

gaze drifted toward the front door. "Quinn has always been mama's girl."

Huh. That explained a couple of things.

Tate studied her profile while she was lost in thought, realizing what a complex woman he'd stumbled over. And what a big hole she was going to leave in his life after such a short time together.

She took a breath that raised her shoulders, then heaved a sigh. "Guess I can't stand out here all night."

When Olivia reached for the door, Tate said, "Hey." She glanced at him. "It's going to be okay."

She smiled, but it looked pained. Then nodded and pushed into the house.

Tate followed, closing the door at his back while he took in the rich wood floors that looked original, the plaster walls, the high ceilings and thick crown molding. A chandelier cast dappled light over the neutral paint. The foyer was generous and welcoming, with a bench, plenty of hooks for winter jackets, racks for winter boots, and an umbrella stand. To the left, a wide staircase led to the second floor, a carpet lining the middle of the wooden steps. The first few stairs were wide and curved, tapering into a straight staircase.

Tate ran his hand over the newel, a pillar where the remaining rail spiraled to begin an elegant curve up the stairway. "Beautiful."

Olivia glanced back at him and smiled, and Tate could see her love for the house in her eyes. "Dad and I refinished the entire staircase. Sanded every balustrade and the entire railing by hand."

Tate's gaze slid up the stairs again, now looking at what had to be over a hundred balustrades. "Oh my God."

She laughed softly. "Yeah. Every corner of this house has a memory of my dad in it. I can't ever imagine it leaving the family. Mom and Dad used to talk about having grandkids running through the hallways the way Quinn and I did. I thought Quinn would have a couple by now."

The image hit at the heart of Tate's own fantasies. At least the ones he'd had when he'd married Lisa. Hearing Olivia talk so fondly of kids was creating a pull inside him that he knew instantly was both illogical and dangerous.

"Why hasn't she?"

Olivia sighed, shrugged. "She's so wrapped up in Mom and Mom's business, but...I really don't know."

"And why haven't you?" There was no possible way for him to keep the question inside.

It made Olivia laugh with real humor. "My life is not conducive to children." She looked around. "The idea of being able to share my dad's legacy with my own children is a romantic one, and I haven't been a romantic in a long time. Realistically, I doubt I'll ever have children."

That news kicked Tate in the stomach. He realized exactly how irrational that was. How childish. And just how infatuated he'd become with her. Because he wanted to expand this little slice of intimacy they were sharing, he forced himself to detach and respond the way he would to a female friend.

"Really? Why? Your life may not be conducive now, but you're young."

She lifted a shoulder and studied the chandelier. "I like kids, enjoy my friends' kids. My secret pleasure is kids' birthday parties, even though I end up barely breaking even on the cost. I just love the kids. Had hoped to have some nieces and nephews to teach French and travel with when they got older, you know? But, me?" She shook her head. "I don't see it. I've never had anyone in my life who changed that."

Tate stuffed his hands in the pockets of his jeans. A dull ache nagged somewhere inside him. He was probably stepping over a line, but hell... "Liv, have you ever been in love?"

She turned a heartbreakingly sad smile on him, one he'd

bet she didn't realize looked so empty, and shook her head. "Can't say I have."

That stunned him. And saddened him. So deeply saddened him, his heart sank in his chest. He was trying to find a response when Quinn called through the house.

"Liv?" She was on the same floor but somewhere deeper in the house. "Everything is in the fridge or on the counter." Her voice grew closer. "But I'm going to have to run out to another market to get you more organic eggs. The one I went to didn't—"

Quinn turned into the foyer, her hand on the doorjamb, and stopped short. "Oh." Her gaze jumped between them, then back to Tate and immediately shadowed with guilt. "Mr.—"

"Tate, please," he said, voice gentle, adding a smile.

She relaxed. "Tate."

Barefoot, wearing shorts and a tank top with her hair in a braid, she looked beautiful and young and fresh, and the thought of seeing the same side of Olivia tugged at Tate's heart.

"I'm sorry, I didn't know Liv was bringing anyone over."

Olivia glanced at Tate, then to her sister, she said, "Tate asked to come over so he could talk with you—"

"Quinn, is that Olivia?" Their mother's voice floated down the stairs. The women's gazes locked, and Tate witnessed—or maybe felt, he wasn't sure—a hell of a lot of silent communication between them.

Olivia, standing at the bottom of the stairs, broke Quinn's gaze to look toward the voice. "I'm home."

"Oh, great. How did your talk with Tate go?"

Olivia shot a death stare at Quinn, who crossed her arms and looked at the floor.

"What did he think of your menu suggestions?" their mother prodded.

Olivia glanced at Tate, but she was putting puzzle pieces together.

When Olivia didn't answer, her mother called again. "Olivia?"

"I loved them, Mrs. Essex."

Tate's answer pulled both Quinn and Olivia out of whatever silent war they were battling.

"Mr. Donovan?" Footsteps sounded on the stairs, and as soon as Teresa cleared the second floor, she bent to peer over the banister. "Well, hello."

He grinned. "Please call me Tate. I was just dropping Olivia home and wanted to come in and tell you myself that I'm completely comfortable with Olivia handling the catering at the banquet."

"How thoughtful of you." She continued down the stairs and moved forward to shake his hand.

"Your home is absolutely beautiful," he told her.

She beamed, and her daughter's blue eyes twinkled back at him. "Thank you. We love this place."

"It shows."

"Well," Olivia said, "I'll just let you three talk. "I'll be in the kitchen."

Olivia's eyes met his for a second before she moved into the other room, but he couldn't quite read her thoughts. Tate slipped into socializing mode, something he didn't love but had learned for the publicity part of his career. He did his best to soothe any nerves the two women might have over his commitment to the project and glossed over the "menu choices" he and Olivia had allegedly been discussing.

Quinn remained quiet, responding only when Teresa cajoled a response.

Teresa's phone rang. "Oh dear, I'm sorry."

"Perfectly fine," Tate told her. "I'm headed home."

She shook his hand and answered her phone as she wandered down the hall and into another room.

"Well, I better help Olivia—" Quinn started.

"One second, Quinn."

She stiffened, clearly locked and loaded for battle.

"I just want to put your mind at ease regarding things between me and Olivia."

"That's none of my—"

"That's not what you thought when you sent Olivia to set boundaries with me."

She sipped a breath and pressed her lips together.

"I've been impressed with the work you and Teresa have done to date. And I've heard nothing but fabulous things about Essex from everyone I've talked to. I hired you before Olivia ever came to town. Nothing that happens with Olivia—good or bad—will color how I feel about your services, your company, you or your mother. I have the ability to see them separately."

She searched his eyes, seemed to weigh her words. "She's leaving. You know that, right? I don't know what you're looking for, but from everything I've heard about you, Olivia's style isn't yours. I hope you're not fooling yourself into thinking you'll change her mind. She never stays. No matter how much we want her to stay, no matter what we do, she never stays."

That knocked a little chunk of his heart loose. But he nodded, accepting reality. "I do know. She's been crystal clear about where she stands. And I've taken that into consideration. But..." He glanced at the floor, not sure what he wanted to say or how to say it, so he just let it come out. "I am crazy about her. And the way I feel when I'm with her is something I don't want to miss out on just because I may get hurt when she leaves."

Quinn looked away, exhaled, and her shoulders slid lower, her whole posture one of disappointment and dismay. "Fine. It's your life. As long as it doesn't affect Mom and the company." She met his gaze once more. "Good night."

Quinn disappeared up the stairs. Tate stood there a second, listening to Olivia's movements in the kitchen just a few feet away and Teresa's buoyant voice muffled in another room, wondering what the fuck had happened to this family.

He wandered into the kitchen and watched Olivia a minute while she glanced at grocery items, reading ingredients and segregating different things in different areas on the granite countertops. Her movements were efficient, her hands quick.

She paused, sighed, and combed her hands through her hair. Then collected the pale strands into a tail, wound it round and round, then pulled an end through the center, securing a bun without a clip in seconds. She'd clearly done it thousands of times.

He walked up behind her and slipped his arms around her. She gasped and jumped, trying to push away, exactly the way he'd expected her to.

"Shh," he whispered at her ear, his eyes sliding closed on the exquisite feel of her against him. Instantly bringing back memories of some of the hottest sex of his entire life just an hour before. "Quinn's upstairs, and your mom's on the phone in the other room. I'm just saying good-bye."

She relaxed against him, slid her hands over his arms, and turned her head, leaning into him. That small show of affection and acceptance opened a stream of warmth through him.

"How'd Quinn take it?" she asked.

"She heard me." He kissed her neck. "But I'd be prepared for fallout. She's as stubborn as you, but not near as easy-going or happy with life."

Olivia sighed. "Well, at this point, I don't think it could hurt much between us."

"I'm sorry, baby. I know how it feels when your sister is shooting daggers at you every time you see her."

She closed her eyes and groaned, then spontaneously turned into him and wrapped her arms around him. The move stunned Tate. He held her tight, soaking in the feel of her face pressed to his neck. The feel of her needing him, even if it was only for a few seconds. Because he hadn't felt this good, this whole, this complete, in years.

"Take me with you." Olivia's whisper was so soft, he would have thought he'd imagined it if he hadn't also felt her breath on his skin. "I don't want to do this alone anymore."

Another chunk of his heart broke away. He was feeling painfully grateful to Quinn at that moment. If she hadn't reminded him of how rooted Olivia was somewhere else, this woman could so easily make him forget she was going to shatter his heart in a couple of weeks. But Quinn was right. Olivia might need a little lovin' to get through the rough spots, but when she was solid, she didn't need anyone.

He hugged her tight. "I'm right here. You're not alone. If you need interference, pick up the phone."

14

Olivia watched Tate's truck pull away from the curb through the side window at the door, with something bizarre gnawing and twisting in her gut. She couldn't reconcile these crazy feelings.

To settle herself, she thought through the segments of her life. She was stressed over school approaching—there wasn't much she could do about that. But just to reassure herself, she pressed her back to the front door, pulled her phone from her pocket, and tapped into the app for her bank account. The payment for a catering job she'd done in Tuscany had been deposited. She had the fifteen percent she needed to live up to her responsibilities in the scholarship agreement. Which was good, because it was due in about a week and a half.

Olivia took a deep breath, filling her lungs. She pushed the phone back into her pocket and looked up the stairs. Quinn wasn't nearly as simple or clear-cut. And Olivia was beginning to realize she and her sister might never reclaim the unbreakable bond that had been so painfully severed a decade ago.

Her heart felt heavy. For the first time, she wished she had someone to talk to about it. Tate would be a great listener. He'd be compassionate, but honest. With his recent problems in his own family, he might even have valuable insight for her. But opening up a personal line of communication like that could lead him to the wrong conclusion, and she didn't want to give him any false hope.

She closed her eyes, dropped her head back against the door, and thought of her tiny flat in Bastille. Of her neighbors, Vivienne and Leila, who were picking up her mail. Of her coworkers, Gautier and Jean-Marc, who were sharing the shifts she was missing by staying longer. Of the cobblestone streets, her favorite cafés, and their owners who'd become woven into the fabric of her life. She longed for the serenity of everything she knew and found comfortable.

But there was no Tate in Paris.

"Livvy?" Her mother's voice startled her. "Are you all right?"

"Sure." She straightened. "Just making a mental list. Hey, do you have a minute? I really need to talk to you."

She took a nervous glance at her watch. "Well, I have a meeting with a senator and his wife about a christening in forty-five minutes across town, and at this time of night..."

"It won't take long."

Her mother smiled and followed Olivia into the kitchen, where they sat at a small table in a bay window that overlooked the backyard where Olivia had played all her young life.

"I was talking to Quinn about the business, and I realized that I may not have explained over the years how much experience I have in restaurant management."

Her mother's gaze was attentive and concerned.

"And I wanted you to know that I've worked with some of the best restaurateurs in Europe over the years. Learned so much about management and finances from top businessmen in the restaurant industry who have huge catering businesses."

"That's fantastic." Her mother's expression brightened. "Honey, I really want you to think about coming home once school is finished. You've been gone so long. If you don't want to join our company, you could have a very lucrative catering company of your own. Or you could get a job as an executive chef at one of the dozens of five-star restaurants in the city. DC is nothing if not a food and party mecca."

Olivia shook her head. "No, Mom, I'm talking about your business. I'm *worried* about your business—"

"No, Livvy, no." She covered Olivia's hand with her own, smiling. "Honey, this is the most business we've seen since we've started. This is fabulous. A huge upturn in our sales and events. Once we get through this first wave, we'll have the capital to pay off debt, hire employees, and expand." She patted Olivia's hand. "Baby, you won't have to send money home anymore." She cupped her cheek. "You're sweet to worry, and there were times in the past when it was hard, but we're on the upswing."

Her mother wasn't hearing her, and Olivia saw the disaster waiting in the road ahead.

She clasped her fingers around her mother's and smiled. "That's fantastic. You and Quinn have worked hard for this, and I'm so happy to see you finally getting some wind beneath your wings. I just want you to know is that growing too fast can be as detrimental to a business as not growing at all."

She gave Olivia a disparaging look. "Olivia, don't be ridiculous."

This. This was the problem. "I'm serious, Mom. I've seen it happen with my own eyes. I've had businessmen tell me it has happened to them. Research it. Ask other business owners. If you grow too fast, if you overcommit before the infrastructure of the business can handle it, you'll topple, and it could take the whole company down."

Her mother sighed, clearly unhappy with Olivia's message. "I know you're worried because you care, honey, but I don't believe in negativity—"

"This isn't negativity, it's *reality*."

Teresa glanced at her watch. "I have to go, or I'll be late."

When her mother stood, Olivia pushed to her feet and stepped in her path. "I've done the numbers. Based on the jobs you've taken on over the last month and the number you continue to add every day, you're already leaning toward catastrophe like the Tower of Pisa."

"Olivia," her mother scolded. "Enough."

She didn't care if her mother was angry, because Olivia was angry too. Angry because she was scared. She saw her mother and sister headed toward the edge of a cliff for the promise of a sparkling diamond on the other side, ready to walk off the edge with nothing to save them but the faith that a bridge would appear.

"It's not enough until you hear me." Olivia continued talking while her mother walked around her toward the front door. "With just you and Quinn running this company, with no financial backing, you're already juggling too many jobs. Every job you take on from this point adds another brick to the top of that tilted tower. All it takes is one job to go wrong and everything—*everything*—will spiral out of control."

When her mother turned the doorknob without acknowledging her, Olivia slapped her hand against the door to hold it closed. This was her only chance to say her piece. She would never forgive herself if she returned to France without at least warning them. Whether or not they took her advice was up to them.

"I know this isn't what you want to hear, but I love you and Quinn, and it's important for someone to tell you that if you don't pull back now, while you still can, you could lose your entire business in the blink of an eye. Think about it, Mom. Then what would you have?"

Her mother jerked the door open, jarring Olivia's arm, walked out, and slammed it behind her.

Pain coiled in Olivia's bicep and shoulder, and she reached around to rub at the burn. "Fuck."

The ache dug deep into the muscle and broke Olivia's last thread of strength. Her pained grimace turned to sobs on a dime, and before she knew what was happening, she was leaning against the wall, her face against her forearm, bawling.

"Livvy." Her sister's soft voice registered first, then Quinn's hand on her shoulder.

Olivia startled and turned while stepping away. She put one hand against the wall for balance, her breathing choppy. "M-mom..." She couldn't get her thoughts together. Couldn't keep the tears from falling. She pushed her hands against her eyes and shook her head. "Mom d-didn't li-i-sten. Now she's ma-a-d."

The overly simplistic words made her feel three years old again, and just as inept. Just as out of control. And Olivia couldn't stop the tears.

"Livvy." Quinn crouched and brushed her hair aside, rubbing at Olivia's wet cheeks. "You did the right thing. You told her what she needed to hear even though it was hard for both of you."

Olivia couldn't think. She was overwrought with emotion. She'd been holding it all in for so long. Too long. She slid to the floor and dropped her head back against the wall, trying to regulate her breathing. Quinn sat next to her and pulled her into her arms.

Olivia rested her head on her knees and Quinn sat with her, hip to hip, thigh to thigh, her fingers combing through her hair, the way they used to as kids—while watching TV, reading books, coloring, trying to fall asleep.

She took a shaky breath. "I miss you." The words came out weak and broken. Olivia cleared her throat. "I miss us. I miss the way we used to be."

"Me too." Quinn leaned her head against Olivia's and wrapped her arms around her shoulders. "I'm so sorry."

Olivia sighed. Just the small break in the wall between them seemed to release pressure in her chest. "Why?"

"Tate said something tonight... It made me realize that I've been pushing you away all these years. I didn't even really know why."

She lifted her head and wiped her face. Quinn loosened her arms, and Olivia pulled back. "What do you mean?"

"He said that the way he feels when he's with you is too good to give up even knowing he'll hurt when you leave."

Her breath stuttered, and another wave of tears pushed at her eyes. "He...said that?"

"Yeah. And it made me realize that I've been pushing you away for exactly that reason. Losing you has hurt so much that when you're home, I don't want to let you in because I know you're going to leave again. But after Tate said that, I realized I've wasted years pushing you away."

Olivia dropped her against Quinn's. "I don't want to do that anymore, Liv."

Olivia hugged Quinn tight. "Me either." She exhaled heavily and spontaneously asked, "Want to come live in France with me? I bet you'd love it."

Quinn started laughing, which made Olivia laugh too. "Yeah, I really do." She pulled away and looked at Olivia. "But let's get Mom on her feet first, so we can just have fun."

"Deal."

Quinn released Olivia and pushed to her feet. Then she offered her hand. "Come on. I'll let you boss me around in the kitchen."

15

Tate wandered among the tables on the covered deck at the Crofts' home and picked up empty trays as inconspicuously as possible. It gave him a reason to visit Olivia in the kitchen, even though every time he did, she told him he distracted her. But as the day wore on and more guests arrived, Tate had discovered more and more men hanging out in the kitchen chatting with her when he wandered in. Men clearly interested in more than her cooking skills.

He felt that little tick festering in the pit of his stomach, a mix of jealousy and self-doubt. And he'd done a decent job of dousing the smoldering ember with logic and rationale. Now, he was just holding out for the end of the party, when he hoped he could convince her to come home with him—if not for the entire night so he could wake up with her, at least for several hours where they could be alone. Where Tate could lavish some attention on her and what would soon be—if they weren't already—sore muscles. Where Tate could get his fix.

Because he needed an Olivia fix.

Badly.

The fact that this was a big problem with her exit coming so soon was a constant thread of tension he just kept shoving to the back of his mind to deal with later. He didn't have a hell of a lot of options.

His cell chimed. He pulled it from his back pocket and found a text from his agent Dave Burnett. *Tiffany and I will be home from Greece in a few days, so we'll be at your Afterschool Advantage dinner next weekend. I bought the tickets online today. Tiff said you have a great party planner. Can I get her info? I need to set up a series of dinners for a handful of college kids I'm recruiting for NBA and NFL in a couple of weeks. Just dinners, accommodations, sight-seeing trips. Thanks.*

He texted his agent back. *Fantastic. Look forward to seeing you both. My planner is great. I'll send her info in a few.*

Pocketing his phone, Tate searched the deck for Teresa. She was sitting in a small group with her back to him, chatting with Tina Croft and Betty Bradfield, a longtime neighbor of the Crofts who occasionally babysat Lily in a pinch. He wandered that direction, waiting for the right moment to interrupt.

At a table nearby, he collected another empty dish and said hello to a couple of the Crofts' friends.

"A lovely couple," Teresa was telling Betty. "It's the first grandchild on both sides of the family, and relatives are traveling from Italy for the christening."

"How wonderful," Betty crooned.

"They've having the ceremony at St. Patrick's—"

Tina gasped. "Oh, I love that cathedral."

"I know," Teresa said. "So gorgeous. It's going to be a stunning event. I've reserved District Whiskey's rooftop terrace for the reception."

"That's one swanky christening," Tina said, an edge of humor in her voice. "Beckett's lucky he made it to the neighborhood church. I'd have been just as satisfied to dunk him in the nearest pond as soon as the ice thawed and make the sign of the cross on his forehead."

Tate was chuckling to himself, already planning how he'd repeat that to Beckett, when Quinn approached the women. Tate saw his opening and started around the chairs toward the front of the seating arrangement.

"Quinn, honey," Teresa said. "Can I have a minute?"

Tate's feet stopped.

Teresa excused herself and stepped just a couple of feet away with Quinn. Tate waited patiently. If he didn't get the information now, he'd forget and never send it. And the way Teresa's calendar was filling up, it would be too late for Dave to get in with her.

"What's up?" Quinn asked.

"I just got an email from Senator Dioli's wife, Angela, with a signed contract. I'm going to pick up the deposit check this week."

"Wow." Quinn didn't sound anywhere near as excited as Teresa. "What's the date of the christening?"

"August—" Someone walked between them, and Tate didn't hear the date.

"Isn't that the same weekend as the Devoy wedding?" Quinn asked.

"Yes, but the wedding's on Sunday, the christening's on Saturday."

"But we'll be preparing for the wedding all week." Stress lifted Quinn's voice an octave. "We'll need Saturday to set up—"

"Honey, don't worry about those details now. With the payment from that christening, we only need one more decent-sized job to pay off the balloon payment."

Balloon payment. The women continued to talk, but Tate's mind rolled back in time. He only had negative associations with balloon payments, because he'd had one on the house he and Lisa had been renovating when they divorced. From what he could remember, balloons were generally used for quick-turnaround sales or less than favorable borrower arrangements. And he knew they carried significant risk.

Now Tate's mind veered to Olivia's love for her childhood home. To how deeply connected the house was to Olivia's memories of her father. A father she'd lost too soon. The thought of how she'd feel if her mother and sister lost that house...

"Excuse us." The voice belonged to an older couple passing between Tate and Quinn and Teresa. Everyone's gazes shifted. Teresa and Quinn locked eyes with Tate, and he instantly saw the oh-shit pass through their expressions.

By the time the elderly couple hobbled their way past, Teresa had collected herself. "Well, hi, Tate. Enjoying the party?"

"Very much." He glanced at Quinn, then back to Teresa. "I didn't mean to interrupt—"

"It's fine," Teresa said, but her expression said something different.

Tate pushed forward. "My agent is looking for a planner to help him arrange some events for a handful of college kids and their parents he has coming into town in a couple of weeks. He says they're being recruited to the NBA and NFL."

"Oh really?"

Tate nodded. "He'll need someone to be the liaison for the families, find them accommodations, create a schedule for them that includes time with my agent and various tours as well as some downtime with tourist-type activities that fit their preferences."

"Sounds very doable." She glanced at Quinn and nodded. Quinn shrugged, nodded. Teresa smiled at Tate. "Yes, yes. If you'd like to give me his number, I'll call him in the morning."

"I'll get you his email and his number. He's vacationing in Greece, but he'll be back in a few days. And I'll pass your information on to him as well."

"Thank you so much for thinking of us."

Tate nodded and started to turn, but Teresa reached out and squeezed his arm gently.

When he met her gaze again, Teresa murmured, "Please don't mention..." She paused, selecting her words carefully, "what you overheard between Quinn and I with Olivia. There's no point in upsetting her so close to her return to France when everything is going to turn out just fine."

Tate darted a look at Quinn, but she was gone. He told Teresa, "Of course."

He couldn't quite describe the bizarre sensations churning in his gut as he picked up another empty tray from a nearby table and started toward the kitchen, only that they were uncomfortable and conflicted.

Quinn intercepted him, also carrying empty trays in the same direction. She stopped and smiled at him. "Great minds?"

She'd been unusually warm to him today, a surprise given the tone of their discussion last night and how coldly it had ended. "I'll go with that. Here," Tate said, gesturing to his arms, "pile those on top. I'm going in."

"Thanks." Once the trays were settled on top of his, she offered a random "Olivia and I talked last night."

Tate wasn't sure if he should be hopeful or wary. "She's been so busy, I haven't gotten a chance to say more than two words to her today. Was it a good talk?"

Quinn smiled. "It was. One we should have had a long time ago. I think things are going to get a lot better. At least... between us."

Relief slid along his shoulders, loosening muscles Tate hadn't realized were tight. He wanted to know what she meant by *"between us"* but this wasn't the place to ask, so he said, "That's great."

"Thanks. If it weren't for you..." She shrugged. "You've been good for Liv."

That took Tate off guard. Olivia had added so much to his life, he hadn't stopped to consider that he might have been good for her in any way. "You think?"

Quinn nodded. "If your banquet had been anyone else's banquet, I'm sure she would have told us she couldn't do it. Staying forced her to look at the situation longer, to stay and unearth some problems. But I think her relationship with you has helped her actually *do* something about it. She's more open. More willing to get involved. So, yeah, I think."

Tate smiled. "Thanks. Hey, about that thing you and your mom were talking about—"

"Honestly, there's nothing Olivia could do to help that she isn't already doing. So telling her about it would only cause useless stress and probably create more problems and set us back rather than move us forward."

He could see how that might happen. But he still didn't like them keeping it from her. Though she'd also moved away and dropped out of their lives, so he wasn't sure she had a right to know. Either way, it was a family matter. So he nodded.

Quinn started back to the party, and Tate headed inside. Even before he got halfway to the kitchen, he heard his father's deep laughter, then Olivia's giggle. The combination turned his mind and his mood in a completely different direction, and he smiled. His father was a people person, generous to a fault, intelligent and gregarious, yet Lisa had never warmed to him.

"Another horrible mistake," his father said as Tate came around the corner, "oh, I think you've heard this one son,"— Olivia turned, took the trays from his arms and put them into the sink while listening to his dad—"was when my reservation at a conference hotel got messed up and I had to take what I could find. It was at a tiny, tiny hotel on a side street."

She nodded to Joe to indicate she was listening, then stroked her hand almost absently over Tate's arm with a soft

"Thanks for bringing those in," before refocusing on his dad, who had continued to tell his story.

"...so I get up to the room, and the air conditioner is broken. All right, no surprise. I go downstairs and find a very pretty housekeeper, early fifties, blonde, beautiful bone structure, anyway, she doesn't understand English." Joe's grin grew, and he glanced expectedly at Tate. "Did I tell you this?"

"I don't think so." Tate rested against the counter, and Olivia did the same, so close her hip pressed against his. And then stayed there for the rest of the story. Such a simple thing, yet such a sign of deep comfort and intimacy. And it felt as good to his heart as sex with her felt to his body. "While I'm trying to tell her about the air conditioner, instead of saying *J'ai chaud*"— he looked at Tate to translate—"meaning I'm warm, I said—"

"Oh no." Olivia's eyes went wide. "You didn't."

Joe laughter deepened. "I did."

Now Olivia was laughing so hard, she bent and crossed an arm over her stomach.

Joe looked at Tate and finished the story, "I said *Je suis chaud*"—he choked on another laugh—"which means I'm horny."

A fresh wave of hysterical laughter rolled out of Olivia. She grabbed Tate's arm to stay upright. Tate was chuckling too, but getting a lot more pleasure from seeing Olivia so happy then out of the joke itself.

"For the longest time," Joe went on, "I couldn't figure out why people would look at me funny when I pronounced *branler* as *branlee* when I asked directions."

Tate had no idea what that meant, but he didn't care. He was loving the sight of happy tears streaming from Olivia's eyes.

"Stop." She straightened, grabbed a napkin, and patted her eyes dry. "Oh my God." She took deep breaths as she tried to get ahold of her laughter. "I'm going to burn dinner if you don't stop."

She checked the oven, adjusted the temperature, and moved to the refrigerator, pulling out bags from every shelf.

While she laid things out on the counter, Joe asked Tate, "How's the camp going?"

"Great. I've got another bunch of awesome kids." Tate gave his dad some of the hockey specifics, lining out the skills he was teaching the kids and where the kids played during the year. "Will you be able to make it for the dinner?"

"I'm planning on it." He grinned at Olivia. "Olivia must not be a hockey fan. She's way too quiet."

She pulled a white casserole dish from the cupboards and set it on the counter, then moved the cutting board so she could face them while she worked. "I told Tate I watched a lot of hockey with my dad as a kid. He passed away and I moved overseas, and I sort of lost track of the sport." She grinned at Tate. "But you can bet I'll be watching this season."

"I'm sorry about your dad, hon," Joe said.

"Thanks. Yeah, great man. I wish I'd had more years with him." She smiled at Joe while she laid out big fat tomatoes and a log of buffalo mozzarella on the cutting board. "You two would have liked each other."

Olivia sliced tomatoes, then moved on to the cheese. Her speed, skill, and grace were mesmerizing, and both Tate and Joe watched her layer a broad basil leave on a thick slice of tomato, all on top of a generous slab of mozzarella before standing it on its side in the dish. She repeated that pattern, filling the casserole dish with two bright rows of red, white and green salad within minutes.

"Are you going to be here tomorrow?" Olivia asked Joe. "I was thinking of making his boys lunch and bringing it to the rink. If you come with me, you could tell me what the heck's going on."

Tate's heart burst into acrobatics. She'd just combined two of the most important things in his life together—hockey and family—in a casual morning outing that held no benefit for her. If he wasn't so jaded, he'd think he was falling in love with her, right there on the spot.

"I have an afternoon meeting," Joe said. "Then I fly out, but I'm free until eleven, and that's the best invitation I've had since I got to town."

"Hey, now," Tate joked. "You're here, aren't you?"

While Olivia washed the cutting board, Joe said, "Now, if you're just starting culinary school, where'd you learned to do all this?"

She grinned over her shoulder. "On-the-job training." She dried her hands and whipped together a vinaigrette dressing, then drizzled it over the top of the dish and set it aside. "I've been cooking for years. I learn as I go."

"Then why school? You're obviously skilled and experienced. Why not just start a catering company?"

"Probably because I've worked for quite a few and I know how difficult they are to run. In fact, the whole event-planning business is a real struggle. I was trying to explain that to my mom last night. Her business has been sort of limping along for ten years. It can often be a feast-or-famine environment. And competitive. Mom and Quinn are really good at what they do, but most of the time, it's not what you can do, it's—"

"Who you know," Joe finished for her.

She nodded. "And thanks to Beckett and Eden and Tate and all these other great people here, Essex has gotten a second wind. But what I learned from living the work and watching the way company after company after company like Mom's and Quinn's ran is that there are a variety of reasons businesses fail, and some of them are the opposite of what you'd expect. Like growing too fast. I'd rather watch others make the mistakes instead of jumping in and making them myself." She wrinkled her nose. "I think that's called *lazy.*"

"I think," Tate said, "that's called smart."

She offered a soft smile and moved to the fridge again, returning with more bags. She drew a pan from the lower cupboard. "I also don't want to get stuck cooking at a greasy spoon all my life because I didn't go after a degree. As a cook, you make a little more than minimum wage. As a chef with a reputable culinary school's name behind you, life opens up. You can work as an executive chef, personal chef, run your own business, develop a food-based company."

"Do you know what you want to do?" Joe asked.

She sighed, leveled a light, careless smile on Joe and said, "Nope."

Joe and Tate laughed together.

"All right, son, we should stop distracting her."

"Thanks for keeping me company," she told Joe. "I'll get your number from Tate and check in tomorrow."

"Perfect."

"Tate, do you have a minute?" she asked. "I had a couple of ideas on the menu for your event."

"Sure."

Joe's gaze cut between Olivia and Tate. A nanosecond of hesitation followed before a big smile broke over his face. "I bet there's nothing like seeing Paris from a local's eyes."

"That's truly the only way to see Paris," Olivia agreed. "Next time you're there, please call. I'd love to get together."

He nodded and glanced at Tate. "Maybe we ought to take a trip later this summer? Before your season starts, son. It's only a seven-hour flight." Joe glanced back at Olivia. "He's never been."

Olivia smiled up at Tate. "I hope we can change that."

His heart surged. Hope tumbled through him. But logic wasn't following. He was wondering why his father would encourage such a thing as Joe wandered onto the deck and Olivia checked the oven one more time.

When she turned toward him, Tate was going to ask if there

was anything he could do to help her, but she grabbed his arm and pulled him toward the back of the kitchen. "Your dad is so sweet."

"What are we doing?"

She pushed open the door to the pantry, stepped in, and pulled Tate in behind her. "I haven't had a minute alone with you. And I'm dying here."

Closing the door, she pushed him against it, then leaned into him. And sighed. "Better."

Tate wrapped his arms around her, smiling. "Yeah?"

"A little." Her hands circled behind his neck.

"Only a little?"

"This will make it a lot better." And she pulled his head down to kiss him.

Tate groaned before his mouth even touched hers, but when he felt her and tasted her, another sound of deep pleasure rolled from his chest. The way she opened to him, the way she tilted her head and tasted him, like she was equally as needy, lit him up instantly. Olivia pushed up on her toes, rubbing all along Tate's body.

Her dress, a loose, thin slip of silky material, helped his hands slide over her effortlessly, enhancing every dip and curve. And while his tongue explored her mouth, his hands memorized her body.

She broke the kiss for air. "Is the night over yet?"

"God, you smell like heaven." He slid both hands up her back and over her bare shoulders. "Can't end soon enough for me. I'm dying to get you alone. But I love watching you work. I love watching you impressing the hell out of everyone."

She sighed and smiled. "You're the only one I want to impress."

"You accomplished that the day we met." He stroked her face. "Hey, are we keeping this thing with us, you know, under the radar? I mean, we never talked about it, and I didn't even think to bring it up until we were already here, surrounded by both our families. That all kind of happened fast."

She laughed. "Everything with us has happened fast."

The insinuation in those words zinged a thrill through his chest. "Everything between us is fucking lightning."

"Yeah." Her response was joy filled and dreamy and threatened to make Tate's head light. "I think your dad's clued in, and Quinn knows, but my mom..." She released a heavy breath and winced. "We're still at odds, and I could see her making a fuss. Thinking I'm tarnishing her reputation by cavorting with a client." She grinned and met his eyes. "Even though we were cavorting before you were a client."

"I love the way you say cavorting."

She laughed. "I love the way you cavort."

And then she kissed him again, and Tate let himself get lost another minute. Her mouth was so soft, so warm, so expressive. When they pulled back, a hot little smile lifted her lips, and her hands stroked down his chest. She pulled away enough to slide her hands between their bodies and all the way down the front of his until she covered his hardening cock. Pleasure surged, and his eyes slid closed on a groan.

"I wish I had time to cavort right now," she whispered.

"Baby, you're going to make this night seem endless."

"Already there." She pressed another sweet kiss to his lips. "I better check the oven."

"My place tonight?" he asked, pretty sure that was the plan but still praying she said yes.

"You won't find me anywhere else."

Tate couldn't stop smiling as he followed her out of the pantry. With his arm around her waist, he snuck in one last kiss to her neck. She giggled, then stopped short and sucked back her laughter.

Oh shit.

The thought registered a split second before alarm buzzed

Tate's stomach. He looked up and found Mia standing in the kitchen, obviously looking for someone. Then he recognized the Rough Riders' jersey in her hand and knew she'd come looking for Olivia. But Mia's sharp, surprised, questioning gaze held on Tate.

"Well, hi there," Olivia moved away from Tate, going straight to the oven and pulling a tray from the rack. She smiled at Mia again, but Mia was still busy giving Tate a what-the-fuck glare. "Mia, right?" Olivia asked. "Rafe's fiancée?"

Mia turned her gaze on Olivia, seemed to assess another moment, then smiled. A little.

She was definitely not Joe.

"Yes," Mia said, obviously unsure how to feel about this revelation.

"Hey," Tate said, wishing he had something to hide behind to cover the hard-on Olivia had kicked up in the pantry. Since he didn't, he stuffed his hands into his pockets. "What's up?"

Olivia used serving spoons to toss what looked and smelled like chicken wings in the sauce they'd been basting in, poured them into a dish, and garnished them.

"I was just coming in to—" Mia said.

Quinn bounced into the kitchen with empty trays in her hands and stopped beside Mia, her face bright with excitement. And she was wearing one of Mia's jerseys. Quinn had worn gauzy black pants and a floral tank to the party, and Mia's design looked great on her.

"Look what Mia gave me." Quinn held her arms out, then turned and used one hand to sweep her hair from the back, where Rough Riders was emblazoned in an arc across the shoulders. "Isn't it adorable? She makes these. A whole line of them for the Rough Riders, and she's branching out with six more NHL teams next year. Isn't that exciting?"

Olivia's smile was bright and genuine. "Oh my God. That is *adorable*. And *very* exciting. Congratulations."

Mia seemed to relax a little, which helped Tate ease back from his defense position. "Thank you."

Olivia took the empty trays from Quinn and handed her the bowl of hors d'oeuvres, saying, "Honey lime sesame chicken wings."

"Got it." Quinn held Olivia's gaze. "I thought maybe Mia's expansion plan could help Mom understand the whole big-picture planning thing."

"Ah, great idea." Olivia nodded. "You always were the smart one."

Quinn gave a superior smirk. "Well, one of us had to be pretty, may as well have been you."

Since they were identical, that was freaking hilarious. Even Mia laughed, and Tate felt the tension in the room ebb.

When Quinn left for the deck, Olivia told Mia, "That was sweet of you. Your whole family is so amazing."

Mia held up the jersey in her hand. "I brought one for you too. It's a different style. I heard you were twins, so I figured they should be a little different."

"Oh..." Olivia stopped what she was doing, her eyes sliding over the jersey. "Oh, Mia..." She cleaned her hands before touching the jersey, holding out the bottom while Mia held the top. It was one of Mia's best-selling styles, and Tate knew from seeing it on models that Olivia would look sexy as hell in it. "Wow, this is too nice to be considered a jersey."

"That was the idea."

"You make these?" Olivia met Mia's gaze. "For a company? Or...?"

"My own company. A huge risk and an even bigger leap of faith," she darted a look at Tate, "but I think it was worth it."

He smiled, nodded. "Agreed."

Olivia took the jersey, holding it up. "I can't wait to wear it." She flashed a smile at Tate. "I'll wear it tomorrow when Joe and

I come watch you and the boys." She hesitated, and her excitement faltered. "If...that's okay."

Fuckin' A. The woman kept sending him head over ass down a hill. Tate grinned. "I think that's great."

Olivia turned it around, looking at both sides.

Mia crossed her arms and leaned her hip against the counter, assessing them. "It has the generic Rough Riders on the back," she met Tate's gaze directly, "but maybe she needs one with Donovan across the shoulders."

Tate's heart flipped. Olivia wearing his name, sitting with his dad, watching him teach his kids. Could life get any more fucking perfect?

Yes. It could—she could live in DC, not Paris. She could be his—long-term, not for only another week.

Olivia's gaze lifted to Mia's, then jumped to Tate's.

Tate met her eyes. "I'll leave that up to Olivia."

He tried to pull up some barriers in anticipation of her backpedaling from what some women—including Lisa—had viewed as ownership as opposed to support.

Olivia's smile was excited and immediate. "Oh, I'd love one with—" She stopped short and looked at Mia. "I mean, not if it's any more trouble. Because I love this one. It's fabulous."

Mia grinned and shook her head. "No trouble. I have some in the car." She glanced at Tate as she pushed off the counter. "I'm a good sister like that. Be right back."

Olivia's mouth was still hanging open when Mia walked out. "Oh, shit." She hung her head. "Your sister?" She pressed a hand to her forehead. "Your sister just caught us in the pantry?"

Tate laughed, stepped close, and wrapped Olivia in a hug. "No, she caught us coming out of the pantry. And believe me, baby, she's got no room to say anything about sneaking around."

16

Tate found it ridiculously hard to leave Olivia alone to work. Especially with all the new thoughts running through his head and the new feelings storming around his body.

He wandered out onto the deck where Beckett's family and friends and teammates spread across the covered porch or kids played out in the big grass-covered yard. Joe was perched on the edge of a chair, chatting with a group at the far end of the deck. Mia was sitting on Rafe's lap nearby. Teresa continued to chat up guests, refill wineglasses, and pick up the occasional plate, while Quinn offered guests the latest morsel from the kitchen.

"Donovan." Beckett sat on the steps leading from the deck to the yard along with three other Rough Riders. "We're trying to pick a date for the guys' weekend." Tate started that direction with Beckett saying, "Can you believe it's been five years?"

"Not for all of us," Andre said in his thick Russian accent. He'd joined the team two years before.

"Thank you," Isaac, who'd been a Rough Rider for three years, added.

Beckett, Grant, Isaac, and Andre were all looking at their phones. Tate leaned his back against the pillar on the deck.

"Let me rephrase," Beckett said, "five years for the *important* members of this illustrious club."

A few choice taunts moved through the group.

Beckett looked up from his phone. "Where's Eden? Eden," he yelled at his fiancée across the backyard. "Your calendar didn't sync with mine."

"Yeesh." Grant shook his head. "That's gotta be ugly. An NHL player and a paramedic with a six-year-old?"

Beckett chuckled. "I'd juggle fuckin' balls of flame for those girls."

Olivia stepped out onto the deck, instantly capturing all of Tate's attention. Her arms were loaded with more trays of hors d'oeuvres, and she wandered from group to group, serving and chatting. God, she looked gorgeous. No different from any other day, just, man, she was radiant. Her hair, her skin, her smile.

Her sweet little slip of a dress was soft navy with a small floral pattern distributed over the bottom of the skirt and bodice, two thin spaghetti straps on each shoulder. And all he could think about was how good she felt underneath.

"Dude, you're drooling." Isaac's comment drew Tate's gaze. "Stop ogling the hottie and check your calendar." To the other guys, he said, "I'm free pretty much all summer. Give me a date, and I'll block it out."

"She and her sister are very beautiful," Andre said, glancing at Olivia, then back at his phone, "but beautiful woman, they bring problem. Headache for sure. I know. My Nika..." And he started speaking Russian. But the emphasis with which he said the words conveyed a message that made all the men laugh.

"I can hear you," Nika sang from the bottom step where she sat playing with her two-year-old son, Dmitri.

"I can't do anything the first part of July," Grant said. "Faith and I are spending the fourth in North Carolina, and we're making some improvements on the store."

Grant's girlfriend, Faith, owned her family hardware store in the hometown where she and Grant grew up. While Faith was more of a do-it-yourselfer guru on YouTube and talk show segments now, she still ran the store remotely, and they took frequent trips there in the summer.

"Count me out for all of August," Beckett said. "After the wedding and honeymoon, Lily starts school, and we'll have to go back-to-school shopping."

A collective groan rose through the group, making Beckett smile.

Tate took another sip of his beer just as Olivia untangled herself from the firefighters Eden had invited from her station, men who'd homed in on Olivia and Quinn as soon as they'd arrived and hadn't stopped flirting since.

Which was probably just another day in the life of Olivia and Quinn Essex. Which made Tate wonder if he wanted to tackle the bi-continental, barely-seeing-each-other-eight-months-of-the-year relationship idea.

Olivia turned away from the four firefighters still talking to her as she walked away, laughing and shaking her head. With one tray left, she scanned the porch until her gaze found Tate's. She smiled and started directly toward him. His heart flipped, and he couldn't stop from returning her smile.

"Yo, Donovan." Isaac's voice yanked Tate's attention back to the group.

"What?"

"When are you going to Ontario?"

"I leave right after the banquet, and I'll be gone three or four weeks." He returned to watching Olivia. "Go ahead and schedule. I'll come if I can."

Isaac followed his gaze. "Bro, she's not a good bet for you."

Grant glanced that direction, then returned his gaze to his

phone with a distracted, "Unless you want to fight those brawny firefighters for her."

"Who's hungry?" Her gaze never left Tate's.

"Me, me, me," Grant said before he even looked to see what she was offering. Prying his gaze from his phone, he twisted and reached for mushrooms lining the tray. "Whatcha got here?"

"Caprese-stuffed garlic butter portobellos," she answered.

"Oh my God." He took one along with a napkin. "Can you come teach my wife-to-be how to cook"—his gaze jumped to Olivia's face, and he grinned—"and not tell her I said that?"

Olivia laughed and asked, "What's this about fighting the brawny firefighters?"

Grant's expression turned guilty, and he quickly stuffed his mouth with the mushroom so he couldn't answer. Which made Olivia laugh.

"Tate's thinking about—" Isaac started.

Tate kicked his shin.

"Ow." He laughed and scooted away as he reached for a big mushroom cap from the tray, met her eyes, and said quickly, "Fighting them for you."

Tate lunged for Isaac, but he'd anticipated the move and escaped his reach. He gave Isaac an-I'll-kill-you-later glare, then darted a look at Olivia. "Sometimes they forget how old they are."

She laughed and stepped closer to Tate. "Well, I'm glad you don't. Because that would be a complete waste of time." With the tray in one hand, she ran her other hand from his shoulder to his elbow. "You'd take them without even breaking a sweat. Besides..." She slid her free arm around Tate's waist and leaned into his side, meeting the gazes of the men around the circle. "Tate's already got me, hook, line, and sinker." Then she smiled up at him. "Those cocky kids aren't worth a second thought."

Right then and there, he knew—he was officially in love with this woman.

And what the fuck was he going to do now?

"Thanks, baby," he murmured.

She offered the tray of appetizers to Beckett. "Can I leave these in your capable hands? I want to put some finishing touches on Lily's cake."

"Got it."

She glanced around the circle, "Dinner in about twenty minutes, gentlemen."

Then she sent one more smile Tate's way before she swayed into the house. And Tate could hear his fuckin' heartbeat in his ears. Christ, she'd just flipped his world upside down.

"Wait." Grant was frowning at different members of the group. "Doesn't she live in Paris? Dude, are you seeing her? Or is she just coming on to you?"

This was where it got dicey.

When he didn't answer immediately, everyone read it for what it was.

"Tate, man," Grant said, "You're dating a woman who looks like that and lives in Paris? I mean, believe me, I see the appeal, but after what you've been through?"

"Shut up," Isaac said. "Who cares where she lives? I'd do that no matter—"

"Don't." Tate's bark cut into Isaac's careless words.

Isaac put his hands up. "Hypothetical, man. I was just sayin' you should totally get some."

"Jesus Christ, Hendrix," Beckett said to Isaac. "Just stop talking. You always make it worse."

Tate didn't want to be here anymore. He pushed off the pillar. "I'm gonna go hang out with the fun crowd."

He jogged down the stairs toward the kids on the swing set.

Tate stared at the lush lawn beneath his feet, grinding his

teeth. He wasn't as mad about what Grant and Isaac had said as he was about the truth of their words. If Tate were advising a friend in his own situation, he'd have the same reaction as Grant. The idea of trying to hold on to her, on to whatever this was between them, after knowing her for such a short amount of time based on great sex was one thing. But doing that while she was in Paris, when her lifestyle overseas where men was concerned was admittedly open and casual?

No. Even the thought of another man touching her made Tate's head buzz with anger. Worse, the thought of her wanting another man made him see red.

"Stop, stop, stop." He ran a hand through his hair, trying to pull himself out from the lingering darkness that obviously hadn't fully cleared from Lisa's betrayal. He'd never been like this before Lisa. Never been a jealous guy. Which was probably why it had taken him so long to see the signs with Lisa.

"Uncle Tate." Lily's call lifted his spirits and dragged him from the pit. "Push me high, push me high."

"Me too," Amy and Rachel called in unison.

He got behind the girls and took turns getting them all up to speed as twilight turned to night. The cool air and the girls' laughter helped Tate decompress and shake off the ugliness. He was going to have to face this and get over it. If not now, with Olivia, eventually with someone else. He couldn't have a good relationship with any woman if the fear of cheating was always lingering on his mind.

Mia strolled toward him across the grass.

"Shit," he muttered under his breath.

She rounded the swing set and took over pushing Rachel. "So. You and the caterer." She glanced his way. "How long has that been going on?"

"Not long, and I don't need any more crap over it either."

"Who's giving you crap?"

"The guys."

"Jealous, most likely."

Tate grinned.

"It's nice to see you happy again."

He nodded, shrugged. "Well, don't get used to it. She's just here helping out her family on a visit. It's not serious."

"You and not serious don't go together."

"I'm trying something new."

"Is it almost present time, Uncle Tate?" Lily asked, her voice rising and falling from the swing.

"Dinner first, princess," he told her. "But soon. And I hear you've got a pretty fantastic cake coming."

All three girls cheered.

"Where is she from?" Mia asked. "And how long is she here?"

"What? You didn't get all the details before you came over?"

She just gave him a look.

Tate sighed. "She lives in Paris, and she goes back right after she caters my charity dinner."

Mia's mouth dropped open. She stopped pushing Rachel and turned to face Tate. "Paris? Are you serious? The first woman you date since your divorce, and she lives in *Paris*?"

"I know. Don't."

"Are you sleeping with her?"

He grinned at her directness. "None of your business."

"No way. You lost the right to tell me it's none of my business when you so totally interfered with Rafe and me. Are you?"

"Aunt Mia," Rachel cried, kicking her feet as she slowed, "push me."

Mia gave Rachel a couple of hard pushes and turned that penetrating stare on Tate again. "Tate?"

He rolled his eyes. "Yes."

"Wow," she said, breathless.

"Jesus, you make it sound like a miracle or something."

"You said it, not me."

He cut her a look. If the kids weren't around, they'd both be swearing a lot more.

She just grinned back at him. "I meant that it's a bold move, to get into something with someone so far away who you can't see very often during hockey season. Does Dad know?"

"He has an idea."

"And?"

"What do you think?"

Mia wore a silly little smile. "Well, he's been in and out of the kitchen all afternoon bending her ear, so I'd say he likes her. Can she travel here?"

"No. She starts culinary school as soon as she gets back to Paris."

"For how long?"

"A year."

"Maybe on breaks?"

Tate shook his head. "Drop it, Mia."

"Why?"

He clenched his teeth.

"Tate?"

"She doesn't want anything serious. When she leaves, it's over."

All Mia's excitement went flat. She pushed Rachel a couple more times. "Did you know that when you got involved with her?"

"Yeah."

"Did you know she lived in Paris?"

"Yeah."

Pause.

"Then...*why*?" she asked.

He stopped pushing the kids, pressed his hands to his hips, and thought back. "She's...different. Nothing like the women I meet here. She's so light, carefree, positive. She's one of those can-do people, but with a level head and serious work ethic. She makes me feel..." He shook his head and looked at his sister. "God, when I'm with her, I'm so damn happy. And I know this sounds pathetic, but she makes me feel special."

"That's not pathetic," Mia said, her voice soft. "That's connection."

His mouth lifted in a small smile. "We definitely have a connection I've never had before."

Tina stood on the edge of the deck and yelled, "Dinner!"

All three girls cheered and squirmed off the swings, leaving Tate and Mia there alone.

"So what are you gonna do about it?" Mia asked, crossing her arms.

Tate wrapped one hand around the swing chain. "What do you mean?"

"I mean this is pretty big. Think about it. How many women have you met over the last year, year and a half since you found out about Lisa? Since you divorced? Hundreds. And don't think I don't know how many of those women have thrown themselves at you. I also know you haven't slept with one of them. Your entire life, you've been a relationship, one-woman kind of guy. So this is big. So what are you going to do about this situation? Are you going to just let something this special slide through your fingers? Or are you going to put the same kind of determination into changing her mind about your relationship as you do maneuvering a puck into the net?"

Behind Mia, her boyfriend and Tate's best friend from childhood approached. "Rafe's coming. Don't get into this with him. Not until I figure it out."

Mia didn't answer before Rafe stepped up beside her and wrapped his arm around her shoulder. "You two look serious over here. It's a freaking six-year-old's birthday party for God's sake. What could possibly be serious?"

Mia smiled up at Rafe and wrapped her arm around his waist. "He's just nagging us about a wedding date again."

"Dude," Rafe said, pointing at Mia. "This is where the problem lies."

Tate smirked. "Let's let Dad work on her over dinner."

17

Olivia glanced around the kitchen to make sure she had everything.

"I hate leaving you with all this to clean up," she told Quinn, who was already elbow-deep in suds.

"Are you kidding? You're the cleanest cook I've ever met."

"Why did Mom cancel the serving and cleaning help?"

Quinn refocused on the sink. "She didn't think we needed them. Liked the idea of keeping it intimate with family."

"At your expense," she said, frowning. "I don't like that. I also don't like the fact that she took on that christening after everything I told her last night."

Quinn's gaze jumped back to Olivia's. "How'd you hear—"

"Tina mentioned it. What I said last night is very true," Olivia told her. "If you want Mom to keep this business, you two are going to have to come to an agreement on how to grow at a manageable rate."

Quinn nodded. "I'll talk to her about it. And she'll get in here and pitch in soon. We won't be here but another hour. Go. You've worked harder than anyone."

Olivia really wanted to go. She was so looking forward to a

night with Tate. Things had shifted between them tonight. Strengthened. And she was anxious to see how that translated into the bedroom. "Okay. I'll see you tomorrow."

In the foyer, a tangle of people were saying good-bye. Lily was asleep on her father's shoulder. Tate was standing near the door. She'd already spoken to Beckett and Eden, Tina and Jake, and received countless accolades and thank-yous from other guests. She really just wanted to slip out the door with Tate now. She'd especially like to slip out the door without explaining to her mother that she wouldn't be home tonight.

She made her way around the edge of the foyer toward Tate. But just before she reached him, her mother turned from saying good-bye to someone and faced Tate.

"Do you have your agent's information?" she asked him.

He pulled a small piece of paper from his pocket and offered it to Teresa. "I told him you'll be contacting him—"

"For what?" Olivia stepped up to them, curious but cynical, and looked directly at her mother. "Why would you need to talk to Tate's agent?"

"Oh, don't worry about—" her mother started.

"He's looking for a planner to help out with—" Tate said at the same time.

Anger shot up Olivia's spine, and she grabbed for the paper. But her mother didn't let go, and Olivia found herself in a tug of war.

"No, Mom," she said, stern but under her breath so she didn't make a scene. "No more jobs until you finish the ones you have."

"Olivia..." Tate said, concern in his voice.

"This isn't your business," Teresa told Olivia. "It's not for you to say—"

"This isn't just your business either. Think of Quinn. She worked her ass off here today because you cancelled the help. That's not okay."

She yanked at the paper, but her mother had a solid grip on it, and the paper ripped. Olivia crumpled the piece, and Tate stroked a hand across her shoulders.

"You don't have to like what I'm saying, but if you want to keep this business, you'd better at least research it. And until you have a full, solid plan set in place, *stop taking jobs.* I'm telling you this because I care."

"It's been a long day," Tate said, his voice soft as he curled her close beside him. "Are you ready to go?"

A wave of regret washed over her, and she covered Tate's hand with her own, turning away from her mother. "Yeah, I am."

She dropped the paper on the way to Tate's truck. He opened the passenger's door, but turned her to face him.

"Are you okay?" he asked.

"I'm sorry," she said at the same time.

He smiled. "Come on, let's get you home."

She slid to the middle of the seat and cuddled close for the drive. The night was warm but not humid, and the night air smelled good. Within two minutes of driving away from the Crofts' home—and her mother—Olivia relaxed. With Tate beside her, her heart filled. It filled and filled and filled until her ribs ached. Until she couldn't get close enough.

Curling her feet underneath her, Olivia moved even closer and pressed her lips to his neck. His sigh was like a drug, making Olivia light-headed. Then he stroked a hand through her hair, but to Olivia, it felt like fire between her legs.

This was crazy. This was wild. She didn't know *what* this was.

"Oh my God," she whispered against his skin. "I want you so bad."

"Mmm, baby." He shifted in his seat. "I'm wishing I didn't live quite so far into DC right now."

The sudden, intense desire was so hot, she didn't know what to do with it. "I can't wait."

He laughed softly.

"No." She pulled away and looked out the windshield, then told Tate, "I mean it. I can't wait. Pull over."

He did a double take. "Are you—"

"Serious? Yes. Here, by the river."

They were just crossing the Potomac. Olivia pushed her sandals off with her feet, then slipped her panties off and started working on his jeans.

Tate took a side road and slowed.

With his button open and his zipper down, she pushed one hand into his pants, under his briefs, and circled his hardening cock.

"Jesus Christ, Liv..."

She framed his face with her other hand, tilted her head, and kissed him, pushing her tongue into his mouth. She *needed* him. And he was way too interested in driving.

"Tate..." she whined. She didn't even care how needy she sounded. "Just park. I don't care if it's in the middle of the road."

The truck bounced a little, and Tate didn't even have in Park before Olivia unsnapped both their seat belts, scooted toward the passenger's side, and pulled on his arm. "Come here."

Instead of scooting with her, he twisted, caught her head in one hand, and held her steady as he kissed her hard. His growl rolled through her mouth down her throat, and she whimpered. She couldn't think. She was on fire. Aching from the roots of her hair to the balls of her feet. She just needed him inside her. Loving her the way only he could do it. So completely.

His hand slipped down her back, across her hips, and pulled her under him at the same time he moved over her. She wound her arms around his neck and pulled him down to meet her open mouth. Spread her thighs to take his hips and lifted toward him. Moaned when he met her pressure.

He tore his mouth away, gasping for air.

"Tate, inside, inside insi—" His heavy hand stroked between her legs, and her mouth dropped open on a cry. He pushed inside her, rough and deep. "Yes."

She arched, fisted his hair, and pulled his mouth back to hers. Then his fingers were replaced by the long hard thick hot glorious *naked* length of him in one hard, swift plunge.

"Ah God..." She lifted into him. "Fuuuck yes."

He paused, and Olivia writhed against him. She opened her eyes, frantic for more. He was looking at her with a wild expression, hair a mess, eyes glittering. "Are you on birth control?"

She shook her head, trying to understand. "What?"

"Birth. Control."

"Oh my God, I can't think." When he growled with lust-filled impatience, she repeated, "Birth control, yes. The pill. Always use a condom too. Always, always, always, always, always..." Until now. "Fuck."

"Want me to put one on?"

"Noooo." She groaned the word, shaking with need. "Want to feel you."

The look in his eyes softened. His slid over her hair and closed on the back of her neck. "You turn me inside out, Liv."

He didn't pull out, but he moved inside her. "Oh my God." Deep inside her. "Ohmygod ohmygod ohmygod—"

He rocked back, easing pressure on whatever had been threatening to rip her open with ecstasy. Her vision blurred. Her heart beat in her ears.

"Did you put an aphrodisiac in my wine?" she asked, breathless. "*What. Is. This?*"

His lips hovered just above hers. "*This. Is. Us.*"

She whimpered, and he moved, rubbing something inside her that made Olivia want to climb the walls. "Ahgod..." She stretched her hands overhead and pressed them against the door. "So fucking good. Don't stop, please don't stop. Jeezus… Tate, Tate, *Tate.*"

The orgasm slammed through her like a bolt of lightning. Tate climaxed seconds later. The power of his body pushed her across the seat until her head was up against the door. And when the storm settled, they were left a panting, sweaty bundle of fatigue.

"Jesus Christ." Tate whispered the words, then pressed his elbow to the seat and dropped his forehead to his arm. "What the fuck, Liv?" He breathed hard and fast. "Where did that come from?"

She lowered her arms, stretched her legs, and felt the burn of him still inside her. And smiled. Smiled the kind of smile that lit her up with joy from the inside out. A laugh of pure happiness bubbled out of her, and Tate lifted his head.

"You didn't turn off the truck," she said, grinning.

He matched her smile. "You didn't give me time."

And they held each other's gaze in what felt like the most intimate moment she'd ever experienced. So intimate, Olivia's heart fluttered. The moonlight streamed through the windshield, making his features sharper and harder. He looked fierce, but his eyes told the whole story. They were flooded with the same kind of affection fizzing inside Olivia.

When their gazes held an extra second, Olivia said, "I've never done that. Any of that." She shook her head, a little surprised to realize everything about her time with Tate was a first—the amount of time she'd spent with him, the problems they'd navigated, how her affection for him made her desire stronger. "It was amazing."

"I'm going to remember this for the rest of my life." The warmth in his voice suffused Olivia.

Tate exhaled and lowered his head, nuzzling her neck

before he kissed her there. "We'd better get moving before the cops come and bust us like teenagers."

He had to coax Olivia a little more to get her to give up their cocoon of bliss. Sliding back into reality was extra painful with the problems involving her mother hovering and Olivia's exit looming.

But once they were back on the road, with her head against Tate's chest and his arm around her shoulders, the night air blowing across her face, Olivia found comfort again.

Eventually, the questions she'd known she'd have to face came.

"I'm glad you and Quinn patched things up." His voice, low and soft, filled the cab.

Olivia instantly flashed back to the night. Yes, she and Quinn had definitely plastered over a gap in their relationship, but she'd noticed tension buzzing in Quinn all night. The kind radiating off a sous chef who'd arrived late and was rushing to complete his job before Olivia found out he was behind. One a waiter got when they were caught eating the last Mango-basil vacherin in the fridge before the dinner rush was over.

"Me too. We have a ways to go, and she has her hands full with our mom. I hope it lasts."

"Liv," he said, almost hesitantly. "What happened?"

She tilted her head to look at him.

"I mean, you all obviously love each other. But this underlying tension, it's long-standing, and I know there are problems with the business, but I don't get the impression that's the real issue."

"Oh, so perceptive, Mr. Donovan." She paused, but with no easy explanation, she said, "It's complicated."

"How 'bout the streamlined version?"

"We had the all-American family," she started, raising her emotional walls as she eased into an abbreviated version of her past. "My dad had a good job, my mom stayed home and raised healthy twin girls. We lived a nice life in the nation's capital. We have extended family in the area, aunts, uncles, cousins. Our backyard used to look very much like the Crofts' did today. When I was young, I always believed my life would be the same when I grew up. I've already told you I was a daddy's girl. He and I were... We were just best buddies. I idolized him. Loved him more than I could ever put into words."

Her heart swelled the way it always did when she thought of him. "When he wasn't working, we were together doing something. We loved all the same things—music, sports, culture, history. I developed my love of travel and cooking from him. We talked about all the places we'd travel when he retired. Had even planned our first trip for the summer between high school and college."

When she paused to collect herself, Tate said, "Sounds amazing."

She nodded. "I planned on going to culinary school. Had been accepted to one of the top schools in New York. And was in a special culinary tract in high school where I supplemented my graduation requirements with culinary courses at a specialty charter school."

"That's cool. I didn't know you could do that."

"Yeah. It was. I first noticed my dad had something going on —something beyond the normal flu or colds or whatever— about two or three months into my senior year. I didn't find out he had cancer until *after* he died of a heart attack two days after Quinn and I graduated."

"Oh God." True dread filled Tate's words, and a ball of anguish sat heavily in the pit of Olivia's stomach. "They didn't know? The doctors didn't catch it? Did the cancer cause his heart problems?"

"That's where the ax falls in our family. They *did* know. Mom and Dad knew at least six months before Dad died, but they didn't tell me and Quinn."

"Jesus..." His arm tightened around her.

"Only, Quinn found out by accident. She heard Mom crying, went to check on her, and overheard her and Dad talking about it. I wasn't home. I was catering an event with my high school class that night. And when I got home, everything seemed totally normal. Even looking back a hundred times, knowing that they all knew, I still couldn't find any sign of it."

"They didn't tell you?" Tate asked, disbelief filling his voice.

"No. None of them. Life went on as if nothing had changed. There were little shifts. Quinn seemed moodier than normal. She drifted away from me. When I talked to Mom about it, she told me it was a normal part of growing up. That Quinn was preparing herself for the day we separated for college. Whenever I asked Dad how he was feeling, he blamed his trips to the doctor, his fatigue, his loss of appetite on stress at work, and said it wasn't something I needed to worry about. I was seventeen, and I was busy. They'd never lied to me before, so I just took them at their word."

She stopped. This was the killer. The other stuff was agonizing, but this cut Olivia open. She let her gaze blur over the streets of DC as they came into the city, her mind years in the past.

"I was out with friends when I got the call that Dad was in the hospital. And even though I was only a ten-minute taxi ride away, he was already gone when I got there."

"Oh no," Tate breathed, his voice pained. "Baby, that's..."

He trailed off. She understood. There were no words.

Over the years, she'd had to find some way of coping, and in a lot of ways, she felt dead inside when it came to this part of her life.

"His heart attack was brought on by the cancer's progression. A shutdown of his organs, they said. In the days that followed, I found out about the cover-up. Logically, I know why they did it. My father didn't want me to give up on culinary school. My mother knew I would have dropped every-thing and spent every minute with him. Quinn...Quinn was just as lost as I was. She did what her parents told her was best.

"They'd planned on telling me that summer, between high school and college, but that choice was taken out of their hands. They robbed me of those last months with the person I loved most on this earth. I didn't get to tell him how much I loved him. I didn't get to say good-bye. I didn't even get to be there with him when he went."

Those thoughts still cut at her, ten years later. "I felt totally betrayed by the people I trusted most. The people who were supposed to love me and keep me safe. And the last thing I wanted to do was stay there. I didn't even want to go to culinary school anymore. Everything that was tied to my family reminded me of my loss and the betrayal."

Tate pulled into his complex. He navigated into his parking spot and turned off the truck. Olivia sighed, straightened, and released her seat belt. Tate did the same but made no move to get out. They sat there a moment in silence.

"In the last few months of his life, my dad had become almost preachy about the value of living life to the fullest and following your heart. He'd gotten me hooked on the idea of never missing out on the adventures life had to offer. So when I felt like I had no one left I could trust and I needed to escape the heartbreak, I took all the money I'd saved over the years from birthdays and part-time jobs and bought a one-way ticket to Paris, because it was one of the places we'd always talked about going. I didn't end up staying there long before I started moving around. And I've lived on every continent, experienced dozens and dozens of cities, but now, coming up on the tenth anniversary of his death, living, working, and soon going to culinary school in Paris seems like...fate or destiny or coming full circle. Whatever you want to call it, it just feels like something I need to finish before I can figure out where I go from there."

Tate stroked a hand over her hair. "He'd be so damn proud of you, Liv."

She smiled. "Yeah. He would. Thanks." She looked down at her hands. "That's why this thing with Mom's company is so... It's troubling and upsetting, and it pisses me off too. From the moment I got here, I've been discovering things I didn't know. Things they've kept from me. And I still don't have the whole story.

"Mom and Quinn used Dad's life insurance and the money Mom and Dad had saved for college to start the company. I couldn't have cared less, but I didn't think that was fair to Quinn. But when I left, they felt abandoned, despite the fact that their behavior pushed me away. It's a huge rift, a decade in the making. We've made small progress over the years, but they've still never visited me once. Never truly valued my abilities until I saved them at the engagement party. Yet, they still won't take my advice. I just don't know if we'll ever be able to mend things."

"Man, baby," Tate commiserated. "That's messy."

"Very messy. Too messy. I can't do it anymore. I can't do lies. I can't do secrets. I need things open and up front so I know where I stand, you know?"

He nodded. "I get it."

"That's not happening with Mom yet. I'm not even sure it's fully happening with Quinn. I don't know if it will ever happen. And, God, I love them, but I don't trust them. It's a horrible thing to say, but it's even a worse way to feel. And *how* do you repair a relationship like that? I just...I don't know what to do with them, and it breaks my heart a little more every time I come home."

"I'm so sorry you went through all that. I can't even imagine how painful and complicated it has to be for you."

She forced a smile to lighten the conversation. "And I'm sorry to turn into such a downer after such a blockbuster start to the night."

He leaned in and kissed her. "You're not a downer. Thank you for sharing it with me."

He kissed her again, sliding his warm tongue into her mouth. Olivia sighed and leaned into him. Pulling back just enough to break the kiss, she said, "Thanks for being so awesomely you."

18

Tate drew Olivia into the master bath by the hand and reached in to turn on the shower. While he adjusted the temperature, she rested against his back, draping herself over him.

Once he had the temperature right, he turned and drew her dress over her head, then unclasped her bra. Olivia dragged off his tee and pushed down his pants, and they both stepped into the steamy shower.

He held her, letting her rest as much of her weight in his arms as she wanted. That was something he'd always wished for in a woman, to know that when things got really rough, the other person would be strong enough to carry you through. Lisa hadn't even come close. But, looking back, she'd never shown signs of having the strength.

Olivia, on the other hand, had more inner strength than anyone Tate had ever known. All she'd done with her life after all she'd been through was a testament to her perseverance and commitment.

Now if he could just get her to commit to him.

In the very next thought, he realized that by asking her to

do that, he'd be asking her to give up something important. Something that made her who she was.

Tate squeezed soap into his hand and stroked it over her back while Olivia kissed his chest and held him close. "You know we only have a few days left."

She groaned softly against his skin. "I know."

"Did you mean what you said to my dad tonight?" he asked. "Or were you just being nice?"

She tipped her head back and looked up at him. Her lashes were clumped with water droplets, her face glowing, her cheeks rosy. "I always mean what I say. I may change my mind about something, but when I say it, I mean it. I loved your dad. Your sister too. And the thought of showing you my little corner of France thrills me."

He breathed easier. But there were still several hurdles to jump. He put them off, focusing on enjoying the moment and soaping every inch of her down, then using her like a human sponge against his own body, making her laugh.

Tate was already aroused when they dried off, and it felt amazing to fall into bed with her, naked. Feel her slide and move against him. Know he'd wake to her in the morning.

The thought of letting her go kept sneaking in and stabbing at him. He tugged her on top of him, twining her legs with his, and brushed her hair back from her face. "Tell me about school. Is it every day? Do you get weekends off?"

"They say its thirty hours a week, but I did their short course in pastry, and it was twice as many hours as they claimed in the brochures."

"Ouch."

"I'll work when I can, nights and weekends, I guess. It's going to be tight. I'd planned on working a solid week before I started so I had some cash on hand, but..." She moved a little south, kissing his chest and rocking her hips against his erection. "I'll get by."

"I have no doubt." His biggest doubts now were about *him* getting by once she was gone.

He shampooed her hair, then shut off the water and wrapped her in a towel. When he picked her up, Olivia crossed her arms around his neck, her legs around his hips, and kissed him the way she always did, with all of herself. All her passion, all her affection. And Tate didn't want to go back to living without it.

He laid her on the bed, hovering over her with so many emotions pushing and pulling at him, he didn't know what to do with them all. He felt desperate and needy. After just two weeks, she'd invaded his heart. A heart he'd begun to think was dead.

"What's going on inside your brain?" she asked, easing her hand between them and stroking his length. "I see you thinking."

Pleasure swamped him, and Tate clenched his teeth. "Just about how good it feels to have your hands on me."

"That's not the look I saw. Do you regret it?"

Fiery tension coiled at the base of his spine. "What?"

"This? Us? Getting involved? When the time for me leaving is getting closer?"

She rubbed the head of his cock over her sweet folds and arched a little, taking him inside. Tate's breath exited on a whoosh. He held her gaze and rocked his hips, sliding deeper. Heat and warmth and softness surrounded him. He tipped his head back, closing his eyes to soak in the perfection of her. Of how badly he wanted to hold on to it.

Deep inside her, he opened his eyes to hers again. Lifted one hand to stroke her face. "I could never regret you."

She pushed up and kissed him. Wrapping a hand around his neck, a thigh around his, she rolled him to his back. With her hands against his chest, she pushed up and used those toned legs and tight abs to rock them both until they were panting.

Tate sat up. Supporting himself with one arm, he wrapped the other around her back and covered her breast with his mouth. Trailed kisses up to her mouth and cupped her head to circle his tongue with hers.

This was a whole different type of sex. Slow and deep, every move calculated on both sides to give pleasure, to express affection, to show, without words, how much they cared. Tate felt it deep in his soul.

"Tate..." She whispered his name against his lips, as if she wanted to tell him something.

"Right here, Livvy," he murmured, kissing her neck, pulling her hips into his. "I'll always be right here for you."

She made a whimpering sound, locked an arm around his neck, and pushed her other hand against his knee, giving her leverage to lift into him. Tate watched her orgasm rise in the pleasure tightening her face.

He needed her looking in his eyes when she came. Needed that connection. Needed her to remember the pleasure between them.

"Liv." He cupped her cheek and pulled her head to his. "Open your eyes." His own orgasm was close, and he ground his teeth to hold it off. "Look at me, baby."

Within seconds of her gaze locking with Tate's, Olivia's pussy clenched around him, her head fell back, and her mouth fell open on a cry.

Tate pulled her mouth to his, plunged his tongue deep, tasting her release before his own ripped through him. He buried his face against her neck and cried her name as it rocked his foundation and Olivia wrapped her arms around him and held him tight.

19

Olivia lifted Tate's arm, draped over her waist, and slowly slid from bed, gently laying his arm down. She stood there, watching him sleep with her arms crossed, the fingernail of her thumb between her teeth, her heart tripping all over the place.

This was a problem.

Worse, it was a problem she had no experience with. One she'd never believed would happen to her and one she didn't know how to fix.

Tate shifted in sleep, rolling onto his back. His white sheets slipped a little farther off his glorious body, displaying one muscular thigh and calf. But what Olivia couldn't tear her gaze from was his face. How calm and peaceful he looked in sleep.

Her chest constricted again with a strength that made her pull in a breath and hold it.

Oh yeah, this was a big problem.

She squeezed her eyes closed and whispered, "Shit."

Turning toward the windows, Olivia wandered across the room and looked out on the gardens. She'd never been here before. Never had these feelings. Since her family had so totally shattered her trust, she'd never opened her heart to anyone.

But here she was. Unable to think about leaving Tate in a few days with no idea when she'd see him again. If ever. And while the thought of never seeing him again was unfathomably painful, continuing to see him was equally as inconceivable.

Aside from the impossibility of solving the problems of distance and time to see each other, it forced her to look at the future. It made her ask hard questions, foreign questions, like what Tate wanted out of this. What she wanted out of this.

If they tried to do something long-distance for the year she was in school, then what? Would he expect her to move home? Did she want that? Was that even an option? He couldn't live in Europe, could he? Did they even have the same level of hockey in Europe? Did it operate the same? Would he even want to do that? And did she want him to do that?

"Liv?" His soft voice pulled her from the vortex. She turned and found him sitting on the edge of the bed, ready to stand. "What's wrong?"

"Nothing. I'm sorry, did I wake you?"

"I can hear it in your voice." He pushed to his feet, and the sheet fell. Even in the shadows, the man took her breath. He came to her, slid his hands over her shoulders, and wrapped her in his arms. "Have a bad dream?"

"No." She buried her face against his chest, swamped with emotion. God, she didn't want to let this go. "I'm...scared."

He pulled away, combed his hands through her hair, and cupped her face. His dark eyes held hers in the light drifting off the city. "Of what?"

"This. Us. You. Me."

"Whoa, slow down." He slid his hands down her arms and took her hands, backing toward the bed. He sat and pulled her into his lap sideways, pressing all his hard muscle and warm skin against her. He circled her waist and cupped her cheek. "What's going on?"

"I don't know. I just...You brought up leaving, and I've been so busy with jobs, and my mind's been caught up with my family, that I didn't think about it. And now I feel like it snuck up on me. It's all I can think about—"

She broke off, unable to put her fears into words. Or afraid to. And even though she knew the fear was unreasonable, she couldn't stem the urge to both run from him and seek safety in his arms.

What she felt like she needed to say wasn't something she should be talking to him about. Not when she was so unsure. She needed a friend to talk to. But she only had Quinn, and her sister didn't understand Olivia's life and wouldn't understand her fears. She also wouldn't be impartial.

"I'm not good at this," she admitted. "And I don't want to say the wrong thing and hurt you or screw things up."

"Knowing you're upset and not knowing why hurts me. Not being able to help you hurts me. Talk to me, baby."

God, she couldn't do it. She just couldn't get it out. "Let's go back to sleep. I'll be fine in the morning."

"Liv," he said his voice soft and patient, "if there's one thing I learned from my marriage, it's that pretending problems don't exist only creates bigger problems. It doesn't make them go away."

Her gut knotted. Her chest squeezed. "I've never felt like this. I've never even imagined feeling like this."

He pressed a kiss to her shoulder. "Like what?"

"This," she said, frustrated she wasn't sure how to define it. "This thing between us. I never look beyond right now. After my dad died, I put one foot in front of the other and just lived life as it happened. No plans, no commitments, no ties."

"No risk," he murmured. "No heartache. I get it."

"The first time I really looked into the future was when I got my scholarship. I've sort of always been saving for it, hoping someday I'd find a way to go to school. So when I found out I'd gotten the scholarship, I already had most of the fifteen percent they require from me in the bank. But not all of it. And I knew I had to have it all by next week or the scholarship would go to someone else and I'd be right back where I started."

She paused to take a breath. Her mind was spinning. Words were spilling. She wasn't even sure if she was making sense. "So even then, I put the future out of my head and just picked up as much work as I could every day. It's what I know how to do, just put my head down and keep going. It was just the other day, when my latest paycheck had been deposited, that I saw my savings account tip over the total I needed. That's when I knew, one hundred percent, that school was real. The first time I knew I was really going to see that dream come true."

He squeezed her. "Congratulations, baby."

She huffed a laugh, but she didn't feel happy. She just felt plain scared. "Now all this is happening with you, and I leave soon, and I can see that I'm not going to be able to just put one foot in front of the other anymore. I've always been able to walk away and return to everyday life without any problem. But I already know I'm not going to be able to do that now. And that creates all kinds of problems that force me to think about the future. And I'm not good at it. I just... It terrifies me." She covered her face. "I feel like I'm going to hyperventilate."

"There's something at stake in life now," he said, his voice calm and quiet. "It's easy to float through life when you don't have much to lose. But the more you want something, the scarier it is to reach for it, because you risk losing."

She dropped her hands. "Maybe if it was just one thing at a time, it wouldn't feel so overwhelming. But now there's school *and* you..."

"Is it me?" he asked. "Or do things with your mother and sister have you wound up?"

When she looked into his eyes now, she didn't just see the physical man anymore. She saw beyond his handsome features. She saw Tate, heart and soul. She saw Tate's essence. And she didn't want to let go.

She broke his gaze on a whispered "Fuck."

"Just say it," he said, an edge in his voice. One that indicated he was preparing for something he didn't want to hear. "Just get it out in the open. There's no point—"

"I...love you." She pushed the words out, sure they'd get stuck if she held on to them a second longer. And, damn, they felt so bizarre coming off her lips. As if her mouth wasn't created to form them with this meaning.

They left Tate speechless. Which only made her nerves jitter harder.

"I mean, I think I do. I don't have anything to compare it to. I just know this whole leaving thing has me really...messed up inside. And I didn't even want to say the words because I know you've been hurt, and I don't want to say things that might mean one thing to me and something else to you. I don't want to hurt you. I just...I just... Shit, I just...*love* you. I love being with you. I love thinking about you. All I want to do is spend time with you—like all the time. And I hate the thought of leaving you, even when what I've been working toward for ten years is waiting for me in Paris. Even when I love Paris. And, shit, this is all just too damn weird for words."

She pressed a hand to her chest and dragged in air to lungs that felt like fists. "I can't breathe. I think I'm having a panic attack."

"Oh, baby." He wrapped both arms around her and lay back, dragging her with him. Olivia rolled to her stomach, stretching over him, trying to press every inch of her skin to his. When he doubled those thickly muscled arms around her and held her tight, it felt so good it hurt.

"It's not real, right?" she asked, searching for some sort of level ground. "This is some weird reaction to stress, right? I mean, we've known each other a little over two weeks. That's not how love works, is it? Not real love." God, her brain was in knots. She pressed her face against his neck. "See, this is why I didn't want to say anything. Because I'm so screwed up. And after what you've been through, hearing this is probably the last—"

He released her and lifted her head, kissing her quiet. A steady, solid, warm kiss that instantly stopped the spin and grounded her. She relaxed. Breathed. And sank into the kiss. Where she found everything she needed—affection, strength, confidence.

When he broke the kiss, he stroked her cheeks and looked deep into her eyes. "I feel the same way, baby. It feels fast, but it also feels right. Life is messy, and love doesn't always come when and where it's most convenient. So, yeah, it's scary. And after what we've *both* been through, it should scare the hell out of us. That means we really care. That means we're serious. If we weren't scared, Liv, it wouldn't be real." He kissed her again. "I love you, Liv."

Panic fluttered beneath her ribs again. "But what about— How are we— This is—" She dropped her forehead to his chest. "*Shit.*"

He started laughing.

A sweet sensation rippled through her, but she groaned in misery over how this would complicate everything. "Shut up. I'm freaking out here."

His laughter faded, and he sighed. His hands slid down her back, over her ass, and held her to him as he rolled. When she was beneath him, Olivia parted her thighs and took his hips snug between her legs.

Tate rested on his forearms, the backs of his fingers skimming her face. "You've made me happier in these two weeks than anyone has made me in years."

"I've pissed you off pretty good too."

He smiled. "Only because it took you way too damn long to realize that resistance was futile."

That made a little laugh bubble up.

"I know you're leaving soon," he said, "And I don't want to stress you out. You've already got a lot going on. Let's just take one day at a time right now. After the banquet, we'll sit down together and make a plan. We have all kinds of time, Liv. Like my dad pointed out, Paris is only a seven-hour flight away."

"But I don't know what I want to do after—"

"You don't have to know that now. I don't know what I'm going to do when my next contract comes up. We can't always know where we'll be a year from now. Nothing that's happened for me in the last couple of years has followed the plan I had in my head. So maybe planning that far in advance and making plans now based on what you think might happen isn't such a great idea. At least for us. And at least not right now."

The fear receded. Olivia could see clearer, breathe deeper. "Really? You're okay with that?"

"What did you expect? That I'd demand you live here when your whole life is there right now?"

"I guess I figured after what your wife did, you'd have issues with me being so far away."

"Ex-wife," he corrected. "And you're right. That's a trouble spot for me. If you're not ready to stay with one man, or if you think your sexual needs are too high to be satisfied in a long-distance relationship, then this won't work, because I could never share you." His eyes took on a dull ache. "And I would definitely want to know either way before you leave."

"That's fair." Her nervous flutters dimmed. "But I can tell you right now I've never been loved like this before. Not in ten years. Not anywhere in the world. So I'm not the least bit interested in trying to go out and search for something I have right here."

Framing her face, he kissed her gently. "You make me feel like more of a fucking superstar than a stadium full of screaming fans."

She lifted her hips, rubbing against his erection, and his eyes closed on a groan.

"Why don't you show me—again—just what a superstar you are, Mr. Donovan."

20

"Water break, guys," Tate called to the kids. "Then we'll finish up with skating skills."

He glided to the bench and picked up his own water bottle.

Beckett slid up beside him. "Who's picking the music today?" he yelled. "I'm tired of Connor's rap crap."

The kids laughed, and a bunch of them called out Derek's name.

"Set it up, Derek," Beckett told the kid.

Derek skated toward the iPod linked to the rink's sound system while they took a break.

Tate glanced toward the end of the rink where Olivia sat with Joe, and Beckett followed his gaze.

"Things are lookin' pretty tight with you two," he said, watching Olivia laugh at something Joe was telling her. "She's hanging with your dad, bringing lunch to your kids, watching your practices, catering your dinner..." He turned a grin on Tate. "And by the smile you've had on your face all morning, I'm guessing she's just as sweet in bed."

Tate squirted water at Beckett. "Shut up."

"Which means yes."

Tate couldn't stop smiling.

"Have you guys talked about her leaving yet?"

"A little last night. I want to get through the banquet. Then the stress will be off, I'll have her full attention, and we can work out the details."

"Details?"

"Yeah." Tate grinned. "She wants to keep it going."

Beckett raised his brows. "You're okay with that? Long distance?"

"It's certainly not my first choice, but she's way too good to let go."

"You feel good enough about things between you that you'll trust her?"

He lifted a shoulder. "Now, yes. Over the summer, yes, because I'll be able to visit her. I hope that by the time the season starts, she'll be so in love with me that she'll let me cover some of her expenses so she won't have to work so much, and she'll be able to come here."

"Sounds like you've given this a lot of thought."

"Not really. Everything's happened so damn fast."

Beckett's face broken into a grin. "Welcome to my world, bro." When Tate laughed, Beckett slapped him on the shoulder. "Ain't it grand?"

He looked over at his dad and Olivia again just as they laughed together. Then Olivia leaned into Joe and rested her head on his shoulder. The sight touched a deep part of Tate. A part Lisa had never reached during a year of dating or a year of marriage. Yeah, it was fast, but even Joe had already taken Olivia on as another daughter. She didn't know it yet, but Joe would be one of the biggest blessings in her life the way he'd been in Tate's, Mia's and Rafe's lives. And Tate loved being able to offer Olivia the support of such a great man.

His grin brightened and reached all the way into his chest. "Sure is."

He called the kids to the top of the ice, lined out the drill order and pattern, then told them, "We've got a special audience today—my dad and my girl, Olivia, who's brought you all killer eats to share after practice." A collective cheer broke through the kids. "Make us look good, will ya?"

Beckett skated along the sidelines, offering coaching as Tate led them through the exercises.

"Cue the music, Derek." Tate faced the kids and shouted, "Who's ready?"

"We are!" they returned in chorus. This was one of their favorite parts of practice. Tate's too.

"All right, Derek." He paused, and the kids joined him, each punching a fist in the air. "*Turn it up.*"

When a song from Nickelback blasted from the speakers, Tate put his hands on his hips and cut a look at Derek. A ripple of laughter rolled through the kids. Even Beckett laughed.

Tate asked Derek. "What part of 'no questionable lyrics' didn't you understand?"

Derek just shot him that mischievous smile and shrugged.

"I'll let you get away with it this time." He pushed into his skates. "Anybody else tries it, you're all getting pushups. Let's go, guys. Impress me."

Tate slid down the ice backward, creating a smooth, slow stroke of his blades for the kids to follow. "Push and cross, push and cross. Derek, go."

Derek turned and followed, then the rest of the kids followed a few feet apart.

"Heads up," Beckett called. "Toby, eyes on the wall not on the ice. Jason, keep your stick centered and still."

At the rink's curve, Tate took the exercise along the wall back to the other end of the ice and continued for three more laps.

Nickelback transitioned into "Hall of Fame" by the Script.

"Now we're talking," Tate yelled, using his stick to point at

Beckett. "Turn that bad boy up." To the kids, he yelled, "At the top of your lungs, guys, let me hear it."

The chorus came on, and together, their voices filled the rink, and Tate felt higher than a fucking kite, dancing on his skates, adding little jumps, because he knew the kids got a kick out of it and it made Tate happy.

"You can throw your hands up, you can beat the clock, you can move mountains, you can break rocks..."

From the side of the rink, Beckett was yelling over them, smiling just as big. "No hot-doggin' it like Donovan. Keep the bounce out of your step. Keep your sticks quiet. You're going for smooth. When you're a hotshot, you can mess around on the ice too."

The kids laughed but kept skating and kept singing. *"You can be the hero, you can get the gold, breakin' all the records they thought never could be broke... Do it for your country, do it for your name, 'cause there's gonna be a day when you're on the wall of fame..."*

On the next lap, Tate dropped his stick by the goal and began a serpentine pattern from wall to wall to work on the kid's backward crossover skills to "All In" by Lifehouse.

"Damn, Derek," Tate called. "You're my DJ for the rest of the week."

"Check your lyrics, Derek," Beckett cautioned like the dad he was.

"Killjoy," Tate hit back, pulling laughter from the kids.

He'd never seen them skate so hard or so well. Tate's whole world felt like it had fallen into perfect harmony.

"Reach for ice, cross under," he called. "Reach, cross." They were nailing the advanced drill, so he added another new skill and had them easing down to their forearms before pulling back to their feet. When they had a handle on that, he added a jump, landing on one skate.

They'd worked the length of the rink a dozen times and had

all the kids red-faced, panting, and dripping sweat before he brought practice to a close.

Beckett tossed each kid a water bottle, and they either dropped flat on their backs on the ice to rest, or propped their backs up against the wall.

Tate took a drink from his own bottle and tugged off his helmet and wiped down while Olivia and Joe made their way toward them.

"That's got to be the best practice I've ever seen, son," his dad said as he followed Olivia to the bench and set down one of the bags of food. Olivia put the other down beside it. "I'm sorry, I've got to leave."

"Already?" Tate asked, stepping into the box.

"I'll be back Saturday for the dinner." He opened his arms for a hug, and Tate looked down at his dad's clean, casual travel clothes, then at his sweaty practice uniform. "Dad—"

"Come here," he ordered, wrapping his arms around him. "You should know better by now."

Tate hugged him back, and over his shoulder, he found Olivia watching, her smile soft, her eyes filled with warmth.

"I just...love you."

Her words from the night before shone in her eyes, and Beckett's heart swelled again.

Tate released Joe, and Joe turned to talk to Beckett.

Olivia stepped up to Tate. "That was beyond amazing," she said, glancing around at the boys still sprawled out on the ice. "You're even better with them than I ever imagined. Look at them. Those are some damn happy kids."

"That means I've done my job right. They'll devour in minutes what took you hours to put together for them."

"That means *I've* done *my* job right." When he laughed, she said, "I'm going to walk to Metro with your dad and head home from there."

"Okay." He rested his butt against the half wall. "What's on your agenda for the rest of the day?"

Smiling, she poked a finger to the middle of his chest. "Your dinner. I'm going to hit the grocery. Are you sure you want to leave the menu to me? This is your last chance to make changes."

He shook his head. "I trust you implicitly."

She leaned into him and tilted her face up to his. "That means a lot to me."

He dropped a kiss to her lips, letting it linger even though he knew one of his best friends, his father, and all the kids in his camp were watching. When he lifted his head, he murmured, "Can I see you later? Take you to dinner? Or for a drink?" He lowered his voice. "Or massage your feet?"

"I think your feet are the ones that will need massaging tonight."

"I won't fight you on that."

She laughed. "I would love to, but I need to try to talk with my mom. It would be good for me to sleep there tonight, even though I'd rather be with you."

He sighed. "I understand."

"But let's find a little window to hook up. Watching you skate seriously turns me on, and I want to reward your body for all that hard work." Her grin grew; her eyes sparkled. "I'm crazy about you, Donovan."

He sighed and dropped another kiss to her lips.

"Okay, kids," Joe said. "Hate to interrupt, but I've got to get going. Sweetie," he said to Olivia, "why don't you stay?"

"*Pffft.*" She waved the idea away. "If Tate had his way, I'd never get anything done."

She squeezed Tate's hand before she followed his dad out of the rink. And as Tate let the kids rest another minute, he watched them walk out together.

"Dude," Beckett said. "I haven't seen that grin on your face for years. She's the best thing that's happened to you since way before Lisa."

Tate nodded and met Beckett's gaze. "Without a doubt."

He teased the boys by opening the grocery bags Olivia left with him, "Let's see what we've got here." He leaned down and breathed deep. "Oh, hell, this is heaven right here. I don't know, Beck. Did they work hard enough for this kind of reward?"

The kids laughed and groaned and shouted.

"Depends," Beckett said. "What's in there?"

"Sandwiches," he said. "All kinds, with all the fixins. And they're on that crusty handmade bread."

"You're right," Beckett agreed. "I'm not sure. Anything else?"

"Ooo," Tate said. "Big, fat pickles. And—oh man—home-made kettle chips."

Half the kids were on their feet, crowding around, shoul-dering each other to get close.

"I think the final call will depend on dessert," Beckett said.

One of the kids reached for the bag, and Tate slapped his hand. The boy pulled back laughing. On the bench, Tate's phone rang.

"Can you take care of this?" Tate asked Beckett. "I'm expecting a call from Dave."

"You got it." Beckett yelled for Derek while Tate retrieved his phone. "Take the other bag. Lunch in the lounge boys." He glanced at Tate. "See you there?"

"Save me something, will you?"

"Eh," he said, grinning. "Maybe."

He answered, "Hey, Dave," while the kids put on their blade guards and followed Beckett into the building.

"Hey. I've just added a kid to my calendar next week. A real hotshot from Canada. I want to sign him in time to pitch him to the NHL in July, and he's a really big fan of yours. I was wondering if you could join us for dinner."

Next week, Olivia would be gone. He'd need anything he

could get to keep his mind busy. "You bet. Just tell me where and when."

"Great. Thanks man. He's going to be stoked. I'll have Teresa let you know the time and date."

Tate's mind scanned Dave's staff. "Who's Teresa?"

Dave laughed. "Little soon for off-season brain, isn't it? Teresa's the planner you recommended. The one organizing your banquet."

He opened his mouth to clarify, but all the synapses connected at once, and he muttered, "Oh shit," instead.

"What's wrong?"

Tate winced. "Man... That's too complicated to explain over the phone. But could I ask for a favor now? Can you find another planner to arrange things for the kids coming next week?"

"That's a weird request. But for you, I would. Unfortunately, it's a little late for that. She's already done with eighty percent of the planning. I've already given her a sizeable nonrefundable deposit. Shit, man, don't tell me she's going to screw me over and leave my people hanging. Let me know if I need to hire a backup."

"No, no, you don't need a backup." *Fuck.* "I've gotta go, Dave. I'll see you Saturday."

He disconnected and planted his hands along the top of the half wall, staring down at the ice. "Well, this is awkward."

Did he tell Olivia that her mother did exactly what Olivia had warned her not to do? It was a little soon to be stepping into family business. Especially when it had such a long, complicated history. He and Olivia hadn't even shored up their relationship yet, at least not in the framework of living apart over the next year. She sure hadn't told her mother about it.

"Shit."

He dropped to the bench and unlaced his skates. Dave's jobs wouldn't even happen until after Olivia was gone. And they wouldn't affect her, at least not as far as needing a high-class caterer went.

Looking at it that way, telling Olivia felt a lot like tattling on her mother. Plus it would only upset Olivia. And they didn't have much time left together. He'd like to see Olivia leave when she was on positive terms with her mother. It would give her more incentive to come back.

He pushed into his running shoes, picked up his skates, and headed toward the lounge for lunch with the kids. Halfway down the hall, his cell rang. He didn't recognize the number.

"Donovan," he answered.

"Tate." The woman's voice was pleasant and a little familiar, but he couldn't place it. "This is Teresa Essex."

What the... He stopped in his tracks.

"Hi, uh..." He wasn't sure what to call her. She'd asked him to call her Teresa, but somehow that didn't feel quite right. "How are you?"

"Fine, fine. I just wanted to thank you again for the referral to Mr. Burnett."

Tate's eyes rolled toward the ceiling with dread before he closed them.

"I just got off the phone with him, and he mentioned you had some reservations."

Dave, you fucking shit head...

"I wanted to reassure you that we will take great care of Mr. Burnett's needs. In fact, I'm making all the final arrangements now. I understand you'll be joining him for dinner next week, and I'll be calling shortly with all the information."

He leaned against the wall. "You know, Teresa, I hate to get into something that's not my business, but I'm sort of already in the middle. I really care a lot about Olivia, and Olivia really cares about you and Quinn. I don't feel right about you taking on this job with Dave when she has so many reservations about it." God, his stomach churned. "I think it would be best for everyone if you found another planner to take over for you—"

"Tate." She broke in with a conciliatory tone, but one with underlying steel. "I'm not sure what you think is happening between you and Olivia, but I feel the need to apologize in advance. From what everyone says, you're a sincere, caring man. Olivia has priorities, and relationships have always fallen to the bottom of that priority list. So while it's sweet of you to consider her feelings in all this, I'd just caution you to hold on to perspective when it comes to Olivia."

Tate's mouth dropped open. Anger roiled in his chest. He was about to jump to Olivia's defense when Teresa went on.

"She does worry about the business quite a bit, but that's because she's not here to see it operate. She hasn't been around to watch it grow or to see how Quinn and I have tackled every obstacle put in our path. Ten years later, we're still here, and we're growing, thanks to referrals like yours. It won't take long for Olivia to see that her worries are unfounded and that Quinn and I are completely stable. So if you wouldn't mind keeping the conversation you overheard yesterday between us, we'd all really appreciate it. Bringing it up would only dig the rift between us deeper just when we're starting to smooth things over. We've asked so much of Olivia this trip, I'd really like her to enjoy her last days here."

He closed his eyes and rubbed at them, torn over what to do, while still believing it wasn't his place to do anything. So he ended up offering a non-answer with, "I understand. Look, I've got to run. I'm at practice. Thanks for the call."

With a hasty good-bye, he disconnected and hung his head.

Fuck. He wished his dad hadn't already left. Tate could really use his wisdom right now.

He pushed off the wall and turned toward the lounge. He'd have to think about this more later, after all these preteen boys went home.

21

"How long is Mom going to avoid me?" Olivia asked Quinn where her sister worked beside her in the kitchen at Andrew Mullen Auditorium.

With two days until the banquet, Olivia was settling into the organization. She was stocking, making lists, creating a work-flow. Quinn was taking charge of supplies, making sure there was enough dinnerware, glassware, tablecloths, centerpieces. Finding and renting the equipment Olivia needed that wasn't already in the kitchen.

Quinn had plugged her phone into portable speakers, and a mix of pop and country floated through the space. While Olivia unloaded groceries into the refrigerator, Quinn stacked dishes on the shelves.

"If Mom's avoiding you, she's avoiding me. I haven't seen her for more than ten minutes over the last two days. We have a lot of new clients. She has to meet them all, organize them, make arrangements. She's as busy as we are."

That was a lie. Olivia had heard them talking downstairs the night before when they thought she was asleep. They'd talked for hours. While Olivia lay in bed, staring at the ceiling, wondering if the secrets in their house would ever stop. Wondering what her life would have been like if her father hadn't gotten sick. Wishing she'd gone to Tate's for the night.

"How are you feeling about this?" Quinn asked. "Feel like you're ready?"

Olivia nodded. "I've done everything we're both doing now and more. I've been a sous chef for years. There were times when I had to fill in for the head chef—when they got sick or hurt or were just plain lazy-asses. Being the one where the buck stops for something this important and for someone this close to me is a little overwhelming. But, yeah, I'm ready. Nervous but ready."

This was a great experience for her, and it would go a long way toward adding to her confidence.

"You know," she told Quinn, broaching a subject that had been on her mind since she and Quinn had their break-through. "Le Cordon Bleu has management courses. Culinary business management, restaurant management, international hospitality."

"Oh yeah?" she said in a way that told Olivia she wasn't really listening.

"Yeah." She finished with one grocery bag and started on another. "They even have a degree in wine and wine management. You used to be so passionate about wine, but I haven't heard you talk about it much over the last few years."

"Oh, you know. No time. No money."

And conversation stalled again.

"Quinn." She stopped putting groceries away and faced her sister. "What's bothering you?"

She lifted her brow and shook her head. "Nothing, why?"

"Because I know you, and I know you get quiet when you're stressed."

A little smile lifted her lips. "Just a lot of work to get done."

Another lie. Yes, there was a lot of work to do, but that

wasn't causing the level of stress Olivia felt rolling off Quinn in waves.

Olivia's mind immediately veered toward leaving. Her escape. Escape from the pain she felt whenever she came home. Escape from the loneliness she felt more with her family surrounding her than when she was alone in her flat in Paris.

She finished emptying the bag and closed the refrigerator door. Picking up her phone, she checked the time, then for a message from Tate. But there was nothing. Which was a little odd since his camp had gotten out about two hours ago.

She texted him: *Hey handsome. Is everything okay? Are we still on to go over the final menu? I have a couple of minor things I want to ask you about.* She paused and the hurt inside her gnawed. She added: *I miss you.*

"I miss you..." she whispered with the shake of her head.

Those words were so bizarre to her, yet they came so naturally with Tate. She had to send the message and shut her screen off so she didn't give into the urge to text him: *And, I love you.*

"Is that Tate?" Quinn asked.

"Yeah. I can't decide if a few of the menu items are too froufrou for his group or not. I was hoping I could get him to weigh in."

"How does he feel about you leaving?"

Olivia looked at her sister. Quinn continued to fill shelves with plates, bowls, cups, saucers...

"Uh...that's sort of complicated."

"Why?"

She took a breath to quell the nerves that came up whenever she thought of the quasi-commitment she'd made him.

"Because we're going to keep seeing each other. Or, at least, try... I guess." She pushed her phone into her pocket and started on another bag of groceries. "We haven't gotten into the details of how that's going to work yet."

"Really?"

The sheer shock in Quinn's voice brought Olivia's head up.

"I just mean," Quinn said, "he's so transparently one of those forever kind of guys."

Written between the lines, Olivia read: *and you're not a forever kind of girl.*

"How would anyone know if they're the forever kind unless they found the right person?" she asked. "Because by all accounts, you should be married with a couple of kids or a kickass career by now. But you're no further along in life than I am."

Irritation flashed across her face. "Because I'm busy. Busy trying to keep this damn company from going under and taking Mom with it. And this isn't about me. I'm not contemplating a relationship with someone on another continent."

Quinn seemed both irritated and genuinely concerned. But Olivia couldn't tell where this was coming from or why.

"I could see you two having a fling," Quinn said, "because that's just how you live and he's getting over a divorce, but taking it further? Are you sure that's not just an easier way for both of you to say good-bye?"

Olivia opened her mouth to say she didn't have a hard time with good-byes, but that wasn't true with Tate. And Tate was, admittedly, actively holding on.

"His life has really been stalled by the divorce," Quinn said. "He's thirty or thirty-one, he wants kids, and his career is here. It's not like he's got a job he can take anywhere. And he makes millions of dollars a year. Holding his position, getting future contracts, making that kind of money, it all hinges on focus. If he's all into you and you're on another continent, how well do you think he'll be focusing?"

Olivia really didn't like all the points Quinn was making. Each one she couldn't battle made her heart drop a little lower.

"You're awfully knowledgeable about in the inner workings of hockey and Tate all of a sudden."

"All I did at the party was overhear people talking and get chatted up by hockey players. You can learn a lot in a few hours if you're talking about the right things and listening to the answer with an open mind."

Olivia read between those lines too and didn't like the insinuation that all she and Tate had been doing was fucking. Which, in part, was true. Another hit to her confidence where Tate was concerned.

"Maybe I'm wrong," Quinn continued, "but I don't see you settling down anytime soon, and I'm having a hard time imagining you coming home." She shrugged and started back on the dishes. "I can see how it would be fun for you to have him coming to Paris to visit, but, personally, I don't think that's worth the consequences of the possible fallout for Tate when you decide to move on."

Olivia didn't respond immediately. She was turning over the very real facts Quinn had just thrown at her and all her ideas of continuing a relationship with Tate shattered into a million little cracks held together by a fragile invisible web.

"I wish you ladies would include me in these conversations."

Tate's voice startled Olivia, and she swiveled toward the door. He wandered in and leaned a shoulder against a bank of cabinets, and he didn't look happy. He also had a bad cut on the side of his chin that was developing a bruising halo.

"I appreciate your concern, Quinn," he said, "but this is something Olivia and I need to decide on ourselves." He looked at Olivia. "We may not have known each other long, but I think we know enough about the important things to make this decision."

"I'm sorry," Quinn said, embarrassed. "Of course, you're

right." She picked up an empty box. "I'm going to take this to the trash and head out to find lunch."

Olivia opened her mouth to say something to alleviate Quinn's unease, but as she turned to walk out the opposite direction, Tate held up a hand.

When Quinn was gone, Olivia moved toward him. "I'm sorry you had to hear that. What happened to your..." She trailed off when she saw the cut had looked so bad from further away because it was stitched closed with black thread. "Oh my God. You got stitches?"

She didn't wait for an answer before she turned and opened the freezer, searching for something to put on it. "Is that where you've been? The emergency room?"

Grabbing a bag of peas, she pulled a paper towel from the roll nearby and covered the bag. She lifted the wrap to his face and gently covered the ugly cut.

Tate winced but laid a gentle hand over hers. "Are you having second thoughts?"

"No, that's not how that conversation started. Quinn asked how you felt about me leaving, and I told her we were going to keep seeing each other." When he didn't respond, she pulled her hand from the cold press and rubbed it along the jeans over her thigh. "I hate to admit it, but she has some valid points. Things I didn't think about."

"Like what?"

She pushed her hands into the back pockets of her jeans. "Was what she said true? Do you want kids? Is having me in Paris going to fuck with your concentration?" Her stomach hurt. "I feel like a selfish bitch for not considering—"

He pressed his fingers to her lips, then set the peas on the counter and wrapped his other arm around her, pulling her close. He was hurting. She could see the dull haze of pain in his eyes.

"Baby, have you taken any pain meds?" she asked. "I've got ibuprofen. It will help with the swelling."

"If you were selfish," he told her, ignoring her question about his pain, "you wouldn't be here right now, and you certainly wouldn't be spending all this time and effort on my dinner. If you were selfish, you wouldn't care what happens to your family's company. If you were selfish, you wouldn't make these trips home to see them when they've never made an effort to do the same for you." He moved his fingers and pressed a gentle kiss to her lips. "If you were selfish, the questions Quinn just raised wouldn't bother you."

She leaned into him, picked up the bag, and pressed it to the cut again. "Keep this on or you're going to swell, and those stitches are going to hurt like a mother."

A little smile tilted his lips. "Sounds like you've been here before."

"I play with knives for a living."

Without warning, he cupped the back of her neck and kissed her. The force of it pushed a surprised sound from her throat. Then his lips parted, and his tongue slid along hers. All her stress melted, she sighed and opened to him. He tried to do the same but made a sound of discomfort and pulled back.

"Sorry," he said, wincing. "The numbing's wearing off."

"What happened?"

"Just one of those things. One of the kids ate it at practice. His momentum carried him into me, and I got the end of a stick."

"Ouch."

"It'll be fine by tomorrow."

They fell silent a minute, and their previous conversation flooded in. She repeated the question he never answered. "Is what Quinn said true?"

"Not about why I slept with you. I've been divorced for a year, over it almost before the final came through. I've had the opportunity to sleep with women since. I haven't because no one has interested me enough to make the jump. So, no, I didn't sleep with you because I was getting over a divorce."

That part didn't concern Olivia in the least. People sought out sex for hundreds of different reasons. The only thing that mattered to her was that once they'd met, they'd forged something beyond a sexual attraction. "What about the rest?"

He exhaled, planted his back against the cupboards, and braced his feet, pulling her into the vee of his legs. "Do I want kids? Yeah, I do. When I want them depends entirely on who I'm having them with and what our relationship is like. I like the whole original divine order to family—dating, marriage, kids. Is that model perfect? No. Is anything perfect? I haven't found one thing yet. But I know, now more than ever, that I want to be one hundred percent solid with a woman before kids enter the picture. The divorce made that nonnegotiable for me. Because if I had a child with Lisa, our lives would be a constant battle. I grew up without a dad for twelve years. I watched Mia grow up without ever connecting with hers. So that's one of my hard and fast values."

Olivia nodded and slid her arms around his waist. "I like that. Your love of family is one of the many things I admire about you. Along with your drive to be the best at what you do. It's one value of many that I think we share. I know how important your career is to you, and I don't want to interfere with that."

"That's *my* job. That's not something you can control. I've been playing hockey for over two decades. Focus is part of the muscle memory that kicks in as soon as my blades touch the ice. I've dated and broken up with women during that time, including marrying and divorcing Lisa. If anything, it made my game better, because I poured everything I had—all my frustration, all my anger—into the game."

She sighed, but felt only marginally better.

"What about you?" he asked. "How will having a long-distance relationship create stress in your life?"

She tipped her head and thought about it. Slipping her fingers under the edge of his tee, she stroked his warm skin. "I'll miss you. I've never missed anyone before. Except my dad. That will make me sad, but I'll keep busy with school and work. I might be more stressed about money, because I'll be trying to save to come back when I can get a break."

"I've been thinking about that. We can talk about it Sunday, after the dinner. What about men, Liv?" A flicker of a shadow passed through his dark eyes. "Your casual relationships have been a big part of your life."

She sputtered a laugh. "You make it sound like I sleep with a new guy every night."

"If you're missing me, stressed and lonely, it wouldn't be out of left field for you to find comfort where you are."

This talk was causing turbulent emotions. "I don't know what you want me to say. I've never done this before. If I wanted to keep sleeping with you *and* other men, I'd tell you to look me up when you're passing through. That's not what I'm doing, Tate. I'm putting all my trust in you. Emotionally, this is like a cliff edge for me."

That seemed to soften his eyes. He nodded and threaded his fingers through her hair.

"One of the reasons I've stayed out of relationships as long as I have," she said, "is because a lot of Europeans have a lackadaisical view of commitment. I can't even count the number of people I know who sleep around even when they're in a serious relationship. Maybe my first eighteen years drilled the American culture into me, or maybe it's because my parents were married so long and loved each other until the very end, but I've never found anyone who made me believe that all they wanted was me. When you're making love to me, I feel so completely..." God, she didn't know how to put it into words.

"Wanted and needed. I never knew how important that was to me until I had it with you."

Emotions flashed across his face with the complexity of a kaleidoscope pattern. His fingers massaged her scalp. "I'm ready to buy a fuckin' plane so I can go home to you every night."

"That," she said. "That right there. That's what I'm talking about." She hugged him close. "I love the way you love me."

His heart beat thumped in Olivia's ear. She closed her eyes, loving the idea of having this to fall asleep to every night. God, this was so crazy.

"Baby?" he said.

"Hmm?"

"I need to talk to you about something."

She pulled back and looked up at him. His expression matched his tone. "That doesn't sound good."

"It's not bad. I mean, it doesn't have to be. I don't even think it's a big deal, and I know you've got a lot going on. It's just—"

Footsteps cut off his words. They both turned toward the door, where Olivia's mother's voice entered before she did. "Olivia? Quinn? I'm here to see how you're—"

She felt Tate stiffen, but Olivia didn't move away from him. If her mother didn't care enough to even entertain Olivia's concerns about the business, she wasn't going to hide how she felt about Tate.

"Oh," her mother said, her gaze skipping from Tate to Olivia and back to Tate. But instead of surprise, Olivia saw alarm before her mother covered. "I didn't mean to interrupt."

"Quinn said she was grabbing lunch," Olivia told her, "but didn't say where she was going."

"I see." Teresa wandered in, her gaze still skipping between Olivia and Tate. And she was acting nervous, which was odd. Then she noticed Tate's cut. "Oh, Tate, what happened to your face?"

"It got in the way of a kid's stick today. I'm fine."

Teresa nodded. "So what do you two have your heads together about?"

Another odd question. "A few last-minute menu changes."

Her mother's expression said she was suspicious of that answer, but she didn't challenge Olivia. "And everything's okay?"

"Fine. I have all the ingredients I need, either way. I'm just fine-tuning for the audience."

"All right, then."

She looked like she was going to leave, so Olivia told her what she'd wanted to tell her last night. "I want to talk with you more about the company's finances before I leave, Mom. It's important."

"Oh, honey. I really do appreciate your concern, but we're doing fine. All these new jobs are covering the expenses, providing a salary for both me and Quinn, and we still have money left over to reinvest."

"But you don't have any cushion. If one of these jobs falls through, it could wipe you out. Things like that happen all the time. You just don't have the capital to risk—"

"Honey. Let's not waste Tate's time. You and I can talk about this later."

"Like we did last night?" These dismissals were making her angry.

"I got home late—"

"No, you didn't. I heard you and Quinn talking. And I know Quinn told you I wanted to talk to you." When her mother didn't argue, Olivia relented. "Fine. Do it your way. Just know this banquet is the last thing I want to be involved in."

"Olivia," she said, in her don't-be-ridiculous tone. "Don't blow this out of proportion." She glanced at Tate. "I'm sorry to be dragging our family business in front of you, Tate." She shot a stern look at Olivia. "We'll talk about this *later*."

Teresa walked out, and Olivia shook her head. "Whatever happened between me and Quinn wasn't as significant as I thought." She lifted her gaze to Tate's, feeling like she'd had the scab ripped off an old wound. "They're doing it again. Hiding things. Whispering so I don't hear. Planning things I don't know about." She lowered her gaze to his chest. "It's never going to change."

Tate wrapped her in his arms and held her tight. "This is a stressful time for all of us. Let them get through this run of events and try again."

She nodded, sighed, and refocused on his handsome face. "I'm sorry. What did you need to talk to me about?"

He shook his head, and a little smile tipped his lips. "You have enough to deal with."

"You look tired," she told him, stroking his cheek.

He grinned. "Stitches stress me out."

"Aw, I'm sorry I wasn't there to hold your hand." She was only half teasing. She really wished she had been in the ER with him. "Go home. Get some rest."

"Are you sure—"

"I've got this. I've got *you*. Nothing to worry about here. Now go home."

"Thanks, baby. You have no idea how nice it is to have you in my corner."

Her heart warmed. She loved being able to do something nice for him. Pushing up on her toes, she kissed him. "Dream of me."

22

Olivia worked into the early morning hours on basic food prep to make sure she and her sous chefs would have enough time to get everything ready. Then she met her assistants at the kitchen and started work again just hours later.

Now, at three in the afternoon, the day before the event, Olivia finally felt confident about the big night. She wandered out of the kitchen, where the other chefs were still working and into a stairway leading to the restrooms to call Tate, but her cell rang.

She smiled, prepared to say, *"I'm ready for our date"* but it wasn't Tate, and she didn't recognize the number.

She turned her mind away from the best French restaurant in DC where Tate had made reservations for them tonight, and took a seat on one of the stairs and groaned at her aching back. There, she answered, "Hello."

"Hi, can I speak with Quinn Essex please?" The voice was female and unfamiliar. Olivia and Quinn often got mistaken for each other, but this was a first.

"No, this is her sister."

"Is Quinn available?"

"I'm sorry, she's not. Can I help you with something?"

"I'm not sure. This is Vera with District Distributing. I need to speak with someone in charge of billing."

"Oh no, I definitely can't help you. How'd you get this number?"

"It was listed as an alternate contact. I'm sorry to bother you. I'll continue to try the other number I have."

"When I see her, I'll let her know you called."

Olivia disconnected and dialed Tate. He'd come in twice earlier in the day to see her, and she'd been too busy to give him much more than a few kisses.

He didn't pick up, which meant he was probably out taking care of the awards he planned on giving out at the banquet.

"Hey there," she said to his voice mail, "I can see the light at the end of the tunnel here. Hope your chin is feeling better. I'm looking forward to a long intimate dinner and an even longer, more intimate dessert. Call when you're free."

She disconnected, spent a few minutes stretching her back, legs, arms, and hands. And went back to work. Setting up the industrial blender, Olivia got started on the crust for the individual key lime streusel desserts. All two hundred and sixteen of them.

Olivia was filling Ziploc bags with the graham cracker blend when Quinn appeared at the door with her laptop in her hands and tears wetting her face.

Olivia froze. Alarm shot an icy-hot streak through her stomach. "What's wrong?"

She set the mixing bowl down with a *thump*, spilling graham cracker crumbs across the counter. Wiping her hands on her apron, she turned to face her sister. But she was frozen, waiting for what had to be devastating news by the look on Quinn's face.

"We have a big problem."

"*We?*" She held up her hands. "You and Mom have resisted

my every attempt to help. What you want is a fixer. I'm not going to keep cleaning up the messes you and Mom make. Especially not when you continue to keep secrets from me. Whatever that's about"—she gestured toward Quinn's tears and the computer—"isn't my problem."

Quinn pulled the computer to her chest and took a choppy breath. "It is if you care about Tate the way you say you do."

All the discomfort in her stomach hardened into a rock. Olivia crossed her arms and tilted her head toward the main dining room, then started that way, her anger growing right alongside fear. She took a seat at one of the two tables she'd set up a few days ago for paperwork.

Quinn sat on the edge of another chair, pressed the computer to her lap, and stared at it. "I'm not sure where to start."

"Skip the drama, just tell me the problem."

Quinn pulled in a breath. Another. She dropped her head, covering her face. "I'm so sorry."

Despite her anger, despite her hurt, Olivia couldn't stand to see Quinn so distraught. She leaned in and wrapped her arms around her sister. "Jesus Christ, Quinny. Life's too short to be so stressed and unhappy."

"You're never going to come back."

Olivia pulled back and frowned at Quinn. "What?"

"After this." She exhaled. "You're never going to come back."

Everything inside her braced for a deathblow. "*What, happened.*"

"The distributor for our liquor called."

Olivia's mind shot back to the phone call she'd gotten an hour before. "District Distributors?"

Quinn gaze her a glassy stare. "Yeah. H-how did you know?"

"They called me earlier looking for you. What kind of problem with the liquor could possibly cause this level of distress?"

Quinn took another breath, then started talking. "They said the payment for the liquor for this event didn't go through. So, I gave them the credit card number again, checked the expiration date and the code on the back, but it still didn't go through. I told her I'd look into it and call her back."

"That doesn't sound like a problem that warrants all this." Olivia gestured to Quinn.

Quinn lifted a finger. "There's more."

Dread collected like a boulder in her gut. She leaned back and crossed her arms.

"When the payment failed again, I called the credit card company. They said we're over our credit limit, but that account has our highest limit. That freaked me, but I figured I'd look into it later. So I paid with another card." She shook her head. "Didn't go through. Credit limit maxed out. I tried the emergency card. Same."

Olivia's mouth dropped open in shock. "Holy shit." She frowned. "Where's Mom?"

"In Chevy Chase with a client. She never answers her phone when she's with a client. So I'm panicking now. And even though I know we shouldn't use cash to pay for things, I went to the bank. The distributer said they'd need cash or a cashier's check since the payment didn't clear ahead of time." Quinn tented her hands over her mouth and shook her head. "There's no money in the business account."

"What do you mean no money? There has to be something—"

"Two hundred dollars."

"*What the hell?*" Olivia's mind was spinning over the debt, the lack of cash. "What happened to all the deposits you've been getting for all these new jobs?"

Quinn put her laptop on the table. The screen showed a Wells Fargo bank account. Essex Elite Events bank account page. Olivia pulled the computer toward her, scouring the numbers.

When her sister started pointing toward the amounts and explaining what they were, Olivia lost her patience and snapped, "I know how to read a bank statement."

Quinn pulled back, cupped her hands in her lap, and stared at the table. And Olivia felt like shit. She stared at Quinn for a moment with a sense of utter and complete loss. Olivia had always believed she and Quinn would eventually find their way back to each other. She'd always hoped she and her mom would find a bridge back from the betrayal they both felt. But looking at her sister now, after seeing what her mother and Quinn had been doing all these years without even telling Olivia about it, she'd never felt more alienated. Or more unwanted.

Unless she could fix the problem.

She lowered her gaze to the computer screen. Her chest ached. Her stomach hurt. And a huge, *huge* part of her, like ninety-nine percent of her, wanted to shove the computer back at Quinn and tell her to clean up her own mess.

But they'd dragged Tate into it. And she wouldn't let him down.

So, she scrolled through the numbers, looking at where the money was coming in and where it was going. Within five minutes, Olivia saw the pattern, and her stomach dropped.

"You've been spiraling for months. Jesus, Quinn, you've been living by the seat of your pants for almost a year." She looked up at her sister. "You're smarter than this. You aced accounting in high school. You did an internship with Boeings finance, for Christ's sake. You know better than to pay deposits for future jobs with final payments from past jobs."

She shook her head and offered a quiet, "I wasn't managing the money. I didn't know."

"Shit." Olivia planted her elbow on the table and propped

her forehead in her hand, searching deeper, trying to find some money. Somewhere. There was two hundred dollars in the checking. One hundred in savings. For a business this size, that was terrifying. "Are there other accounts?"

"No."

Olivia's stomach squeezed tighter, and she exhaled on a groan. "What about personal accounts?"

Quinn scraped her upper lip between her teeth and stared at her hands. Then just shook her head. And the fear dug deeper into Olivia's gut. This was bad. Really bad. Like bankruptcy-bad.

The overwhelming financial disaster unfolding in front of her eyes pushed panic into her throat. She moved her hand there, swallowing back the burn.

And dug into the vendors and venues that had been paid in search of money they could get back, orders they could cancel.

"How much do we need for the liquor?" she asked, clicking on the number of the last check written to open an image of the check itself.

"Twelve thousand," Quinn said.

Olivia exhaled hard. She'd known it would be high for the number of people attending and the caliber of the crowd, but that number still took her breath. Not because it was unreasonable, but because she couldn't imagine finding that kind of money in an account this bone dry. She knew she could cut three grand off the top by substituting well liquor for quality name brands. Normally something she'd never consider doing, but right now, she was in survival mode. Right now, she wanted to pull this out of the fire for Tate.

She focused on the last check written for two thousand dollars to O'Conner's Tavern. The memo line read "Burnett/Thompson dinner" with a date for the following week.

She clicked on the next for the same amount to a different restaurant in downtown DC. The memo line read "Burnett/Washington dinner" and another date for the following week.

"What are these Burnett dinners?" she asked, continuing to click through the checks.

Quinn didn't answer, and Olivia forgot her question as she counted eighteen thousand dollars paid out to various high-class restaurants in DC over the last three days. A week earlier, she found an eighteen-thousand-dollar deposit into the account.

The deposit was electronic, but when she clicked on the details, the notes read "Final payment Afterschool Advantage."

"Fuck." She'd used Tate's final payment for the venue to fund the deposits for this Burnett deal, but hadn't gotten a deposit check from Burnett yet. A spark of hope brought her gaze to Quinn. "Is she holding a check? This Burnett guy's deposit check?"

"N-no," she said, her voice breaking. "He's in Greece. Was supposed to be back yesterday or today, but something happened with his flights, and he won't be in until Monday."

Her options for pulling this from the fire for Tate were narrowing. And she felt physically sick at the prospect of telling him that her family had fucked up. In essence, fucked him over, and if he wanted alcohol at his celebrity hockey-studded event, he was going to have to dole out another ten grand.

Shame and anger and hurt coiled tight at the center of her body. She covered her mouth and absently let her eyes roll over the debits and credits as she searched her brain for some other solution.

At the bottom of the page, she found a two-hundred-fifty-thousand-dollar line of credit. The available credit on that line was zero.

"What's this?" she asked. "Where did this line of credit come from? Is this right?" She cut a look at Quinn, who was leaning on the table, her head in her hand. "Is this quarter of a million-dollar line of credit *maxed out?*"

Quinn's lashes fluttered, then closed. She nodded.

"*Quinn.*" Olivia had always been good at scraping money together. But this... "How did you guys qualify for a line of credit that big when the business wasn't even in the black?"

Quinn licked her lips and kept her gaze down. "The house."

Olivia frowned, "What hou—" She sucked a breath and shook her head. "No. *No*, you didn't."

Quinn's gaze lifted to hers with a spark of defiance, the one she got whenever she felt unjustly challenged. "I didn't."

Which meant their mother had.

"It was *paid off.*" Everything inside Olivia crumbled. She slammed the laptop and shoved it away. "Dad worked his ass off and sacrificed so they'd have that house paid off in fifteen years. He knew how much that house meant to us, and he never wanted Mom to have to worry about finding the money to pay for it if something happened to him."

"It's not our house, Liv. It's Mom's."

Olivia shook her head. "You're going to lose it, aren't you? I don't see any money anywhere to make the next payment."

"We won't lose it if we can keep these jobs through to the end. When the money starts coming in, we'll be able to pay everything back."

"To what end? Just to make the same mistakes over again? *Two hundred fifty thousand dollars,* Quinn. How in the hell are you going to pay that back?"

"In payments, the way everyone pays house loans. With the income we get from the company."

Olivia put up her hands, palms out. "Whatever. I can't talk about this now." She pushed to her feet, one hand on her forehead, one at her hip. "When does the distributor need the money?"

"By five thirty."

Olivia looked at her watch. "In an *hour*?" This just got worse and worse. "Are you serious?"

"It's Friday. They're closed tomorrow."

"Fucking sonofabitch." She squeezed her eyes closed to focus. "I have to find Tate." She dragged her phone from her back pocket, tapped into Tate's number, then just stared at it. Another wave of nausea rolled through her gut. "Oh my God, how am I going to explain this?"

She exhaled, closed her eyes, and tried to form a concise way to tell him about this mess. It was a mess for him. A catastrophe for her.

"You won't have to." Quinn's words pulled Olivia's eyes open, and she swore the last two weeks fell on her shoulders all at once.

"What?"

"You won't have to explain much. He already knows most of it."

Her dazed brain didn't absorb any of what Quinn just said. "What? What does he already know?"

"About the house. About the company struggling."

Olivia shook her head at the ludicrous statement. "How could he possibly know that?"

"He overheard Mom and me talking at Lily's party."

No, she wasn't hearing this right. She couldn't be hearing this right.

"Okay..." She shoved her phone back into her pocket. "You're telling me that Tate knew that the company was leveraged against the house and that the company was in trouble?"

Quinn nodded. "Mom was telling me that after the senator's christening, we only needed one more job to get enough to pay off the balloon payment coming due."

Olivia shook her head. "You only thought he heard you. He wouldn't keep that from—"

"Mom asked him not to tell you."

Olivia didn't respond. Her mind was spinning, her world shattering.

"It put him in a really bad position," Quinn said. "Mom did exactly what she did to me, snowed him with the assurance that it would be fine. That the new business would solve all our problems."

Olivia felt a time bomb at the center of her chest. *Tick, tick, tick.*

She crossed her arms and reset her feet. "You're telling me that Tate knew all this and kept it from me because Mom asked him to?"

Quinn lifted a shoulder. "Mom said it would cause more stress for you and more problems between us. And that's true. It's not like you could have done anything—"

"Don't." She put out a hand. "Just don't. This isn't about whether or not I could do anything to help. This isn't about the money. This is about being honest with the people you love. Or in this case, claim to love. I've told you and Mom this over and over. I resigned myself to the fact that we have different values. That we would never have the relationship we had before. But to ask Tate to keep something like this from me? When you both know how this kind of..."

She stopped talking. Closed her mouth. Shook her head. "This is pointless." Tears burned her eyes. "God, I should have known he was too good to be true." She lifted her gaze to Quinn, but felt more pity for her than anger. "Should have known...nothing would change."

She pushed her hands into her back packets and turned for the exit.

"Olivia," Quinn called. "Where are you going?"

She had no fucking idea. She'd already learned that no matter where in the world she traveled, pain followed. She only knew she needed to get away from the people hurting her. "Away from here."

Quinn ran in front of her just as she reached the door. "Liv, Mom and I are the ones to blame for this. Tate was caught in the middle. He didn't tell you because he loves you."

"No, Quinn. People who love you don't keep parts of their lives secret. People who love you don't shut you out. People who love you stand up in the face of the hardest choices and choose you. Not only didn't you and Mom do that for the umpteenth time with me, but Tate didn't do it either."

Olivia held it together until she'd reached Metro. But waiting for the next red train gave her too much time to think. And, as if her mind had been just waiting for the opportunity to ambush her when her walls were down, everything hit her at once. Years of lies and loneliness. Years of grief over the loss of her father and her family. Years of taking care of everything on her own. Even trying to take care of her family from a distance the best that she knew how.

But none of it had been enough.

By the time the train pulled into the station, she'd shut down. Gone into survival mode. She stepped onto the red line train at quitting time and found herself stuffed into the car like a sardine. Olivia kept her eyes on the floor while the car swayed, trying to untangle the knot in her head. But it was useless. The pain created a haze she couldn't think through.

She only had to endure the sardine can for three stops, then she collected herself on the short walk and paused outside the office of District Distributing. Olivia wiped her face one last time, took hold of her emotions the way she'd taught herself over the years, and looked up at the sign over the door. She took several deep breaths of the summer afternoon air, and once she could take a full lungful without a hiccup, she blew it out slowly.

Olivia pushed through the front door, praying the negotiation skills she'd learned bartering in the streets at markets all over the world would come through for her now.

23

Tate climbed the grand concrete steps of the Andrew Mellon Auditorium and threaded his way through the lobby and halls toward the kitchen, feeling jittery. He felt guilty about how excited he was to spend time with Olivia tonight, because he knew the problems with her mother's company would upset her.

He still thought it would be better to tell her about it tomorrow night, after the banquet, but Joe had convinced him the sooner the better.

Pushing into the kitchen, he found the sous chefs gone, the kitchen clean, and all kinds of things stacked on counters in bowls and pans, covered in clear cling wrap. Man, this woman impressed the hell out of him.

"Liv?" he called, then wandered into the storage room and found her standing at some shelves with a clipboard, taking notes. She'd taken her hair down from the knot on the back of her head, and it skimmed just past her shoulders. "Hey, this place looks amazing."

She turned, and the instant her eyes met his, he knew it

wasn't Olivia. He also knew Quinn had been crying. "Oh, hey Quinn. Where's Olivia?"

Quinn lowered the clipboard. "I don't know."

When she didn't expand, Tate's unease deepened. "Okay. Maybe she went home to change for dinner. I'll just—"

"No," Quinn said. "She didn't go home to change."

Tate exhaled, pressed a hand to the wall and asked the obvious question. "What happened? Did you two have another fight?"

Quinn cleared her throat and came a little closer. "I have some bad news."

Tate listened as Quinn explained the liquor fiasco. And how the liquor fiasco had led to exposing the company's troubles. Tate was vibrating with stress for Olivia when Quinn finally dropped the bomb.

"She knows you knew," Quinn said. "About everything."

Tate's breath froze in his lungs.

"We were both so upset, and she was stressing over how she was going to tell you. She's tried so hard to make this perfect for you, and I couldn't stand to see her twisted over one more thing."

"Oh my God." Tate's heart dropped clear to his feet. He closed his eyes and planted a hand over his face. "Oh my God."

"I can't tell you how sorry I am," Quinn said. "I've put in a few emergency calls to chefs we've worked with in the past, but I haven't heard back yet. I'm trying to get a handle on the food. Olivia had everything prepared. She's been working with the sous chefs for two days and has full, detailed recipes for every course. I've asked the sous to come back so I can see how much they feel they can handle on their own. It might not be—"

"Stop, Quinn. I don't want to hear about the banquet. I want to know where to find Olivia."

"I don't know. She left and wouldn't tell me—"

The rattle and shake of glass bottles echoed in the main kitchen followed by "Hello? Anyone home?"

Tate turned into the kitchen to a delivery man with a hand truck loaded with boxes that read "Wild Turkey".

"Oh my God," Quinn said behind Tate. "She...she... How did she...?"

The guy unloaded the boxes and handed over a clipboard with an invoice. "If you wouldn't mind signing for the receipt, I'll grab the rest from the truck."

Quinn looked past Tate's arm to read the invoice, stamped with a big red PAID at the bottom next to an amount just shy of ten grand. Next to the words *Paid in Cash*. Next to Olivia's signature.

"Cash? Where in the hell would she—" Quinn sucked an audible breath and took a step away. "Oh no." Her blue eyes flew wide. "Oh shit, no."

"What—" Tate started, but the delivery guy returned with another load, and Tate held his questions for Quinn.

The delivery guy pointed to the bottom of the form. "If you could just sign there, beneath the other signature."

Tate scribbled off his signature. Something he'd done thousands of times. But when he saw it there beneath Olivia's, a weird buzz kicked off in his head. It reminded him of his signature on his marriage license with Lisa's. Then on the divorce papers with Lisa's.

Tate had failed. Again.

He handed the board back and asked, "Do you know anything about this delivery?"

"Only that the lady gave me a hundred-dollar tip for staying past quitting time to deliver it." He tore off the top sheet and handed it to Tate. "Have a great weekend."

As the guy walked out whistling, Tate was sure this was going to be the worst weekend of his life.

24

Olivia was sitting at the kitchen table, rubbing one of the dog tags from her father's military service as a young man between her fingers, when her mother arrived home.

She came into the kitchen from the garage door just like she had for decades. And as soon as she lifted her gaze and saw Olivia sitting there, Olivia knew Quinn had told her everything.

"Olivia." She was shocked and a little breathless. "Oh, I'm so glad you're still here. I thought you'd be gone."

The pain that had receded over the last hour collected again. She didn't respond, not sure what she wanted to say caught between the desire to rehash every moment of the last ten years and never speaking to her mother again.

Her mother dropped her purse on the kitchen island and took a seat beside Olivia, pressing a hand to her knee. "Honey—"

"Do you remember these?" She lifted the metal tag with a sad smile. "Remember how Dad gave this to me for a metal shop project?"

"And you made a key ring out of it," her mother said. "You still have that old thing?"

"Yep. It goes everywhere I go. I always sort of felt like he was traveling with me, getting to go all the places he always wanted to go, but never got the chance."

Her mother smiled and pressed her fingers to her lips. "He would have liked that."

Olivia nodded. "I think he would want us to figure this out, mom." She closed her hand around the metal and crossed her arms. "I think the way we've been living would break his heart."

Her mother's eyes closed "I—I thought I had everything handled."

"If that lie is for me, it's dead on arrival. You don't take out a two hundred and fifty thousand dollar mortgage to save a flailing company and call that handling things. If the lie is for you, that's up to you."

"I meant now." She opened her eyes. "I thought I had everything handled *now*. Before, I borrowed to cover expenses, invest in equipment and marketing to get the bigger jobs, cover some living expenses, but never caught up."

Olivia sighed a choppy breath and nodded. "You have to start working with an accountant, Mom. Get some business counseling. Something. No one can do this themselves. That's why people take on partners and investors. You won't succeed as an island."

"I know. And I will get help, I promise. I'm going to make this right, Livvy." She reached out and covered Olivia's hand, squeezing it. "I stopped by the senator's home and picked up a deposit check from his wife. I don't have twelve thousand dollars to spend on liquor, but I have five. I know a good discount store that will give me a deal. You don't have to worry about Tate's party. I'll make sure it's fine. I always come through, Livvy."

She smiled, exhausted and aching. "You usually do, Mom. I know you try your best every time. But I gave Tate my word, so I already took care of the alcohol. When you get the money, you can just send me a check."

Her mother sat back. "Where did you get twelve thousand dollars?"

"It was ten, and that doesn't matter." She lifted her gaze to her mother's. "I want you to know that I'm sorry for my part in this distance between us. I feel partially responsible for the trouble you're in now too, and that if I hadn't left after Dad died, we might have made different choices as a family. As much as I felt betrayed over the rest of you keeping Dad's cancer secret, I know you felt hurt and abandoned when I left."

She cleared her throat. "I want you to know that I believe in you. I believe you have what it takes to pull this company out of the fire. And I also want you to know that no matter what happens or what you have to do to survive, I love you. I may not like what's happened or how it's happened, but I'll always, *always* love you."

"Oh, Liv..."

She tapped her Uber app on her phone and stood, pulling her rolling suitcase from behind her chair.

"What—" Panic lit up her mother's eyes.

"I need some time, Mom."

"But where are you going? What are you going to do?"

"I'm going to do what dad would want me to do. I'm going to do what I've always done." She leaned in and kissed her mother's cheek.

Her mother closed her hand over Olivia's and met her eyes. "This is my fault. Tate is a good man, Liv. He only did what he thought was best for you, because I told him it was best."

Her heart twisted. "I know."

"He called and asked me not to take the jobs with his agent. He was worried about how risking the house would hurt you because of how much you love it. He wanted our family to heal,

Liv, because he knew it would make you happy. That's why he didn't tell you."

She smiled, but her heart felt like it was in a vise. "He's a good man." She pulled her hand from her mother's. "I love you, Mom. See you soon."

She walked to the car stopped in the street and climbed in. And as she pulled away from the curb, with her mother standing in the doorway of the only home Olivia had ever known, in a lot of ways Olivia felt like she had when she'd been eighteen, driving to the airport after her father died.

Only this time she could make better decisions. Decisions her dad would be proud of.

25

Tate tipped back his sixth beer, wishing the painkilling effects would kick in. He glanced at his phone again, squinting because his vision was a little blurred.

Eden stood from the sofa in the condo she shared with Beckett and Lily and took the empty bottle from his hand. Tate didn't even feel it leave his fingers.

He turned his phone toward her. "Is that a new message?"

"No, handsome." She ruffled his hair the same way he did with Lily. "That's the old one."

The old one—the one and only text Olivia had sent after Tate's dozens of calls had gone unanswered—was something to the effect of "*I need time.*"

He exhaled and dropped his head back against the chair. Looking up at Eden, he said, "This is your fiancé's fault. You know that, right?"

"So you've said." She gave him an affectionate pat on the cheek. "I'm going to let you boys talk. Good night." She leaned down and kissed Tate's forehead. "I'm sorry, Tate."

"Me too," he said, looking out at the night beyond the windows of Beckett's luxury apartment as Eden walked through the kitchen and into the bedroom. "I'm one sorry sonofa—" He caught himself, because he couldn't remember if Lily was in bed or not. Hell, Tate didn't even know what time it was. "Where's Lily?"

"She's been in bed for two hours," Beckett said from his spot in the corner of the sofa.

The television was turned to some type of game, but Tate didn't even know what sport was playing. "That's shitty beer you got, man."

"Oh yeah?" Beckett asked, amused.

"Yeah. I'm drunk off my ass, and I can still feel a hole the size of Texas in my gut."

"Mmm," Beckett mused. "Sorry to tell you that's not likely to go away anytime soon, bro."

Tate rubbed his eyes, then looked at his phone again, checking the time. It was 10 p.m. He tapped the redial button.

"Tate," Beckett said.

"This is the last time, I swear."

"You said that two times ago."

"Hi," Quinn answered.

"Hey. Anything?"

"No. I'm sorry. I haven't heard from her. If it makes you feel any better, she's not answering my texts or phone calls either."

No, that didn't make him feel any better. It only meant she'd lumped Tate in with the other people in her life who'd hurt her. So he turned to his next most pressing issue. "Any bites on a caterer?"

"I'm sorry to say, nothing good on that front either."

Fuck.

"I guess if we don't hear back by tomorrow, I'll call everyone and cancel."

"I can take care of that—"

"No. That's something I have to do personally. Assure everyone they'll get their money back. You could contact a few charities, see if you could find someone who could use the food."

"Sure. I'll do that first thing." She paused. "Tate, I'm really—"

"Please don't. I've heard enough sorrys for a lifetime. I'll talk to you tomorrow."

He said good-bye and disconnected, then went back to staring at his phone. "Man, what a fucking failure of a year."

"If you're giving up on her already," Beckett said, "then you deserve to lose her. Maybe you should be thinking about how to make it right with her when you do figure out where she is."

"Or maybe if she walked away so easily, I'm better off without her."

"All right." Beckett pushed to his feet. "Now you're just being an idiot." He stood over Tate with more pity than anger. "Because now you're just questioning my ability to read people. Maybe *she's* better off without *you*. Ever think of that?" He started toward the bedroom. "You know where the extra blankets and pillows are."

Tate threw his arm across his eyes. "Fuck me."

26

Olivia felt like hell.

She leaned her head against the wall of the Metro car and closed her eyes. This was going to be one hellish, horrible, very-bad, no-good day. But the sooner she got started, the sooner she could finish. The sooner she finished, the sooner she could go home.

For the first time since she'd moved overseas, the thought of going home brought pain instead of pleasure.

Thankfully, her stop came up, and she focused on the sidewalks, quiet at this hour of the morning, as she made her way through town to the Andrew Mellon Auditorium.

She approached the front glass doors and spied the security guard the coordinator said would be here this morning to unlock the doors for her. Once she was in the kitchen, she settled into the silence and familiarity. Instead of comforting, today it felt hollow.

Olivia took a deep breath and pulled the ingredients she'd prepared for the crab cake appetizers from the fridge and started working. The sous chefs would be here in half an hour, and things would get rolling. She'd feel better once she was in the swing.

She had half the first batch formed into mini flying saucers when the first chef arrived. Olivia greeted him with businesslike efficiency. She didn't have the energy to pull up the light, fun woman who usually lived in the kitchen. Not today.

Olivia looked up with a basic hello and a list of things she wanted prepared in order, but she found Tate standing there instead of her sous chef, and her words vanished. The simple sight of him punched her low in the gut and everything she'd prepared to say, everything that was logical and sensible and the right thing to do, flittered into the wind.

"Liv?" He stood across the kitchen, eyes narrowed as if he couldn't quite believe what he was seeing.

"Hi." She hadn't been expecting to do this so early, and with the flood of emotion filling her from the feet up, she was afraid she might not be able to do what she knew was best for them both.

She stepped to the sink to wash her hands.

"What in the hell?" She wasn't sure if that edge in his tone was disbelief or anger, but he was entitled. "I thought you went back to Paris."

She turned, putting the sink at her back, and found him closer. And he looked like she felt. His hair was all over the place, his face rough with stubble, the side of his chin marred with the stitches and a purplish bruise. His clothes were wrinkled, like he'd slept in them.

"I...thought about it. A lot." She swallowed, trying to look him in the eye and finding it more difficult than she'd imagined. "But I know how important this is to you. To the kids. And I promised you... So I wanted to see it through."

"Where the hell were you?" He put his hands on his hips. "Did you get my messages?"

The quake in his voice slammed her with emotions that

closed her throat. Memories of the pleas and apologies he'd left on her voice mail burned her eyes. She blinked quickly and fought to find the script she'd created for this moment.

"What are you doing here?" she asked.

"I came to put the food in boxes. Quinn found a charity to take everything." He lifted his hands out to the side. "I was going to call everyone this morning and cancel dinner. I didn't think you were coming back."

She should have called. Or at least texted. But she hadn't made her mind up until the last minute.

Script. Script. What was the damn script?

"I think we let things between us get too serious." She forced her voice light, as if her heart wasn't breaking. "But that's obviously not going to work, and I'd like to be able to get through today so we can move on without anger and regrets."

"Not going to work? How can you stand there and act like a mannequin after you told me you loved me?"

She closed her eyes, sucking up the pain.

His hands closed on her arms, and she opened her eyes to his.

"You said you loved me, Liv. What I did was a mistake. Poor judgment. Call it what you want, but it doesn't change the fact that *I love you.*"

Her barriers crumbled beneath the pain of hurting him. Of losing him. "Love doesn't justify lying. Or keeping secrets. Especially given what you know about my family."

She pulled out of his arms and stepped back. So she could breathe. So she could think. Because the pain in his eyes threatened to crush her.

"I trusted you," she said. "I lay in your arms and told you every detail about the lies and secrets my family created that drove me away. And even knowing that, you went and did the same thing."

"I didn't mean to—"

"But you did. It still happened. I'm still hurt. And if we don't have trust here, when we're together, we're not going to make it living apart. I won't do it again. I won't live that way."

He lowered his head, ran a hand through his hair, and when he looked at her again, he was...different. He was hidden behind some kind of wall.

"So that's it? The first bump in the road, and you're done?" He straightened and shook his head. "Then you were right. You and I do have very different meanings for love."

Footsteps sounded at the back door, and both sous chefs walked in, chatting.

"Morning, Olivia. Morning, Mr. Donovan." Greetings peppered the air. Olivia glanced at the men to return their greetings, and when she looked back, Tate was walking away.

27

Tate held a drink in his hand. He wandered through the crowd. He made polite conversation. He'd been here before. He knew how to pretend he wasn't heartbroken.

What he didn't know how to do was stop thinking about Olivia.

This was his fault. Tate knew that. She had every right to be hurt and angry. What kept him out there instead of back in the kitchen was the fact that she wanted to jump ship because he'd made a mistake. He'd made a conscious decision to keep the information from her, and that had been wrong. But he hadn't hurt her intentionally. In fact, he'd been trying to do just the opposite.

He kept trying to tell himself it was better this way. And, maybe in time, he'd believe that.

Teresa and Quinn were on hand to make sure everything with the event was perfect. And every time he looked at Quinn, he ached for Olivia.

"Penny for your thoughts." Mia appeared at his side. Leave it to his little sister to sneak up on him.

"No, thanks."

"Did you find out she's a serial killer?"

He cut a look at his sister. He didn't even wonder where Mia heard. He knew it had gone straight from Eden to Mia. "Shut up."

"Can we play the cold-hot game? It will go a lot faster."

"Go away."

"All right, fine. Let's do one blink for yes, two for no."

Tate sighed and took his first sip of whiskey. A thousand fiery needles pricked his mouth, then followed the liquid down his throat, leaving a searing path.

Oh yeah. That felt good.

"She cheated on you," Mia said.

"Mia." Tate gave her the look his teammates swore could peel paint. Evidently, Mia had seen it too many times in her life, because she laughed.

"I figured I should go for the obvious first. Since that's out, I'll go in decreasing order of most deplorable characteristics. Is she a gold digger?" Mia asked. Tate ignored her. "Okay, let's see, no values or morals? Hmmm, how about a liar?"

Tate frowned at her. "Why is liar so high up on the list? What about ex-con or, I don't know, racist or something."

"Because without trust, you have no basis for a relationship. Trust touches everything, and no one can trust a liar."

A hot knife cut down the center of his chest. Tate tossed the rest of his whiskey down his throat.

"Looks like we're sitting down to eat," Mia said. "You get a reprieve. But be prepared for the third degree after. Because, bro, I've never seen you as happy as you were for the short time you were with her. So if you haven't figure out some way to mend the rift by dessert, I'm going to hound you until you strangle me." She smiled sweetly and patted his cheek. "Then I'll sic Rafe on you."

As she walked away, Tate said, "I'm going to tell him you referred to him as a dog."

She just laughed.

Tate had already traded his place-setting card with someone else's so he was sitting at a table where everyone would talk about nothing but hockey. The world could be on fire, and they'd still be talking hockey.

But he knew it was going to be one long-ass night when the first course of ahi tartar with avocado, ginger, and sesame hit the table and everyone stopped talking to ooooooh at the presentation. Even Tate, who had absolutely no appetite and never ate raw anything, was tempted.

Delicate chunks and strips of ruby-colored meat lay on a bed of sliced avocado and sprinkled with sesame seeds and scallions.

Tate got away with not eating anything by saying he was allergic to seafood. He managed to take only a bite of the second course, fettuccine vongole, which was so good, it made his eyes roll back in his head, by saying he was saving room for the main course.

So when the table was served either oak-fired swordfish or an A3 New York strip with endive marmalade and truffle crust with a red wine jus, Tate's appetite came back with the intensity of his feelings for the chef.

The first bite of his steak actually made Tate moan. No one noticed because everyone else was doing the same. And, now, at the table that talked nothing but hockey, the conversation was all about the food and the chef. And Tate was peppered with questions about a woman he was trying to let go.

"Well," the wife of a Rough Riders' sponsor mused as she took her last bite of swordfish, "she has definitely found her calling." She smiled at Tate. "Like you've found yours. That happens so rarely, it's a true blessing to see."

As amazing as the food was, Tate's stomach was too twisted with loss to eat any more. And while the others around the table continued to obsess over Olivia's food, Tate obsessed over

Olivia. Instead of trying to push her out of his heart, he started thinking of ways he could turn this situation around. But how did you convince someone they could trust you if they wouldn't let you? And how could he possibly prove it to her if she was in Paris and he wasn't?

When the woman beside Tate excused herself for the restroom, Quinn took her seat. Gingerly propped on the edge of the chair, facing Tate, she leaned toward him and spoke in an undertone at his ear.

"Liv used her money for school to cover the liquor."

Shock blasted Tate's gut. His face chilled as the blood drained. "No."

"I thought that was the case yesterday, but I wasn't sure." Quinn kept her eyes on her hands, her lips compressed as she nodded, obviously trying to hold back tears. "I feel... God, I can't even..."

Tate's stomach ratcheted down so tight, a wave of nausea swept through. "Oh my— *Why?* Why would she do that?"

Quinn lifted her gaze to Tate's, and the sight of those blue eyes—Liv's eyes—made him ache. "Because she always keeps her word. She always follows through. Because she loves all of us, and she never bails on the people she loves."

Quinn huffed a sad laugh. "Even when she's mad at them. Even when she has to live across the world for us to get along." She paused, sighed. "I realized tonight that Liv's always been the rock in our family. I thought it was my dad, but now I can see Dad only nurtured Liv. She's the real foundation of our family."

She'd been his rock too. Maybe more like a pebble, considering the amount of time he'd had with her. But he could clearly see she could have been the rock he'd always wanted in his life. And he'd fucked that up.

Tate buckled, trying to cover with an elbow on the table to prop him up.

"Talk to her again," Quinn said. "She made peace with Mom and me. Working our way back to a family won't be easy, but she's really trying. And I know she loves you."

Servers swept away dinner plates and replaced them with dessert, a key lime streusel. Individual circular delicacies with a graham cracker crust and a layer of key lime pie beneath a decadent layer of streusel drizzled with icing and topped with a lime wedge. And a tented card stood on the side of each plate.

Tate's name was hand lettered on the front of his. His heart jumped. Then he darted a look at the other cards to see if those were also named for their owner. But the others were blank.

He darted a look at Quinn, and she immediately answered his unspoken question. "I have no idea what those are."

People around the table picked up their cards and, delighted, read a handful of quotes about food. Some funny. Some simple truths. Nothing earth-shattering. But somehow, Tate knew his would mean something.

"Read it," Quinn urged softly.

Tate's walls crumbled away, and emotions rose to the surface. He picked up the card and opened it.

"Food is symbolic of love when words are inadequate." —Alan D. Wolfelt

Without a word, Tate pushed his chair back and stood, starting for the kitchen. He needed her. He needed her in his life. He needed her to be his rock. He had no idea how he was going to make her see how desperately he needed her, wanted her, loved her, but he pushed through the doors to the kitchen in search of her.

The sous chefs and service staff hummed through the space like bees. In comparison to the relaxed, light atmosphere in the dining room, this space seemed to be on fast-forward. He scanned the space for her.

One of the sous chefs caught his eyes. "Hello, sir." He wiped his hands on his apron and faced Tate with a smile. "What can I do for you?"

"Olivia. Where is she?"

His smile faltered. "Oh, she, she had something important to take care of. She had to leave. I assure you, we have everything under control—"

"You're doing a great job," Tate interrupted. "Did she say where she was going or what she had to do?"

"Oh no, sir. I'm sorry." He shrugged. "As soon as she finished with dessert, she left."

28

Olivia stared out at the tarmac, but she didn't see it. All her focus was on the voice of Le Cordon Bleu's financial aid coordinator in her ear.

"I'm so sorry to hear you won't be joining us," Bijou said. "We miss you here. Albert and Fitz will be sad."

Olivia smiled. The classes and seminars she'd taken at the school had led to a lot of work for her, so she knew most of the staff personally, which was why Bijou was calling her on a Sunday after getting Olivia's email.

"I'm sad too. Very sad. But I'm sure another lucky person will benefit from the scholarship, and I'll continue to apply. Eventually—"

"Actually, I talked to Lourdes last night after I got your email. She looked over the candidates again and didn't feel any of them rose to the level of consideration necessary for her to take the scholarship from you. We can't change the due dates or starting dates, but Lourdes has agreed to hold the scholarship for you if you can start in the next session and if you can secure the scholarship with your portion of the total within two weeks."

Olivia inhaled sharply. Heat burned along her ribs. "Oh my God." She pressed her fingers to her lips. "Are you serious?"

Bijou laughed. "*Oui, mon cherie.*"

She closed her eyes tears burned behind her lids. "I can't thank you enough. Please thank Lourdes for me. I promise you, you won't regret it. I will make you all so proud."

"Oh, *cherie*," she said with affection in her voice, "you already make us proud. Very proud."

Olivia disconnected and held the phone to her chest. Gratitude welled inside her until she ached with it.

Her first thought was to call Tate and tell him.

That dragged her down a little. Okay, a lot.

Olivia collected her suitcase, moved to a corner chair in her gate area, and curled up. Holding her phone close, she watched the jets take off and land and taxi. Carts and people trailed over the tarmac.

Her life was on target once again, on an even better trajectory than when she'd come. Her cooking and catering skills had taken a leap in the right direction. She'd broken through that ugly barrier standing between her and her mother and sister, and they could start rebuilding. She'd get the money for school back from her mother in a few more days when she'd collected final payments from several clients, and Quinn had promised to get her mother to a business consultant even if she had to drag Teresa by the hair.

Olivia had also fallen in love.

And she had the broken heart to prove it.

She closed her eyes and dropped her forehead to her knee.

Maybe her life wasn't aimed at that bull's-eye quite right after all.

29

Tate wandered toward his gate with his duffel over his shoulder, his head down, reading a book on his phone, muttering to himself.

When he nearly missed running into someone, he lowered his phone. "Fuck it."

He'd study on the plane.

He wandered into the TSA pre-check line and breezed through security. He loved flying out of Washington National. With only three wings in the main terminal, it was so much smaller and quieter than Dulles.

He looked around for somewhere to eat. He was starving, and he needed a drink. He'd barely eaten anything all day yesterday and hadn't been able to work up an appetite for anything but Olivia today.

Now his body was demanding fuel. Tate wandered toward his gate, the very last in the terminal, checking menus of eateries as he passed. But he still couldn't find anything that interested him.

"Drink first," he muttered to himself. Maybe that would help him relax. Then maybe he could eat.

He turned the corner in the last section of the terminal and found the American Tap Room. Tate found a table, dropped his duffel on a chair, and sat. When a waitress came by, he said, "Bring me your favorite beer on tap."

She grinned, nodded, and moved to the bar.

Tate planted his elbows on the table and rubbed his face with both hands. "*Je suis désolé.*" His pronunciation sucked. "*Je t'aime. Je reste jusqu'à ce que vous voyez que vous pouvez me faire confiance.*"

"Here you go." The waitress's voice brought his head up. "Devil's Backbone."

He smirked. "Sounds good. Thanks."

She moved on to the next table, and Tate wrapped his hand around the cold glass and inhaled the rich scent. "*Je reste jusqu'à ce que vous voyez...*" His tongue got all tangled. "Goddammit."

He lifted the glass to his lips, inhaled deeply, and filled his mouth with the bold beer. As he set the drink down, he watched people wander past on their way to their gates. During a lull in foot traffic, his gaze moved deeper into the seating area of the gate beyond, which was empty, and the windows that looked out onto the tarmac.

He wondered if Olivia was already back in Paris. Wondered how long it would be before she'd talk to him again. He'd texted and called her several times last night, but she'd never answered.

Movement in the corner drew his gaze. Someone was sitting there, looking out the window. A little haven in a sea of strangers. When they left, maybe he'd do the same until it was time to board.

He took another drink of his beer, trying to relax. Trying to let things fall where they should instead of always forcing them. Across the way, the person stood and paced in front of the window. It was a woman, and she was silhouetted against the bright sunlight outside.

Tate sighed, thinking of Olivia. Of how badly he wanted to feel her in his arms. Of what a long road it could be back to trust between them.

Behind him on the television, an ESPN sportscaster interviewed an athlete. Around him, people chatted or worked while waiting for their flight. But Tate was restless. Anxious to board his flight and get on with his life.

He left a twenty on the table beneath his half-empty beer and strolled into the aisle. Hudson News drew him. A magazine or a novel might keep his mind busy. He started that direction. The woman haunting the empty gate wandered back to her seat in the corner. Something about the way she curled her feet under her and dropped her head into her hands stopped Tate in his tracks.

He couldn't get a better look at her without walking into the darkened area, and the thought of interfering in her little haven pushed his feet toward Hudson News. But no magazine caught his interest. Every novel seemed too intense.

"I'm just screwed," he muttered to himself, leaving with nothing but two bottles of water.

Before he knew it, he was wandering into the empty gate area. And halfway to the window, his feet stopped dead again. The woman's chin rested on her bent knee, where she stared out the window. Familiarity zinged down his spine.

"Olivia?" He thought the word more than spoke it, but she responded, glancing toward him.

Olivia.

His heart rate spiked. His stomach flipped.

Ah, fuck, he wasn't ready. *Je...something. Je suis...something.*

She twisted in her seat to face him. "H-hi." Her gaze darted behind him, then around the gate, as if that would explain his presence. "What... Oh." Some excitement or shock or something seemed to leak from her demeanor. "You must be headed to Ontario."

He shook his head, but his feet carried him straight to her. She'd been crying. Her eyes were swollen and red. Her cheeks blotchy. Her hair was up in a messy bun.

She looked vulnerable and sad.

His heart surged. He dropped his duffel and crouched in front of her. "What are you doing here?"

Her gaze darted away, and she shook her head. With her legs still curled under her, she was tucked into a safe little ball.

"She's just a little lost."

Quinn's words floated into his head, and he knew in that moment, she'd been right. Olivia, for all her strength, her ambition, her drive, was also a little lost. Which was exactly how Tate felt right now.

"I, um..." She sniffled. "Missed my flight."

Suddenly, Tate couldn't think of what to say. Didn't know where to start. He put the water bottles on the floor and clasped one hand over her thigh, the other over her bare foot.

"Did everything go okay yesterday?" Her eyes lifted to his. "After I left? The guys I was working with were really experienced. I knew they could handle plating desserts. I talked to Mom this morning. She said you told her it was a record-breaking—"

He cupped her face and leaned in, kissing her. After a second, Olivia sighed, and a little whimper carried from her throat. He pulled back, met her eyes, and found tears sliding down her cheeks.

"Baby, I'm sorry." He wiped at her tears, and she curled her hands around his wrists, the move so sweet, he felt his love for her blossom in his chest. He kissed her again, gentler. Sweeter. He felt the moment Olivia let go of her barriers, leaning into the kiss with a moan of relief. Tate opened to her and she responded. Just like that, they were in sync. They were connected. They were communicating.

He pulled back and stroked the stray strands of hair away

from her face. "I have so much to say, but I wasn't expecting to see you for at least another ten, twelve hours. Now my head's all jumbled, and I can't think."

Her brow pulled. "What?" She looked around again. "Aren't you going to Ontario?"

He laughed, lowered to his knees, and pulled her into his arms. She locked her arms around his neck and buried her face against his throat with another whimper that tugged at his heart.

"No," he said, holding her tight. "I cancelled Ontario. I'm on my way to Paris."

She pulled back. "What?"

He exhaled. So much to say. But his brain was floating on a rush of endorphins that made thinking extremely difficult. "I canceled Ontario. I want to spend the rest of the summer getting to know you. I want to spend the next few months showing you who I am. I'm going to earn your trust back, Liv." He pulled his ticket from his pocket and pushed it into her hands. "One-way ticket, baby. I'm not coming back until we are as solid as granite."

"Oh my God..."

More tears spilled. He couldn't tell if they were happy tears or sad tears or frustrated tears, but it didn't matter. Nothing would change his plans of spending the rest of his free time proving to her that they were meant to be together.

"Did you get another flight?" he asked. "What time does it leave? Maybe I can change flights."

"No." She wiped at her face and laughed. "I didn't really miss my flight. I mean I did, but not by accident. I was here, ready. Everyone boarded, but I couldn't make myself move. I couldn't make myself get on the plane, so I didn't bother rescheduling."

"Baby, why?"

"I didn't want to leave you."

His heart split wide open. He pulled her back to him and wrapped her tight. "Shit, I love you so fucking much, Liv. Wait, wait." he pulled back, squeezing his eyes shut to pull up the memory. then opened his eyes and held her gaze. "*Je t'aime.* That's all I got. I would have had more if I'd had some time to study on the plane."

She laughed. "I love you too. And I've been sitting here for an hour trying to figure out what to do and what to say to fix—"

"There's nothing to fix. We just need time to get to know each other. And we have months to do that now." Guilt seeped in. "I'm so sorry about school, Liv. I can't even believe—"

"It's okay." She shook her head. "It turned out okay."

"No. You're going, and I'm paying for it. I can't tell you how many people raved about you last night. We can argue all you want about the bill, but I'm—"

"No. You're not," she said with that steel streak of hers. Then her lips turned in a little grin. "I am going, but you're not paying for it because you don't need to. They're letting me keep the scholarship. I just have to start next term."

"When is that?"

"Three months."

The smile that took over his face sank all the way to his core.

"Well then, baby..." He cupped her face. "Let's go sync our tickets. Because we've got nothing but you, me, time and Paris in our immediate future. How does that sound?"

She kissed him, long and sweet. And her blue eyes sparkled when she met his gaze. "*Ça sonne comme le ciel.*"

He grinned and pulled her close, squeezing his eyes closed and absorbing all the joy and love she'd brought to his life. "Sounds like heaven to me too."

ABOUT THE AUTHOR

Skye Jordan is the *New York Times* and *USA Today* bestselling author of more than thirty-five novels.

She and her husband have two beautiful daughters and live in Oregon.

Skye loves to learn new things and enjoys staying active, so when she's not writing you're just as likely to find her in the ceramics studio as out rowing on the nearest lake or river.

Connect with Skye online

Amazon | **Instagram** | **Facebook** | **Website** | **Newsletter** | **Reader Group** | Tiktok

ALSO BY SKYE JORDAN

ROUGH RIDERS HOCKEY SERIES

Quick Trick

Hot Puck

Dirty Score

Wild Zone

PHOENIX RISING

Hot Blooded

Shadow Warrior

Hell Hath no Fury

Wicked Wrath

FORGED IN FIRE

Flashpoint

Smoke and Mirrors

Playing with Fire

WILDFIRE LAKE SERIES

In Too Deep

Going Under

Swept Away

NASHVILLE HEAT

So Wright

Damn Wright

Must be Wright

MANHUNTERS SERIES

Grave Secrets

No Remorse

Deadly Truths (Coming Soon)

RENEGADES SERIES

Reckless

Rebel

Ricochet

Rumor

Relentless

Rendezvous

Riptide

Rapture

Risk

Ruin

Rescue (Coming Soon)

Roulette (Coming Soon)

QUICK & DIRTY COLLECTION:

Dirtiest Little Secret

WILDWOOD SERIES:

Forbidden Fling

Wild Kisses

COVERT AFFAIRS SERIES

Intimate Enemies

First Temptation

Sinful Deception